WHO KILLED THE HUMMING BIRD

BOKLIM CHOI

I have read Mr. Boklim Choi's first novel [The Mountain Rats]. It is a collection of his six stories. Among them, I found the last story was most fascinating and unique in concept. In it, the author invites his family and friends to The Last Dinner before he leaves this world. This blurb site is no place to give you the spoiler. I can only say that his first novel [The Mountain Rats] was a robust introduction of Mr. Choi's literary authorship.

I recently had an honor of reviewing the outline of his second novel [Who Killed the Hummingbird?]. It gave me the impression that it would be even more fascinating than the first book. I will be one of the first who would read the book soon after it leaves the publisher's deck.

I am certain that [Who Killed the Hummingbird?] will present a very interesting reading experience to a wide readership.

Han Soo Lee, M.D.
Author of *Dream Wafer*

Overall, I was very impressed. The story (Who Killed the Hummingbird?) was moving, the characters well developed, and the pace was perfect from start to finish.

Patrick Linsenmeyer
Professional reviewer

Praise for Boklim's previous book,
The Mountain Rats

Bolkim Choi's stories live in the sublime realm some-where between fiction and non-fiction, and pass along flavors of Korean-American life in New York, sometimes on a very personal level.

– Donna Deedy, journalist

I spent my childhood in the Catskills. Your story is not only informative, it's beautifully written. I truly loved your stories.

– Adrian Leslie, author of
Alice Again and two other novels

Your stories evoked so much emotion for me, which I think is what a writer wants. You wrote about things very close to me. Your perspective to make the Catskills house a reality is awesome.

– Sandra Foley,
Harbor View Book Club

ISBN: 978-1540585233

Contents

Introduction

April is not December. In December, people hurry. Something chases them. The last page of the calendar makes them haste. The glittering lights of shopping malls entice them. As the end of the year approaches, people feel nervous and look back at the long shadows they have left behind. December is one of the coldest months. The naked trees shiver. Winds hit them with knife-stabbing blows. Some trees fall, some barely stand, but most of them endure harsh winter months. They have hopes. They wait for the spring's warm weather to defrost their frozen body. January is long and cruel. When short February comes, trees and grass dream of spring. February is like a small wooden bridge. People attempt to jump over it or wade through the frozen water. The calendar says March is the beginning of spring, but people don't believe it, and the trees and grass don't feel it yet. They have hope, but the wind reminds them winter is not over. It will eventually retreat, but slowly and reluctantly.

Occasionally snow comes. It's a warning: Folks, do not rush; they wait patiently. Nature never hastens, it follows the same pace every year.

When April comes, the landscape suddenly changes. The remaining snow mounds disappear; the sea changes its color and birds sing loudly and happily. The trees are budding, and fallen grass begins to lift their heads. Winds don't trample them down. As warm sun lingers, they gain strength; it calls people to the parks. Hungry golfers flock to the courses. Golf balls fly in the sky, and people are making noise in excitement. Spring awakens everything. In April, nature resurrects.

In churches, April is like December. December is a month of Christmas. People rejoice in the birth of Jesus. Churchgoers gather, they sing Hallelujah; people hug each other and watch holy play. In early April, people enjoy special Easter church concerts. Easter and Christmas offerings are a paramount source of the annual that is the church budget. It's a season of sharing. In April Jesus resurrected. He was crucified for all people, rose from the tomb, and ascended to Heaven. It's a month of resurrection. Jesus promised eternal life to whoever believes in Him. April is December for believers.

Chapter 1

The Easter Storm

Westchester, New York
On Easter Sunday, 2006
Elena Reynolds

It was more than an April shower. It was a downpour. Dark clouds gathered in the morning. It started pouring at six o'clock. I woke up at 6:00 a.m. and I took a long shower. At 7:00, I opened the windows and looked at the sky. Winds ripped trees and birds flew away.

"What an unfriendly day! Why today? Why God doesn't tame bad weather?" I murmured.

I turned on the Weather Channel. The weather map showed a severe storm approaching from the Ohio Valley that would linger in the New York metropolitan area. It will rain much of the day and then gives way in the late afternoon. I thought about the inconveniences people face today. The clock on the microwave oven said it was almost eight. It was wet and cold. The temperature hovered in the low forties. The wind chill made me feel freezing. I put a warm coat on to cover my shivering body. I looked at my face in the mirror. I looked pale, a bit sad, but not terribly bad. I opened the garage door and got in my Toyota Avalon.

When I arrived at the church, it was quiet. Not even the Korean church clerk was there yet. The first Korean service starts at 9:30 a.m. I put the heat on to warm up the place and dispel the damp air. At 8:30 a.m., Min Jung, the Korean missionary came. She complained of the storm, almost cursing.

"It should rain yesterday or tomorrow. Why today? It rained on Easter last year, too. Again, this year? Something is wrong in the sky."

She pushed the door of her office open and flipped the light. As time passed, the elders fought the rain and arrived. Their bodies dripped with rain. They said "Happy Easter!" to brighten the mood. At 9:00 a.m., assistant pastor John Kim came.

He said to me, "Pastor Park is not coming for today's service. I am delivering the Easter message."

I was shocked to hear that. It portended something apprehensive. I entered Park's office. Everything looked normal, at first. His desk was clean and his books were in order. And then I noticed his waste basket was deeper than usual. I picked up a piece of crumpled paper. He had scribbled, *Resurrection—His Second Coming—Conscience—Sinner*

I was stunned. I knew something bad might have happened to him. I sobbed for a minute before collecting myself. There's no time to spare. The phone was ringing. It was the pastor's wife. It was the first time I had heard her voice.

"Is my husband there? I was waiting for him until midnight and fell asleep. He still hasn't come home." "No, he is not here. We were about to call you. Oh, my God. If he is not home, where is he? Today is Easter Sunday." I was almost crying.

2

"Is it really? Isn't his car at church? The Hyundai Sonata." She asked me. "I already checked, it's not here. Why did he suddenly disappear? Did you notice anything unusual?" I was demanding her answer. Her voice grew testier, "Not really. He doesn't talk much, especially at home. He has been in a bad mood recently. He didn't eat much and stayed up until the wee hours the last few days. By the way, if he doesn't come to church who's going to deliver Easter sermon?"

"Pastor Kim will. He said Pastor Park told him yesterday to prepare a sermon." She said, "Everything seems weird. I will be there soon."

She hung up hastily. When the assistant pastor appeared in the podium people looked perplexed and whispered to one another. "Where's Pastor Park? Why Pastor Kim today?" Kim seemed nervous. "Pastor Park should give you the sermon. Unfortunately, he is sick. I have no idea how serious, but he couldn't make it." He delivered his prepared sermon.

Thousands of thoughts crossed my mind. More people started to come to the service through the storm. It still rained in long and hard sheets. If it were not Easter some people would miss the service. It's Easter. Every Christian should come to church today. Devout Koreans will never miss it. Men wore their best suits and women dressed up in this wailing storm. They looked gloomy at first, but happy when they crossed the threshold and entered the main church. Congregations hung their rain gear and sat on their usual long chairs. Holy songs filled the church.

At 10:30 am, the larger second service started. Since it was Easter, most of the congregation from the first service also participated in the second. We didn't hear anything about Pastor Park. At that time, Tom Curtis, the English mission elder came to the church. He said he received a

3

text message from Pastor Park last night asking him to deliver Easter sermon for him. Mr. Curtis didn't know why Pastor Park couldn't make it. He guessed pastor Park had an illness.

It was about noon. An American churchgoer rushed to the church and said he just heard the radio news that a man's body was found at Catskills. According to the news report, it looked like he had committed suicide. Police located the car in a deep valley. It was a Hyundai Sonata. The police moved the body to a local hospital.

This astonishing news sent shocks through the whole church. Everybody knew the Sonata was pastor Park's car and, most importantly, he has been missing since last night. There was no possible reason why he would miss the most important service of the year. It was beyond everyone's comprehension. I couldn't stand and listen to all of the increasingly ominous talks. It suffocated me. I rushed to the church office, closed the door and sobbed. At that moment, the phone rang. I hesitated then answered.

"This is Detective Tom Murphy from the Sullivan Police Department. Do you know Mr. Young Min Park? He was found dead in his car. We checked his plate number and found out the car was registered to the Westchester Korean Church. I am so sorry to inform you this bad news on Easter morning, but that's what had happened. Is he a church member, or staff? By the way, who is answering?"

I was unable to answer his question immediately. I was crying. "My name is Elena. I am a volunteer. He is the pastor of this church. This is a Korean church as well as an American church. We have both English and Korean services. We were anxiously waiting for him this morning." I said.

"I can imagine. It's very sad and unfortunate. But,

what happened is what happened. His body has been moved to the County Hospital morgue. His car was totaled. Do you know his family? Why don't you let them know and tell them to come over?"

He gave me the contact information and a brief direction. I could not believe what I had just heard, but I couldn't keep this sad news by myself either. I rushed to his family members to share the horrible news. At that time, the congregations were still at church, and the church choir members were preparing the Easter concert. The assistant pastor called an emergency meeting. They decided to send people to the hospital. The pastor's wife, her son Tim, an assistant pastor, and the English mission elder went to the hospital. I was not invited to join. I hesitated for a moment but decided to leave with them. I wanted to see with my own eyes what had happened in his final hours. He meant a lot to me. I have been one of the very few to understand his inner world. I knew how much he was in agony. I could imagine why he would choose to kill himself on this holy Easter Sunday.

When we arrived at the Saint James Hospital, Detective Murphy was waiting for us at the entrance. He was not wearing his police uniform. He looked in his late 40s. He had a sincere gaze, but he dealt with the case matter-of-factly. He was a detective more than an emotional individual.

He said, "I am sorry for what happened to him. This should not have happened on Easter Sunday Eve, but —.Would you like to see his body? There was no immediate witness. One driver called police early this morning and said he saw a car in the valley and went down to the scene to check it out. He was shocked to find a man sitting bloody in the driver's seat. We sent an ambulance and confirmed the man was dead. His body is waiting to be autopsied, but it appears he took his own life. If you had any doubt in your mind, then we can start an investigation."

We didn't say anything. We didn't know enough to question his judgment. We lost our minds, felt numb and frozen. The detective led us to the morgue. It was dark and damp. An African-American man showed us his body covered with a white sheet. We hesitantly looked at the dead. It was him, the principal pastor of the church. His face was all broken and bruised, and there were still splotches of dried blood.

The medical examiner said," I could not touch his body before you saw. With your permission, I can clean his face."

The pastor's wife didn't say a word. Her crying broke the heavy silence.

She said, "How could this happen? Why did you kill yourself? You are too selfish."

Tim sobbed. I lost words. There was a tightening in my heart. The others in our group didn't say much.

The medical examiner said, "We'll need you to contact your funeral home to take him. I am sorry to say this, but we cannot keep him here long."

One elder whispered to the pastor's wife and gave a Korean funeral home address.

Mrs. Park told the medical examiner, "We will move his body soon."

I asked the detective whether we could visit the tragic scene. Detective Murphy agreed and said someone in the police department would guide us.

As the storm system departed, dry air began to move into the Catskills. It was still foggy and drizzling. The police escort entered Route 28 West and headed toward Margaret County. I opened my eyes wide and studied the landscape. It looked familiar to me. Then I realized I had come here with him only a few weeks ago. I was shocked. It seemed more than coincidence. He must have chosen this road deliberately. I closed my eyes. I recollected the happy moments we had together. Our secret.

Only Heaven and Earth know what had happened that day. I felt a tremor deep in my lower body. I pushed my head into the back of the seat and tried to stop thinking. The police car stopped at a side road, and we all climbed down.

"Watch out. It's slippery after heavy rain. We don't need another misfortune." The police officer said with cautious voice.

His Sonata was by the creek. It was covered by mud; the front portion was almost gone, and the rear bumper had fallen off. He killed not only himself but also his beloved car.

I can remember he had said this, "Oh, I love this car. I feel like this car is me, a central part of my body and soul. This car served me for the last fifteen years. His eyes, legs, feet, and arms were replaced, but he had the same strong heart. I will die with this car when that last moment comes."

We didn't need to stay there and look at the car long. The scene told us everything about what had happened. I tried to find any trace he might have left, his fingerprints or even his last breath. There was nothing I could grasp.

His driver's license, registration, and insurance card were taken by the police. When his family didn't raise any questions, the officer said, "As you have witnessed, there doesn't appear to be any foul play. I cannot figure out his motive. You know the circumstances more than we do.".

I looked at the surrounding area. I saw the lake where

he and I were together at an abandoned house where we had snuck in. But I couldn't think about that today. It was way too much for his family.

When we arrived at the church, many elders and deacons were still waiting for us. They knew what had happened to Pastor Park, but didn't know the details. They said the Easter service went okay and reported most of the congregation still didn't know what had happened. They preferred to trust what they had originally heard: Pastor Park was too ill to deliver Easter sermon. His death, that was too much to believe. It was the last thing in the world they wanted to know. It was unimaginable, absolutely beyond their comprehension.

It didn't matter how he died. What is important is that he was no longer in this world. We could not see him again, could not talk to him, unable to touch him. We could no longer listen to his sermons, delivered in his sweet, baritone voice. Oh, people loved his manner of speech. His sermons were well thought, beautifully crafted, intellectually rich, sonorous and delivered masterfully. His usual twenty-minute sermon was like a good piece of music. What is cruel is that the dead cannot belong to this world. Whether they ascend to Heaven or are buried lifeboats, the ground depends on each person's faith.

Park's final farewell service took place five days after his body was discovered. The funeral was held at the church where he had served for the last twenty years. The church was packed; most of the Korean congregation came to pay their last tribute. As tradition dictated, most of the male mourners wore black suits and dark ties, women dressed conservatively. Assistant Pastor Kim officiated the service. The church choir sang gospel songs and senior elder Chung delivered a eulogy in Korean then elder Tom Curtis delivered his in English. The pastor's wife Won Oak, his son Tim, and daughter Sarah sat in the front seat with their heads down. Pastor Park's mother sat with them. At 78 – year old, she is too fragile to stand long at this sad moment. She kept crying and moaning in Korean. At the end of service, people formed two lines and paid their final tributes. Everybody stood in front of the coffin, dropped their heads and said goodbye. Some said their final words with tears. They hugged family members. The widow and children sobbed with mourners, who they knew well.

I was one of the last people to say the farewell. I wanted to say thousands of words to him. Nobody knew him more than I did. The eulogy didn't echo because the elder didn't know him enough, his love of literature, his love of nature, his true personality, his childhood and most importantly his recent struggle. I couldn't stand there long, people behind me were waiting for their moment. When the wake was over people stood up to watch his casket as it was driven to the funeral home. Many people sobbed and cried when the pastor's body left the church. I tried to hear his last words: he seemed whispering, "I am no longer with you. I am sorry. Please forgive me. I truly loved you."

He was buried the next day. It didn't rain, but it was blustery and cold. People wore heavy coats to protect themselves from both cold and sorrow. A good number of Koreans and more than ten non-Korean church members watched his last moment in this world. As his body was sinking into the ground slowly, everybody sobbed. The widow staggered, her son supported her. One by one, mourners threw dirt upon his casket. It was the final moment. The long funeral process came to an end. Everybody was exhausted. They were sad but relieved.

He is gone, and we stay in this world. People left the cemetery one by one. Not many people looked back. The grave was not properly made yet. The grieving family will return in a few days to check on everything.

After Pastor Park's passing, the church was in turmoil. People couldn't believe what had happened to the church. They couldn't bring back the dead pastor. The church elevated pastor Kim as the Principal Pastor. Many Korean congregations left the church citing various reasons. I came to understand that's the history of the Korean immigrant church. When a church grows fast, every kind of conflict occurs.

The day after the funeral I opened my laptop. I hadn't checked e-mails the last few days. My mind was frozen. There was no room for other people or other matters to invade my heart. Surprisingly, I found an e-mail from him. I quickly looked at the date. It was sent to me on Easter Eve, the day he died.

Dear Elena,

This is the last and only mail I am sending while I remain in this world. It happens to be you whom I love the most. I am sending this at ten. I will be gone when you open this. I know you go to sleep early and check your mail in the morning. I am leaving and not coming back to you. I am embarking on a long, long journey. I will not come back even as a ghost. As you know, I don't believe in resurrection.

In retrospect, meeting you in the Amazon was one of the most important occasions of my life. I still remember you clearly when I first saw you. You were the perfect reflection of nature. You were the morning dew, deep Amazon fresh water, gentle breeze, jumping dolphin, a redwood which had a watermark. Your face was as clear as the Amazon and your speech sounded like the music of the Andes water current. You met me there, a complicated man, one who loved literature and adventure but could not concentrate on writing, a pastor who preached God's words without confidence. You also had seen a man of contradiction. But, somehow you tried to understand me, a tender-minded, awkward individual.

I was driven into your world gradually as our stay continued. The day we left the Amazon we hugged. We didn't say to meet again, but my instinct said I would see you again someday. I believed it's our fate and you seemed to agree. My life had changed since that day. You stayed in my heart and never left. You visited me like the wind and were singing to me like a bird. You had knocked on my bedchamber during the night and sang with a sad voice like a hummingbird. You come to me like an Amazon bird, then become a member of the congregation and eventually to work for me as a volunteer for the English service. Those days were the happiest time in my life.

In the meantime, I reached a certain point in realizing who truly I was. I was an unrecognized novelist more than a pastor, a middle-aged man who denied the presence of God. I was not able to ignore my conscience, deceive congregations, and distrust God. I have been a hypocrite all my life. I have preached Jesus' Resurrection even though I was not convinced. I have been a sinner. I decided to pay for my sin by giving up my life to those who had been misguided by my false faith.

Dear Elena,

I am leaving you. I cannot come back. We will not get

together in Heaven. I am going with your memory. I loved you more than anybody else. Elena, please do not cry for me. I return to nature. My dear Elena, you deserve to be happy, with or without me. So long, Elena. I love you.

Young Min Park

He said not to cry, but I couldn't stop crying. He left his last mail not as a pastor, but as a caring man. Without him, I am nothing in his church. I started to work as a non-paid clerk because he wanted me. I stopped working for the church. I am returning to Elena Reynolds, an English teacher. I have to live a new life, with the beautiful memory of him. He was my soul and my love.

Chapter 2

Mother's Wish

Seoul, Korea
Young Min Park

In 1977, I graduated from theology school and worked briefly as an intern at a small church in Inchon. I was only 22 years old. People called me a pastor, but I felt like a student. Many of my friends were graduate students. I was young, naive and inexperienced. I didn't know how to associate with congregations and never delivered sermons. I was a shy young man who liked to read literary books more than the Bible. I liked to travel every corner of the Korean peninsula rather than mingling with church people.

Young Soon Choi, my mother, told me every day," Now you are a pastor. How proud I am. Be a good pastor. That's one of the best jobs in the world. It's more than a regular job. It's God's calling. You can help many people: you can save their souls, awaken their self-confidence, and lead them to God's world." And she continued, "A good pastor can do more than a politician. You are more important than political leaders and businesspeople.

They don't care about people. They only believe in power and money. You can lead people to the right direction. Take the road Jesus Christ took. That's my wish."

Chang Sung Park, my father, was a teenager when the Korean War broke out. They had lived in Wonsan, South Ham Kyung Province. My parents' family had deep Christian roots. My paternal grandfather accepted Christianity at a young age, influenced by an American missionary. He taught Sunday school and became a deacon. He tried to flee to the South but was caught by North Korean agents and sent to prison camp. My father had not heard from him since the war. He presumed his father was dead.

My mother's mother was a woman elder in Won San. She sent my mom to the Christian Girls' High School there. Her mother couldn't escape North Korea. It is a tragic story that millions of Koreans suffered. My parents were able to take the last rescue ship carrying thousands of refugees leaving Won San. My parents believed God saved them: gave an answer to their earnest prayer. She used to tell me and my sister, "Without His blessing, we couldn't have survived. Thousands of people missed the last ship, tens of thousands of families were separated, and many people died during the escape. It was chaos, a real tragedy; the civil war inflicted deep wounds in our hearts. But, God saved us for use in His Kingdom. We should not forget His blessing so we should pay Him back." I could not understand her reasoning, but couldn't say otherwise. They had to flee again further south as the Chinese Red Army pushed back the allied forces. They arrived in Busan, one of the southernmost cities in Korea. I was born there in 1955. I went to the elementary school there. It was a tent school. We didn't have desks or textbooks. About half of the students were refugee kids, and it was a big class – more than 80 students per classroom.

My parents moved to Seoul and started a business. They worked hard, from dawn to late evening and saved enough money to buy a decent house. My parents always read us Bible, even in the midst of the chaos. They prayed before every meal and went to the early morning service with their exhausted bodies. They firmly believed as long as they worshiped God they would be okay and their children would succeed. Faith had been the pillar of their lives. She didn't give me greater independence and time for wild imaginations. I was taught to be compliant, deferential to adults, and most of all – to follow Bible. Bible is everything for her. She read Bible to me and wanted me to join in night prayer before sleep. She believed God guided our daily lives and that as a family member, I should follow the family tradition. When I didn't listen to her, she turned visibly angry. She didn't spank me, but scolded me and gave 10-20 minute lectures. My mom didn't realize that early childhood experiences could be consequential for children's long-term social and emotional development, and cast a lifelong shadow.

I was not born strong. According to my mother, it took me two days to arrive in this world. My mother was exhausted and feared both she and I may die together. She constantly prayed, "Lord, please save us. When my son survives, I will raise him to devote his life to you,".

Mother believed God answered her prayer. I was born without defects, and my mother recovered her strength eventually. As a child, I did not sleep through the night. We lived on the northern outskirts of the city. It was a small village compared to the bustling city center. There was a wide creek and plenty of woods to wander around. I had a buddy of my age. We two boys went fishing with loose nets and plucked grass and flowers. We liked nature and playing outdoors because our houses were too small to stay inside all day. We didn't care much about a change in weather. Other people shivered and rushed to their houses when the rain came. I longed for snow in winter and heat in summer.

In the night our village was pitch dark. The air was fragrant and heavy, perfect for dreaming. As soon as the nightfall came, I could hear the swift movement of lizards rattling through the leaves. I heard the different noises of insects. When I came home, I was dreaming of what I had seen and heard during the daytime. I had all kinds of dreams in my sleep. Some of the dreams really scared me, especially snakes. My mom told me I was growing whenever I had horrible dreams.

As I learned how to read, I stayed home most of the time and read fairy tales, Aesop's fables, and other books. My mother wanted me to read the children's Bible, but it didn't catch my interest. When my mom stayed home, I pretended to read Bible. Sometimes she quizzed me on the Bible; I stammered answering her questions. She seemed disappointed but didn't scold me.

My father liked fishing. He was as busy as the bees but found time to go fishing. One weekend he took me to go fishing. We got up early, took the bus and arrived at a big lake. We didn't catch any, bought some fish from other people and brought to my mom to cook. I still remember what my dad told me on that day. He told me that no matter how comfortable, we must live like fish. "The water is the home for fish, unattached to any land. Wherever there was water, they could survive, and escape the hazards. We are smarter than fish so not to be caught by fishers. We have to stay in the mud sometimes until the high tide. We have been through all kinds of hardships, the war, poverty, isolation, and anxiety. It's not over yet: You will face more challenges. Don't be afraid. You will get over it. Always remember who you are. You are a fish." On that night, I had a dream. In the dream, I caught some fish, but the fish slipped away from my hands and jumped into the water. The dream woke me up in the middle of night. It was three o'clock in the morning.

I was seriously ill when I was ten years old. Fever soared over one hundred degrees. I couldn't eat or sleep. It was hard to breathe. My parents were afraid. They brought me to a nearby hospital. The doctor recommended going to the big hospital in the downtown. He suspected I had pneumonia. My mother sought advice from her pastor; the pastor referred to his friend who was a well-known internal specialist and I was admitted to his hospital. He diagnosed my disease pneumonia, prescribed a strong antibiotic and put me into the intensive care unit. My temperature didn't drop for several days. My mother was greatly concerned. People suggested herbal medicine, but she didn't listen. She stayed up by my bedside, read Bible and kept praying. She asked the pastor to come and pray for my recovery.

It took me three weeks to be stabilized before I slowly began to recover. I stayed another week in the hospital and then discharged home. I couldn't go to school for two months, and my parents couldn't take care of their clothing store. When my fever dropped, and I was able to move around slowly, my parents returned to work, and my sister stayed vigilant. When I was completely healed, my mother said, "Lord saved you again. You owe too much to God. You have a mission to accomplish. Give your life to the Lord.". I was happy to be alive, but not sure whether God saved my life or the doctors did.

I couldn't dispute my mother and make her mad. I was my mother's only son. My father who was an elder in his church didn't seem to agree one hundred percent with his wife but didn't say anything to dispute her strong belief. They were all devout Christians.

My sister was a pretty girl. When she walked on the street boys stared at her. She didn't seem to care. She'd briefly give a look and pass them with no hesitation. She was much braver than I. When she became a teenager, she was so beautiful that my mother had warned her not to be friendly to any unknown boys. Some of my mother's friends said she looked like her mom, but neither my mom nor my sister agreed. She was taller than mom, and her voice was stronger and sweeter.

My sister had a talent in music. Her singing was second to none in the church choir. She had a high-pitched, powerful voice. She was a leading soprano in her music class. She was dreaming of becoming a famous singer. She wanted to go to music school in one of the best universities in Seoul. My parents didn't say no, but they worried it would cost them too much and it would be hard to support herself as a musician if she were not world famous. Mom wished she could find a good boy in the church, and marry young. Mom wished her daughter to be a pastor's wife but didn't say that to her. She knew her daughter would not be pleased. My sister had a strong character. She usually respected her parents, but when she disagreed she said so with a forceful voice. As she went on to high school, she conspicuously disdained her mother's unwelcome meddling. She wanted to get out of mom's shadow. She thought if mom said something right, it turned out wrong. She always wanted to have second thoughts. She also thought mom pushed me too much.

I remember my sister occasionally telling mother, "Mom, don't tell Young Min what to do and what not to do. He is a smart, mature boy now. If you interfere too much, he might go the wrong way. Let him be himself."

My mom wasn't pleased to hear this, "Shut up. Your brother is a tender boy. He daydreams. If we don't watch him, he might move adrift toward a dangerous path. God saved him twice. He should go to church, join the Bible class, and become a Sunday school teacher."

My sister agreed I was a bit of a drifting boy, but not as dangerous as our mom thought. She always protected me. Sometimes she tried to draw our father to our side. My sister simply refused to be controlled by her mom. She wanted to be her own. She strongly believed that her generation was different from mom's. She was looking far beyond mom's horizon.

I happened to discover that my sister had been dating a handsome boy. He was not a church boy as mom wished. He was a college freshman and a rich boy. My sister said to me, "Don't tell mom. I don't like the church guys. They are weak, too religious and not ambitious. I may try to be a world class singer. How could a pastor or missionary support me? I need a rich man. I am starting to shop for my future husband. And of course, I have to like him. Love is more important than anything else. I don't care about religion. God doesn't feed us. We, the churchgoers feed the clergyman and support the church."

At that moment, she heard mom's footstep. She signaled Hush! And hurriedly said, "Mom, are you home? How was your day? Young Min studied Bible, and I practiced gospel songs.". Mom seemed happy. Dad followed mom and said, "Yun Hee, you have to apply for a good college next year. You need to study math and English. Spend less time on singing. And Young Min, concentrate on school subjects. You will have plenty of time to read Bible. The Bible is an ever-lasting book." We both laughed.

We loved mom, but we thought dad was more generous, not demanding. He was a broad-minded man. While mom had been a relentless pusher, my dad had been a good listener and moderator. He might have seen mom's strong approach to her children and determined it could cause a serious problem in the future. All he wanted was the happiness and harmony of our family. He believed nobody's talent should be denied to satisfy other family member's selfishness. He thought we were all equal. My sister and I totally agreed with our dad's view. We had a fabulous dinner that evening. My sister poured a glass of Korean wine for dad. It was a token of appreciation for his understanding.

Chapter 3

A Cuban Girl

Havana, Cuba
Elena Reynolds

I am a Cuban girl. I was born in Havana in 1959, the year Fidel Castro took control of the island country. I was too young to remember our family's exodus from Cuba. My parents told me how we escaped communist Cuba when I was two years old. They reminded me so often as I was growing up.

You may wonder why my last name is Reynolds. It's an English name, not a Cuban name. Robert Reynolds, my grandfather, was an English sailor. He had worked for a British shipping company. The cargo ship transported daily commodities to the Caribbean Islands and brought rum, coffee, sugar and cigars to Europe in the late 19th century

My granddad was a poor, but decent and religious man. He embarked on cargo carriers to support himself and his ailing parents. At that time, ships were not as big as now, and navigation systems were not as sophisticated. The cargo ships were vulnerable to storms and often sunk. My granddad's vessel met a hurricane one summer. The cargo ship disappeared into the water. My granddad and a few other sailors took lifeboats and reached the shore. They landed at Oriente, a southern tip of the Cuban island. They were exhausted and hungry.

According to my father, a Cuban girl of Spanish ancestry took care of my grandfather. Why him? "Because he was such a handsome guy. And he was speaking pure English. He was a polite man. His parents always taught him to be nice to women. The Spain-Cuban girl fell in love with him, and they had a baby out of wedlock. That was me. Later on, they officially married, and my name was registered, and I got my birth certificate. Angela Morales, my mother, your grandmother, was a brave woman. She didn't heed what other people said. She had snatched my father because she loved him. This is our family tree. We had lived in Cuba for over eighty years. If the 1959 revolution hadn't come, we would still be living there happily. My parents once considered moving back to England, but they ultimately decided to settle here. My mother liked to live in London socializing with upper-class English women, but my father liked the quiet and warm weather. He promised my mom they would visit London every other year. He kept his pledge and traveled Europe with your grandmother. He passed away in 1940, and my mom followed him five years later. I think they reunited happily in Heaven."

Hunter Reynolds, my father, met my mother, Sarah Orlando, at a Catholic church in Havana. My mom said years ago, "Your dad was the most charming guy in the youth group. Every girl chased him, white girls, mulattos, even black girls. Some girls intentionally passed him with their tight hips. Some followed him to his house, and a gave him a love letter. I was the only cool girl who didn't express interest. Of course, I liked him, but I didn't want to join them. I was proud of myself. I was not a beauty, but beautiful enough to attract the boys' attention. One day he asked me to meet at a waterfront restaurant for dinner. I pretended I was not ready, but couldn't say no because I was waiting for the moment. Since the first date, we became close and visited each other's homes. My parents liked him. He was exceptionally well mannered, brilliant, and from a well-off family. He was from a Caucasian minority family, but well accepted by the Cuban elite community. Your dad's family loved me too. My father was a big shot in Havana. We had a big sugar plantation and a trading company. Your dad's father was running a shipping company. So, the two families knew each other. They believed it was a perfect match. We got married when we graduated college. Your grandfather was a friend of Ernest Hemingway. The two had something in common: They both liked to drink and go fishing. Hemingway was older than my dad. My dad often visited Ambos Mundos, the Earnest Hemingway Hotel, and they went for a drink at Sloppy Joe, the Hemingway Bar, near the beach. My dad didn't drink as much as Hemingway. Whenever my dad came home late, your grandmother looked visibly unhappy. She yelled at him, "I don't care you drink with a world-famous writer. Modest drinking is no problem, but never excessively. It will kill you. I want to be with you for a long time. If you keep drinking with him, I will yell at him. I don't care who he is. You are my husband and a lot more important than him." Your grandfather listened to his wife. He maintained a friendship with Hemingway but kept a certain distance at night. Earnest usually drank at night and slept in the morning. I have no idea how he could manage his time for writing 'The

Old Man and the Sea' and 'For Whom the Bell Tolls.'"

Everything was perfectly okay for my family until the 1959 Revolution. Cuba is geographically considered part of North America – like Mexico, but culturally considered part of Latin America. Cuba remained a colony of Spain until the Spain-America War of 1898, which led to nominal independence as a de facto U.S. protectorate in 1902. As a fragile republic, it attempted to strengthen its democratic system, but mounting political radicalization and social strife culminated in the dictatorship of Fulgencio Batista in 1952. Further unrest and instability led to Batista's fall in January 1959 by Fidel Castro. The revolution uprooted my family's foundation. It brought chaos and bloodshed. At that time, the only radio broadcasts were government controlled. Only military anthems and patriotic songs were allowed.

Everyone was on the street, red and black armbands and bracelets hanging from their wrists. My parents hid in their wine cellar and turned all the lights off. They believed darkness could chase the unruly gangsters away. As time passed, my parents realized the circumstances were not on their side. Our family belonged to a kind of bourgeoisie. Revolutionary guards would often confiscate our possessions. Nationalization of all property was one of the first steps they took after the uprising. My parents were at a crossroads; which way should they go – staying in Havana or giving up everything and leaving their home? They had to take the route for existence. On the morning of one spring day in 1961, while my mother prayed at her altar, my father anxiously looked at the sea beyond. He visualized the escape route. As the owner of a big shipping company, he knew lots of people who sent migrants to the U.S. There were Cubans leaving the island on anything that would float, looking to the skies for signs of salvation. The revolution was almost two years old and already defying expectations. People just didn't trust their new government. The fear of communism was hanging over the horizon like darkening storm clouds. The U.S. embargo was a distant concern, while the persistent rumors of invasion and imminent combat swept Havana. The time to make a decision was approaching in each passing hour.

Key West is only 90 miles away from Havana. People can clearly see the other side on a cloudless day. People can sail from one side to the other with a small yacht, or even a canoe when weather permits. Miami is further, 220 miles from Cuba.

We decided to sail to Miami with our friend's yacht. After hours of battling our way through Havana's chaotic streets, we arrived at a marina known as Hemingway's marina. We had a late dinner composed mostly of snacks. As night fell, we slipped into the small-keeled yacht and cruised out of Cuba into the pitch dark ocean. Soon the yacht was headed northbound, which would take us out of Cuban territorial waters. My mother's hair danced in the air. She read Bible and prayed for a safe journey. It was the first serious challenge she was facing in her life. My father looked calm and didn't seem to worry. I sat on my mother's lap and began to fall asleep. As a little girl, I didn't quite understand what was going on at the time. All I wanted was a nice dinner and a good night's sleep.

When our yacht passed under the moonlight of Havana, my father said to mom, "We are leaving Cuba where my father first set foot as a sailor. Cuba is a beautiful country, but the revolution kicked us from the land. We are swimming like fish toward a land of freedom. We have nothing to cry for; we are strong. We can overcome whatever hardship we might face and start new lives in the new world. The darkness was all encompassing. Enrique, the crew, said, "There's nothing ahead. It's pitch black wilderness. Look at the stars. They will guide us and tell us how long it'll take us to get there. Miami is somewhere far north. Winds push our yacht in that direction. We are lucky. We will be there within five hours. Don't worry. Somebody will welcome us. There are lots of Cubans in Miami, and they hate Fidel."

My father assured us that Cubans would welcome us with open arms. He also said Cubans are receiving special welfare benefits, even financial aid packages to help us settle down. My family had left our properties in Cuba, but he wasn't worried. He had a good connection with some Americans in Miami and had considerable amounts of saving in U.S. banks. His only concern was our safe arrival on U.S. soil.

While I was struggling to sleep, my father was nervously watching the darkness. He was looking for the light. He believed only light promised hope. He had been the English-Cuban all his life, but he seemed to have forgotten his heritage. The Reynolds family longed for a new life in the United States.

Dawn broke. As darkness lifted, the water changed its color. It was glowing in reds and ocean itself radiating golden light. It was so peaceful. Seagulls circled the sky. Enrique said," One more hour, then we will be in Miami. It's a long voyage but is worth it. It was a freedom ride – from communism to democracy, from dictatorship to popular rule, from nationalization to all the enterprises to private ownership. "The world had been changed overnight. Our yacht glided toward the Miami port. Surprisingly a thick throng of people was waiting for the new arrivals. They waved Cuban and American flags, hugged the tired and hungry people, provided coffee and snacks. These Cuban-Americans welcomed the defectors from their home country. Miami has the largest Cuban community in the United States. There are more Spanish-speaking people than English. Miami was a Havana within the States. Most of the professionals had left the island over the decades. Many of them ended up in Miami. Dr. Mara Martinez, a dentist who was a friend of my mothers, had been a staunch supporter of the Revolution, but gradually became disillusioned as she received her new paychecks. Her monthly salary of 200 U.S. dollars was not enough to support herself. Even Venezuela was paying more than 2,000 dollars per month for dentists with their doctorate. She felt like a modern-day slave. In this manner, the U.S. had won over Cuban talent since the Revolution.

Doctors were not the only ones to seek a better life in America. A human exodus, tens of thousands of Cubans embarked on the perilous journey between Cuba and the U.S. every year. The water between Miami and Havana is rough. There have been waves, sometimes high, other times not so treacherous. Strong winds sank fragile boats. Some of the passengers swam to the shore and were rescued. Some never made it. The wave of Cuban migrations is driven by hopelessness and fear. For those who did make it, Miami was a kind of halfway house or way station. Immigrants unpacked their baggage here, took a deep breath, and headed to other parts of the country.

Havana and Miami are close, but life in the two countries is nothing alike. In Havana, rain falls in spurts, then clears to double rainbows shimmering on the horizon. Fried pork flanks sizzle in fat inside open windows. People dance and sing on the street. They were poor but happy. They only care about today; tomorrow is one day too far. Havana is a noisy city.

An ocean away, Miami boasts of its shiny steel towers along Brickell Avenue. Miami is a much quieter city. It is as hot and humid as Havana, but people feel much more comfortable here because every building has a good air conditioning system. As soon as we arrived in Miami, we can feel the huge difference between the two cities.

My father made some phone calls, and one of his business partners came to the port to pick us up. His name is Jose Hernandez and looked about the same age as my dad. He praised our adventure, gave us a brief update on the Cuban situation and took us to a rental home. It was much smaller than our house in Havana but luxurious for a refugee family. It has two bedrooms, a modest living room, a decent kitchen, two showers. I was the first to jump into bed and soon fell asleep.

My parents were busy looking over every corner of the house. When my mom opened the refrigerator, she was surprised to find milk, some meat, and other food stuffs. My parents rushed to the market to purchase clothing, shoes, and other necessities. That night we had a very nice dinner in another country. I didn't understand what the circumstance was. I vaguely thought we were on vacation.

My family went through the long immigration process as refugees. My father's friend helped us with all the necessary steps. Jose was born and raised in Miami and had solid connections. At that time, the U.S. government was very friendly to the Cuban refugees. One day, we were summoned in front of an immigration official. He seemed quite surprised to hear my parent's perfect English. After reviewing all the application forms, he said to us, "Welcome to the U.S. We need people like you. Make this country your home." And extended his hands to us. We were legally accepted as residents of this great country,

My father soon found a job at a shipping company in Miami. Miami is the window to Latin America. It is the largest southern port in the country, and cargo trade was brisk. My mom couldn't go to work right away because she had to take care of me. When I turned three years old, she sent me to a nursery and started to work as a saleswoman in a large department store. Soon she was promoted to the assistant manager and worked longer hours. As our family income grew, we moved to a better neighborhood where non-Hispanics were the majority.

I enrolled in a private Catholic school. An after-school program picked me up from the school, and I waited for my mom. My dad came home late from work. We had lived in Miami for five years before my parents felt the need to move to North. Miami was a beautiful, vibrant city, but the climate was very similar to Havana. They wanted to live close to New York. I was seven years old when we packed again and headed to Connecticut. Our new home was close to Westchester and only about 40 minutes by train from Manhattan. This was the dream place my parents wanted to settle in for the rest of their lives.

At a Crossroad

Seoul, Korea, 1973
Young Min

My mother's nagging continued. I was sick of her unreasonable demand to become a pastor. I was a voracious reader. There were novels on my desk, classics and modern, but no Bible. Whenever I heard my mother's footstep, I pretended to read Bible. It was the least interesting book I could think of. I liked western stories more than oriental ones. My imagination traveled to England, Germany, France, Spain, and the United States. China and India were not of any interest. I read books translated in Korean because my English was not good enough then. I knew those translations might not be accurate, but I had no choice. I was hungry for story books.

I didn't neglect my studies. I didn't make the top 5 percent, but always stayed in the best ten percent. My average test score fell between 85-90, and my teachers said I could apply for one of the top-tier colleges in Korea. I excelled in languages; I never missed an A in English since middle school. I was well read in Korean literature and German too. At the time, we were required to choose one foreign language. I chose German, but didn't study hard and forgot most of it after graduation. And I liked history, geography, and social studies. I wasn't particularly good in mathematics, chemistry or physics. My school advisor suggested I should pursue a study in humanities in college.

The third year in high school is one of the most difficult times for us in Korea. Students are under enormous pressure, stayed longer at school, went to private tutors, and constantly consulted with advisers to choose the right college. In Korea, which college one graduates from is one of the most critical factors of success. All high school third graders took the standardized test given by the government, and the score was one of the most important elements of acceptance. My combined score was good enough to make so-called "good colleges." My mother had different thoughts about my college education. She blatantly insisted I should study theology to become a pastor. One night we had a heated argument after dinner. I said, "I don't want to go to a theology school. Mom, you go, why do you push me?" "Young Min, you shouldn't be rude to your mom. Do you know who had saved your life twice? God saved you. You should study His words to pay Him back. That's God's wish, more than my wish." My sister protested "What are you talking about, mom? Why do you believe God saved Young Min's life? Doctors saved him, not God. You believe in ghosts. You are not a rational person, poisoned by misguided faith. Don't try to insert your faith into Young Min's brain. That's his choice. You can't push him."

My father didn't join the argument at first, he was standing between mom and us. He was an elder, but he wasn't very religious. He didn't believe earnestly that I should study theology and practice ministry. But he didn't want to dishearten his wife.

He said," I know you'd like to be a writer or college professor. Look, some of the greatest modern writers are pastors. They are respected because first; they have a good number of followers. Second, they studied philosophy, psychology, literature and communications. That made them write well and become persuasive. Memorizing Bible and learning theology alone cannot make them good pastors. This is my suggestion. Instead of going to the Presbyterian or Methodist Theology School why don't you go to Yonsei University to study theology and other areas of your interest? It is one of the top colleges as you know. After graduation, you can become a pastor if you like to be or you can take the writer's path."

It sounded reasonable to me. It was a Christian college founded by American missionaries over one hundred years ago.

My mother jumped in again," You are capable of

becoming a good minister. You are sincere, intelligent, and you speak well. Most importantly, you have His calling. God needs a young man like you for His work."

My sister disputed, "Mom, how do you know he got God's calling? He didn't say that, did you Young Min? Young Min is your son, but he is not your property. He is his own. Mom, don't push him. That's his life, not yours. You will greatly regret if something goes wrong in the future. Mom, don't go meddling him. Let him make his own decision."

Mom started to cry. My father tried to console her, but couldn't control her explosive emotion. My sister and I retired to our room. I couldn't sleep that night. I toured Yonsei University the following week. I didn't like the idea of studying theology, but I liked the campus and the environment. And I had choices. They had a wide range of curriculum. I knew I had to study Christianity, but I could study literature too.

I announced to my family, 'Yes, I will apply for the school."

My mom looked happy. My father seemed relieved. My sister was very unhappy. She blamed my mom for my choosing theology school. She shut her door and screamed, "Mom, you pushed him to study the God damned theology. You will ruin his life." Mother was astonished but didn't pick a fight with her only daughter. She thought she won the battle and believed God was pleased.

The theology class was small, about half the size of the popular department such as business, English, political science, and communications. The class was made up of two groups of people: those from very religious families and not-so-smart students. So-called the cut-line for accepted students in Theology school was close to the bottom.

To my surprise, my score on the entrance exam was the highest in my class. My parents were happy, but I wasn't pleased. I knew I would not be a good student. It gave me an additional burden. The first year was especially hard for me. I was doubly embarrassed. My fellow students were all ardent Christians, and I was not able to recite popular verses of Bible. They prayed constantly and everywhere, on every occasion. Of course, they prayed before each meal, early in the morning, before going to bed, but it didn't stop there. They always dropped their heads, prayed in a low voice and said "Amen." Amen, Amen, too much Amen, I was sick of them. (I shouldn't say this to my mom. She will be extremely upset because she believed we should pray more than five times a day and say Amen).

To my surprise, there were three female students. I considered asking them questions like, "Do you want to be a woman pastor? I've never heard of it here in Korea." "Is your mom a crazy Christian like my mom?" "Do you want to marry a pastor?" I guessed it was not a bad idea studying theology because of a pastor's wife associated with women congregations all the time. I didn't ask these questions to them. We will find out as time passes.

Smoking and drinking were not allowed on campus, but it seemed like everyone ignored those regulations. The smoking ban was no problem for me because I never started smoking. Drinking was different. Even though I didn't drink much, I enjoyed having drinks with my buddies and talking about books we had read.

Before long, I was one of the worst students in my class. The curriculum was designed to deepen students' interest in ministry and Biblical studies and strengthen our understanding of Christianity. The whole program was tailor-made to introduce us to the key figures, places, events, and themes of the Old and New Testaments. I was not interested in these core courses with the exception of church history. My classmates were puzzled. I performed best on the acceptance exam, but one of the worst in the class. The curriculum couldn't draw my interest. I liked other courses which I took outside theology department. I studied American literature, communications, English, and psychology. I made a few friends in those classes. I barely maintained my credits in core studies, but I got all A's in selective courses.

When my parents asked me how I was doing, I said, "I am not doing well, but not failing either." The last thing I wanted was to be kicked out of the class. It would hurt my pride awfully as well as my parent's confidence in me.

My sister was still rebellious in my favor and tried to protect me from mom's relentless attacks on me. My sister was studying voice at Ehwa Woman's University which was in walking distance from my school. She understood her brother's complicated character and what I had wished to be. She was dating a business major defying her mother's wish. He was not religious at all, didn't go to church even on Christmas or Easter. That didn't bother my sister. She was in love with him, and she was sure he could help her career as a singer.

When our mother found out her daughter had a non-Christian boyfriend, she was visibly disappointed. "Why do you date a non-believer? There are hundreds of good Christian men in the neighborhood. My sister shot back without hesitation, "Mom, it's none of your business. I will never ask your support once I graduate. Mom, don't you believe you are living behind the times? Please change your attitude. You cannot force us anymore. Leave Young Min alone. He is unwillingly studying theology. You can go to church ten times a day, even sleep there, but don't tell us what to do. The more you push, the more we will be defiant. Mom, please stop interfering with our lives."

My mom lost her words and went pathetically silent. She turned her back and cried, but my sister didn't care. She was a real fighter. She had fought not only for her but also for me. My sister intentionally brought her boyfriend home, locked her door and spent time together. She was no longer mom's daughter.

At the end of my first year, I received the report card. English-A, communications-A, church history-A, psychology-A, New Testament-D, Old Testament-D, counseling B. My average was okay, but as a theology major, D for old and new testament study was fatal. I anticipated them to be worse than D because I didn't read Bible at all. I guessed most other students got A's for Bible study.

I considered giving up theology and transferring to an English major. I met a chairman in the English Department seeking the possibility of moving. He reviewed my record and said, "It's okay with me. Your English is excellent. However, you need to get permission from your department chair. As you may know, the English department is highly competitive and has a narrow opening."

I couldn't figure out how to approach my chairman in the theology department. The next day I knocked on the chairman's door. He welcomed me and listened to my plea patiently. When I had finished, he seemed much perplexed and said, "You are a brilliant student. You were the number one placed in our department. Unfortunately, your grade in Bible study is unacceptable. Bible study is the heart of theology school. I guess you lost interest for whatever reason. Rekindle your passion for Bible. Please read Bible every day. That's the bread and butter of Christianity."

I said in an unconvincing voice, "Mr. Chairman, can you allow me to transfer to the English department? I think I can do better in that study." He didn't answer right away. "It's too early. You and I should try harder. Many students didn't do well in the first year. Clear up your head and take a fresh start. Theology study is like a marathon. Not doing well now doesn't mean you cannot become a good pastor or a scholar."

I kept quiet for a moment and said, "Mr. Chairman, I might well be a good scholar, but not a good pastor. I don't believe in some parts of.... the Bible."

The chairman looked surprised, "What? You don't believe the Bible? That's why you got D's. What part of the Bible don't you believe?" He stared me in indignity.

I stammered. He got serious and demanded my answer. I struggled to elaborate. At the very moment, someone called him, and he had to leave his office hurriedly. I was sweating, and I took a sigh of relief.

After a few days, one of the three female theology students, Won Oak, approached me after school.

"Young Min, happy birthday!" She said, "Do you have time? Let's celebrate your 20th birthday. I won't hold you long."

I was surprised. I considered her the best of the three female classmates. She was a smart, charming, and caring woman. I had heard she worked in the theology department as an assistant after school.

"How did you know today's my birthday? Even I forget sometimes. I am not in the mood, but I cannot refuse your request. You are the only theology student who has shown interest in me, and somehow I have favorable feelings for you."

Soon we were sitting together at a café. She ordered a coffee and asked me what I wanted. "Can I have a glass of white wine?"

"Wine? Theology students shouldn't drink at school. We are outside of campus, but people know us." After some hesitation, "Okay, I will cover for you. Young Min, you need my protection. You are like a baby, vulnerable, fragile, wayward, and unpredictable. I am a watch-woman. I should keep an eye on you. You are brilliant, but you wander too much, looking too far ahead and daydreaming. I am not an attractive girl, but you need me. I will stand by you and when you astray I will pull you back."

I was astonished to hear her say that. "Won Oak, what made you say that to me? How much do you know me? Sounds like you know me more than my mom or my sister." I said. "That's exactly right. I have watched you for a whole year and found out your strengths as well as your weaknesses. I admire your intelligence, your love for literature, but I also have come to believe that you are dangerously sensitive. I am sure you need me, and I am happy to stay close to you." Won Oak continued.

I responded, "You talk like my guardian or girlfriend without my consent. Ask yourself if you are sane. I think you are not yourself tonight."

"I know exactly about what I am talking. You were No. 1, and I was the No. 2 student when we started. Now you have almost failed Bible study and are trying to move to another department. I know you met the chairman. He will never allow you to transfer. He believes we need a brain like you. I am not particularly interested in Bible study either, but I tried. I got a B+. It's not very good, but it is acceptable. I know what you got. You got a D. The Bible professor said you didn't read Bible at all. You deserve an F, but he gave you D to save you. They don't want to see you kicked out from the theology school. I will teach you, and we will upgrade your test score. Do you understand Young Min? You can't do anything without me. You cannot run away from me. You are fastened to me."

I almost lost my words, but insisted, "I want to be kicked out, then I can move to the English department." Won Oak retorted," You think you are smart, but you are a fool. Nobody accepts a failed student to its department. Just be quiet and do what I tell you. O.K.? Let's get up. Your mother is waiting for you. You will have a hard time again with your mom tonight, be prepared. Don't fight her. Listen to what she says." She paid for the drink and shook my hands. I felt her hands warm and soft. She was right.

As soon as I got home, my mother called me in her frustrated voice. "Young Min, the pastor of our church called me. What do you have in your mind now? I can't understand at all. Why are you trying to give up theology and moving to another study? Why do you go the other direction every time? The dean and our pastor are friends of more than 40 years. They both defected from communist North Korea and studied theology at the same school. Our pastor recommended you to the dean. Of course, you were good enough to get accepted, but his letter of recommendation helped you. Your dean called our minister about your attempt to transfer. Please don't hurt me, my son. You have a potential to become a great preacher. You speak well; you have a strong voice, and you are good-looking which is important in the new age. You will be a prominent TV evangelist. That's my dream. I can happily close my eyes to the world when you make it."

I was thinking about what Won Oak said about an

hour ago. She must have known what was coming.

My mother continued," It's okay to be a late bloomer. Flowers blossom early go first. Just stay on track. Don't desert. By the way, your father is complaining dizziness and chest pain lately. I told him to visit a doctor, but he is not listening. If he knows your problem, he will be upset, and it makes his health worse. Pray for him and be a good son. Please."

I couldn't say much after hearing about my father's health issue. I hurriedly left the living room. I didn't eat dinner. It wasn't a hunger strike; I just didn't have an appetite. I wanted to see Won Oak, but I didn't call her.

I met Won Oak two weeks after we had had our first discussion. I asked her, "Why are you trying to help me? Are you happy studying theology?"

She responded "I expected you to raise that question. My parents are Christians. My dad is an elder, and my mom is a deacon. I believe it's similar with your parents. My parents don't have a son if they did they would push him to study theology just like your parents. Our parents' generation is crazy about Christianity. It's kind of a blind faith. I considered studying nursing and go to the United States. My mom had different thoughts. A nurse can take care of a few patients at a time, but a pastor's wife can do a lot more. I liked church. I didn't like to read Bible, but I like choir, church people, and the environment. I agreed with my mom and applied for theology class. You know what, I don't like the courses that much so far, but never neglect my studies like you have. Now I have a very important task: help you finish college."

I said, "Why would you do that? I am not your brother and wasn't one of your friends until a few weeks ago. You have nothing to do with me."

She replied, "Really? Somehow I feel saving you is my calling from God. I am the right person to save you because I know you. We are classmates. More importantly, I am fond of you. You cannot get rid of me. I am very determined. We go together towards the same destination. Okay?"

I was speechless. I was a bit scared. I gazed her face carefully and said, "Do you really like me? I don't have a strong personality like you. I am deeply emotional and tender-minded. I feared no woman would like me."

She said, "Not this woman. I like you because you are honest, delicate, sincere and thoughtful. You are a complicated but pure man. You are my man."

"I guess you know me quite well. What compelled you to study me?" I had to ask her.

She said without a pause. "I told you. You have a unique personality, and that drew my attention. Don't worry; you are the only guy I care about. Other boys are all parrots, oh, Jesus Christ! Jesus Christ! Holy Spirit! Holy Spirit! Amen, Amen! Their mouth is like a machine. You are different. You never say something you don't mean. You are responsible for your words. You are an alchemist of language. That's one of the reasons I like you."

I asked, "what are other reasons?"

She responded, "I just like you. That's the reason. You are fortunate to have me." She approached me closely and enticed my kiss. I held her hands and studied her carefully. She looked innocent, and sincere. She was not a strikingly pretty woman but had an air of plain beauty. I pulled her and kissed her. It seemed she waited for my initiative. Her face was shining under the warm sky. We came across in classes often but never gazed intently. It was a secret partnership of love. Because of her love I studied Bible and didn't receive another F or D. I got C and B, it wasn't great but much better than failure. Won Oak bought me dinner and congratulated me. I received A's in other subjects.

I was still an outcast in theology class. Many students looked at me weirdly, but I didn't care. As long as she didn't complain, I was okay. I felt lucky to have her. She was my savior. The dean of theology school didn't call my pastor again, and my mom stopped bothering me. My father's health deteriorated. He had breathing problems and couldn't sleep at night. We took him to a hospital, and he was diagnosed with early stage lung cancer. He had smoked most of his adult life. The blackened image of his lung proved it. It was a shock to our family. His CAT scan showed his right lung was infected. The doctor believed he could remove it. The doctor said my father might not need chemotherapy. My mother still worried greatly because her brother had the same diagnosis several years ago and had surgery. He was close to seventy then. He was okay immediately after surgery, but a blood clot blocked his stomach, and he died two days later. My father's situation was very similar to that.

We got a second opinion from a different doctor, but no one assured us he would be fine. They say every case is different and nothing is guaranteed. After serious discussions, he agreed to have the surgery. My mother's deep concern appeared as a reality. My father looked fine for two days, but then developed a clot which blocked his circulation. My mother, sister, and I kept vigil around the clock and greeted visitors. My relatives brought soup and ginseng teas constantly. His condition did not improve. That was a bad sign. When I looked at him on the fourth day, he looked like a dead man. He couldn't recognize people and eventually fell unconscious. Doctors performed another surgery in a hurry but were unable to save his life. My father passed away in the hospital. My mother cried and regretted making him have the surgery. If he didn't take surgery, he could extend his life a few more years.

His funeral was held at the church. Most of his close friends, as well as the congregation, came to his wake to pay tribute. My father was buried on a winter day. It was cold and very windy. We put dirt on his coffin and sobbed. He was 60; he deserved a much longer life. It was a devastating loss for our family. He escaped communism and built his small business all to support his children's education. My mother believed he was accepted by God. Won Oak came to the service, threw a flower on my father's coffin, and hugged me. My sister later asked me who she was. I said she was my best friend from class.

My father's sudden departure changed the whole dynamic of our family. My sister and I noticed mom was often crying in front of my dad's picture. She wasn't as vigorous as before and didn't eat. She occasionally visited dad's grave without telling us. My parent's business was in trouble too. My mother couldn't manage it because everything was depended on dad's long business experience, connections, and his business acumen. After his passing, everybody turned their back. It was awfully hard to maintain a prosperous business. Our family income continued to shrink and mom worried about our college tuition. She said the worst scenario was to sell our house.

My sister changed her approach too. She was no longer defiant to mom. She found a part-time job to alleviate the family's financial burden and helped with mother's domestic work. She didn't bring her boyfriend home anymore. She was once again our mother's daughter. I started to work as a student librarian and applied for scholarships. My theology grade was bad, but the department chair managed to find a decent scholarship to make up our lost income. My sister and I did not have the luxury to hang around. We had to support ourselves. We had feared for our future. There was no simple answer for these complex issues. We all had to rely on one another and support our family. We had to survive. We couldn't throw in the towel. It was no time to fight each other, and we realized that this support was what my father had wished for so earnestly.

I Dreamed of Color

New Haven, Connecticut
Elena Reynolds

Florida is not Connecticut, and Miami is not Hartford. My parents escaped Cuba to live like Americans, not like Cubans. Florida is a micro-copy of the United States. There are not many genuine Floridians: most of its residents moved there from other states, mostly from the cold Midwest and the east coast. Unlike most of Florida, Miami is not American. It's much more like a Latin American city. 77 percent of Miami's population is Hispanic, half of which are from Cuba. About 70 percent speak Spanish at home, while only 12 percent speaks only English. Miami-Dade County is the home of many Cuban immigrants and an enclave of the huge Latino population. Connecticut is different. It is a central part of New England and grouped with New York and New Jersey as the *Tri-State area*.

Most of the western and southern counties, Greenwich, Stamford, New Canaan, are strongly associated with New York City. My parents wanted to live in a quiet, true American city, not another Havana. They moved near Hartford to live like European-Americans, not Latino-Americans. More than 75 percent of the Connecticut population is white, with Latinos composing less than 5 percent of the population at that time. My parents also wanted to enjoy the culture of New York City. Manhattan is about 50 minutes away by train. My father started to work for an insurance company as a certified financial planner and was promoted to a managerial position quickly. My mom worked for a big department store as a sales manager. She had worked the same position in Miami. We lived in West Port, about a 40 – minute drive from Hartford and New York. I came to Connecticut at the age of seven.

My mother used to say that I was a wild girl. She tried to tame me. She always told me to stay home and read books, but I loved to sneak out and wander around. We lived one mile away from the Long Island Sound, within biking distance. I liked the sea just as much as I enjoyed the mountains. My friend Abby and I biked to the beach. We picked up pebbles, chased ducks, and watched the changing colors of the sea. My father told me the sea could be used as a clock, just like the sun. We could guess the time from the tide of the ocean. When it got dark, the sea told us it was time to go home. Abby and I biked home hurriedly before our parents got home. My mom was always worried about my safety. We lived in a good neighborhood, but in her mind, anything could happen. From my childhood, I loved nature. Everything was curious to me. Every tree, every blade of grass, every stone was different. There was a small pond near my home. I picked up pebbles and studied them carefully. Each is unique. No two stones were the same. I listened to birds singing. Each bird had its distinctive voice. I was fascinated by the wonder of nature.

Most of the kids in the neighborhood were afraid of the foul weather, but not me. I loved every aspect of weather – shine, rain, snow, even severe storms. Each condition creates a different image, and I tried to paint what each one meant to me. After we had moved from Miami, my mom sent me to all kinds of classes – piano lessons, art classes, dancing and even martial arts. I was only interested in the creation of arts.

My mom sent me to a good art institute when I was ten years old. I excelled. When my mom picked me up at school, she always looked at my drawing in the hallway. She was very proud of my work and it clearly made her happy. My art teacher told her that I was a great prospect. My mom bought me all the tools I needed.

When I was in high school, I visited museums in NYC on every last Saturday of the month. The bad weather couldn't stop me. Some days the weather couldn't make up its mind: it rained in the morning, cleared in the afternoon, and snowed in the evening. As long as the metro train was running, it didn't really bother me. I took the train at West Port and got off at Grand Central Terminal. Then, I took the subway to MOMA, the Metropolitan Museum of Arts, and stayed there all day. I purchased an annual ticket for students. I especially liked painting. As a high school student, I didn't know much about art history or all of the different genre. I relied on audio guides and plaque explanations, but couldn't comprehend the more complex works.

I came across a throng of foreign tourist groups every day. They stayed a short period of time, looked at the masterpieces, took pictures, and abruptly disappeared. There were some serious artists. I met some of them and even had lunch together, making sure to ask as many questions as I could think of. This line of communication was an enormous help in grasping the complexity of creating true pieces of art. I discovered some of the most important elements of painting: light and color. I was thrilled to realize this and hoped it would help me improve my artwork. Even with their help, I could not quite understand paintings from different times – the Classical, the Hellenistic age, Romans and Contemporary art remained a mystery. To me, the gallery was a meeting place for art lovers, and I enjoyed the environment, dreaming of becoming an artist. I knew it was difficult, but it was my dream. I wouldn't give up easily.

I was a dreamer. I dreamed mostly at the wee hours. I had the same kind of dream over and over again. When I was happy, I dreamed about a handsome boy. Sometimes he kissed me. When I was in emotional trouble, I was encircled in weird and horrifying dreams. I was kept in a cell, trying to escape and screaming for help. After I had found the magic of light and color of paintings, I dreamed of color. Dreaming of color was an individual thing. I didn't need a companion. I stayed home or went out to the beach alone. The world was full of colors, and they were constantly changing its landscape. I became a sleepyhead. I could nap anywhere with ease. My mom found me dozing on a bench in the backyard. The wonder of color had opened my eyes. I could notice that all the trees, houses, lakes, and birds looked different. Each had their distinguished color. In cold winter months, I was dreaming of snow and ice, how they transformed other objects. In the hottest months, I dreamed of green. I carried those colors with me and kept them in my memory bank. In the spring, I dreamed of flowers.

My severe allergies kept me indoor, but I couldn't

stay inside long. I ventured out, discovering how the grass and trees added to the color of the world. Oh, I loved autumn leaves. Falling leaves told their life stories, their sprouting in the spring, vigorous growth during the summer, finally the time came to part from their mother. Changing color and falling represented the final chapter of their short lives, but they always said, "We are going, but not forever. We are coming back."

I often used planks of wood as my canvasses. I used a knife and created my image in slices. I learned much about dyes from trees. The color of the water was more dynamic than that of plants. The wind changed its colors. When the sky was blue, the water was blue. Gray sky made the bay gray. When winds blew, waves started a wild dance and changed the water contour and color. The seagulls and gliding white swans added dimension to the surface of the water.

I liked to walk the nature trail. The trail was narrow and stretched along the bay. It took me 80 minutes to complete the trail and return home. Some people jogged, some biked, and the elderly strolled with their dogs. Reeds were tall in the summer, became shorter in the late autumn, and fell in the winter. There were three storm shelters along the trail. I always stopped there to watch the bay before walking on. I occasionally visited state parks and the distant Long Island Sound on the Connecticut side. Every park had its character and secret. Every curve of water contained a different landscape and color. It amazed me. The desire to travel was in my blood. As a young girl, I couldn't travel far, but in my dreams, I traveled distant unfamiliar territory. To me, traveling was to chase the light and color, experience the primitive cultures, walk the unspoiled land, and meet the unsophisticated people. I was longing for unadulterated nature and the people in it. Nature doesn't lie. No need. Nature just shows what it is. No disguise, always revealing its true face. I wanted people as pure as nature. I dreamed of meeting such a man someday.

My aspiration as an artist didn't flourish as brilliantly as I had wished. I was one of the best artists in my high school, and all of my school friends admired me, but I didn't win the County High School Art Contest. I advanced to the final stage, but I failed to win the exhibit spot. I was deeply disappointed and cried. My art teacher soothed my pain.

She said, "You might have tried too hard. You tried to make it too cute. Too many elements are in your artwork, which made it hard to communicate. It would be better to make it simple. You're obsessed with light and color, and that diminishes other features. Don't worry you will make it next time. Nothing comes easy, especially in the art world. Ninety–nine percent of people fail, only one of the hundred wins. Let's start fresh." Despite my art teacher's encouragement, I lost confidence in myself.

At the end of my time in high school, I had a difficult choice to make — go to an art school or take a more professional course. My dad said, "Elena, I am an insurance guy. Everybody needs insurance: life insurance, flood insurance, fire insurance. Even good athletes insure for their unseen injuries. We need a Plan B. There is no guarantee that you will be a good artist. Of course, we want you to be, and we will support you all the way, but you never know what's coming. As you know, the art world is super competitive. If you don't succeed, you will starve. Let's have a backup plan. Why don't you apply for English and Art jointly? The last thing I want is for you to get out of the college and not find a job. We will feed you, but you will not be happy."

My parents, my counselor, and I discussed my future. The persistent question was, "Am I exceptional?" One day I considered myself excellent, the next day, I was nothing. I decided to take the safe path, to buy an insurance policy as my father suggested. I submitted my application for English-Art combined study at the University of Connecticut in Hartford. I felt both bitter and relieved. On that night, I didn't have a nightmare. I slept like a rock.

Welcome to U Conn. I was excited to be a college student. I lived within a bus ride, but I chose to live in the dorm like the other students. I liked to live like a fish, swimming the ocean without interference. I didn't want to be caught by a fisherman. Freedom was the lifeline for my art and literature. I divided my time between English, Arts, and writing. I spent a chunk of my extra hours on my painting.

To my disappointment, my art career didn't continue to bloom. It was stuck somewhere between mediocre and quite good. That was not sufficient to reach the top level. My artwork was declined by prestigious galleries. I was furious with myself. I kept asking myself, "Am I a gifted painter or do I just wish to be one?" I looked myself in the mirror. I didn't look like a genuine artist. I was a daydreamer. One day I was wandering through a museum in New York. I watched the photo pieces carefully and was suddenly drawn in. Photography was a new discovery. I instantly began to imagine myself as a photographer – carrying a set of heavy cameras and traveling the world looking for best images. Unlike painting, pictures are a reflection of existing images. I didn't have to create images on canvas from scratch. Instead, I could locate the best scene and grasp it with my camera. I began looking at historical pictures and artistic photo images in the museum. I was happy to have another dream.

Photograph, Photograph, Photograph! I was rejuvenated. My eyes were wide open, and my heart was pounding with excitement. I was now obsessed with the photo image. I was a fish which had found the water again. I wanted to swim the Atlantic Ocean like fish. No one could stop me. My parents looked at me with wary eyes. They knew I was wild again. I set up a darkroom in the basement. The camera lens was my second set of eyes, much bigger and more accurate than my own. I was the girl on the train again.

I registered for a photography class at the Metropolitan Museum of Arts. It was open to all levels. It was more of a creative rather than technical class. It was a relatively small class of twelve students, seven women, and five men. They were all ages and came from all over – Manhattan, Queens, Brooklyn, and Connecticut like me. We met every Saturday for three months. It was focused on the differences among looking, observing, and seeing.

After each class, I wandered the museums, concentrating on photographic works. I saw many different kinds of photos – historical, industrial, wild animals, urban life, scenery, and many others aspects of life. The instructor encouraged us to get out and take one picture every single day, then post that online to invite comments. It was a fantastic way to improve our shooting skill. He advised us on the next steps to developing shooting technics, creating images, and storing them. I started to recreate significant moments of my life: the image of a baby, childhood, high school graduation, going off to college.

The next stage was to find one location where I enjoyed shooting the landscape and then visiting that location over and over. I chose West Port Marina. I photographed the same location in different weather conditions, different light, using new creative ideas. I also took pictures of the homeless. Whenever a poor person asked me for money, I made a deal: Pay two dollars and pose for a few shots. I felt a bit uneasy with the trade, but they consented. I created a series of homeless images to exhibit in the future. Next, I walked all over the city to take pictures of architecture. I went shooting the landmark buildings in New York City at different times of the day, in different weather, and different seasons.

I was particularly interested in photojournalism. Every day I saw spectacular photos on the newspaper and TV. I saw beauty as well as danger. The photographers gave everything they had for this brave shooting. Whenever I watched historical photos, I felt awe. I knew some of them paid the ultimate price to record one chapter of world history. I didn't think myself a coward, but I was not brave enough to jump into the field. I was a fearless girl to my parents, but still, I was a girl, tender-minded, highly emotional, longing for love.

Plan A and Plan B reversed in in the final year of college. I poured my energy into photography, but my chances steadily slipped away. Again, I was quite good, but not exceptionally talented. My photo work was not accepted by exhibitors, and I became depressed. I had to consider becoming an English teacher upon graduation seriously. I had to take more education courses to get the teaching license. Finally, I had no choice. I neglected art to prepare for my teaching career.

At age 24, I became a teacher after one year of internship. I started to teach English in a black neighborhood in Bridgeport. Beginning a teaching job in the inner city was good and bad. It was good because I felt less pressure from teaching and bad because I had to deal with tough, unruly students. My colleagues warned me to be careful and not get too aggressive. I was advised to call campus security immediately if anything happened. As time passed, I felt less danger. I began to embrace the students and earned their respect. I was not a chicken by any means.

I moved out of my parents' home and rented a decent apartment in New Haven. Once I got settled, I had a strong desire to pursue writing. I started to read a variety of subjects. My English professor once told us repeatedly that, "Writing comes from reading. If you don't read, you cannot write." I joined two book clubs, one in my community and the other at the public library. Most of the book club members were retirees, but there were a few young people my age. Surprisingly most of the book-lovers were women. Only a few men came to discuss what they had read. I had to read two novels a month for book clubs, which consumed a big portion of my available time. The book talk broadened my horizons and awoke an interest in literature.

Still, art was my secret love. I couldn't get away from it. I attended art shows, and photo exhibits often in Connecticut and NYC. One day I went to a photo exhibition in Hartford. It was a big show, and thousands of pictures were displayed. When I was strolling around the hall, I came across a tall young man. He looked familiar and seemed to recognize me. He said, "I think I met you. You and I took the photography class at Met. Museum. Didn't we?"

I replied, "I guess you are right. When was it? It's been a while. Have you kept shooting? I've almost given up."

He paused a moment and said, "It's my hobby. I couldn't make money as a photographer. I still shoot sometimes, but not seriously."

We continued our conversation over coffee. That encounter had changed my fate. I was crossing a threshold into romantic life.

Chapter 4

She Snatched Me

1982, Westchester
Young Min Park

It was raining. It was cold. It was dark. It was meant to be a happy day, but I was not excited at all. Won Oak and I were in a small restaurant on the outskirts of Seoul. We were there to celebrate our graduation as well as my ordination as pastor and her confirmation as a missionary. My mother was happy.

She said, "Young Min, you made it. It was a bumpy road, but you've overcome all hurdles. It opens a new life for you. Now you have to work for His world. Congratulations my son. I am very proud of you. You will be a great minister."

I answered mom's wish with deep silence. I could not say too much because I maintained a complicated, uncertain relationship with her. My sister seemed to have mixed emotions. She was relieved because my struggle was finally over but worried about my future. She knew I didn't really want to be a pastor, and that our mom pushed me.

My sister extended her arms to hug me and said in a low voice, "Young Min, don't take it too seriously. Take it easy. Spend time with Won Oak." My sister pulled mom by her sleeve and went home. After Won Oak had said her goodbyes to her parents and friends, we took the subway and headed to our safe haven – a small café in the quiet neighborhood near our school.

"Congratulations pastor park! Or 'baby pastor.' Won Oak teased me.

I smiled shyly and said, "Stop calling me a pastor. You deserve to be called a missionary. Not me. I am not there yet."

She answered, "Whether you like it or not, some congregants will call you pastor. Especially women. They like a novice pastor."

I said, "I can't stop it then. By the way, what are you going to do now? You need a job. My mother found me an internship in a small church in Inchon. I will start soon. I'll stay at the caretaker's quarter with a deacon. I will get a minimum salary. I want to study abroad next year, hopefully in the United States."

She seemed surprised, "Going to study in the U.S.? Who's going to support you? What do you want to study?" "I already got permission from my mom." I replied, "We will sell the business, and she will support me. My sister agreed. Maybe she is happy to get rid of me. I've been her headache for so long. I don't want to study this boring theology anymore. I need to broaden my horizons studying other subjects like literature, communications, sociology, and history. I want to be an intelligent, renowned preacher if I decided to be a pastor."

Won Oak said, "How about me? Will you abandon me? I have been loyal to you. I saved your theology study.

You cannot leave me behind. I will go to the U.S. with you. Don't underestimate my resolve. I am a stubborn girl. I will hold your sleeve."

She looked so serious that I didn't know how to respond. Won Oak quickly added, "My family can send me to the U.S. You need my support. You cannot survive without me. You are smart, but not street smart. You're also unstable. Without me, you can't do anything. I am coming with you. Okay? We are in the same boat. Remember what I told you when you were struggling? We are partners. We signed a verbal agreement. Our kiss sealed the deal."

We drank Korean wine, and we got drunk. She held my staggering body and pushed me to a cab. She kissed me repeatedly in the dark corner near my house. I knew at that moment that she could save me from danger. She snatched me. She was a strong woman, physically and mentally.

Faith

Inchon, South Korea
Young Min Park

Faith is to believe what we do not see; and the reward of faith Is to see what we believe. – Saint Augustine

The Inchon Church was a medium sized urban church. The service started at 11 am, and the majority of the congregation were young. The city's big churches provided three services on Sunday. Rev. Chung, Sung Jae started this church fifteen years ago from scratch and the church had grown steadily. He graduated from Yonsei Theology

College and the dean of the school had recommended me as an assistant pastor. I considered myself not a pastor, but rather an intern. I didn't have the slightest idea how to run a church and deal with diverse parishioners.

The Sunday after Christmas, the principal pastor called in sick and told me to deliver the sermon. After the busy holidays, the parishioners were very quiet, some fell asleep and snored, others dropped their heads and dozed. Even the children were still. It was a time of rest from the season's whirl, and everybody was inclined to sit back and relax. I was not in the mood to give my first sermon, but I had no other option. Won Oak was sitting in the middle pew listening to my inaugural preaching attentively. I prepared a 20-minute sermon. I needed to wake them up. I started my speech in a measured firm voice. I knew how to choose the right words to describe the right circumstances and draw attention. I noticed people shake off their sleep, look around, and try to pick up some words. I gave specific examples in the middle part of the sermon and closed the speech with this –

"Congregants, believe in the presence of God. God is everywhere, in Heaven, here on earth, in the woods, in the water, and of course in your minds. God listens to what we say, sees what we are doing, and oversees our every single action. God guides our lives. God awakens us when we fall asleep. The Lord is the Savior, the Light, and Jesus is God's own Son. As Mary rocks her baby boy, she's filled with joy. Her heart is filled with a mother's glow, and she longs to keep him safe. Then, she sees him on a cross. She feels his pain and feels our loss. She knows his life must come to this. She sheds a tear and gives him a kiss. Jesus life won't be an easy one. His destiny as God's own Son is a burden. Parishioners, Christmas is not over. Every day is Christmas because

we keep His birth, His death and His resurrection in mind every day. Today, tomorrow, and forever. Amen."

When my sermon was over people gave their ardent approval. I could see from their facial expressions and smiles that they accepted my sermon wholeheartedly. Won Oak looked extremely satisfied. She stood by me as we greeted the congregation. I passed my first test as a pastor. The contents of my speech might not be very good, but I delivered it in the most effective way. When service was over church elders and deacons congratulated me.

That night Won Oak and I argued. We shouldn't have brought up the issue, but it happened. Everybody said my first sermon was very good, but I was in a sullen mood. Won Oak prepared dinner at my temporary residence for the two of us. The caretaker had taken a week of Christmas holiday.

"Why do you look so bad? What are you thinking? You did very well. You've proved yourself. Do I believe you can be a good pastor? Absolutely. No doubt." She said.

I shouldn't say anything about my faith, but I did. "I don't feel particularly happy about my sermon. I said something beyond my belief."

Won Oak was mad to hear this, "What? Please stop saying that. You mentioned Jesus's birth, His death on the cross, and His resurrection. You delivered God's words. It's in Bible. You didn't make up the story. It's the belief of all Christians and has been for thousands of years all over the world. It's the belief of the Vatican, Protestants, and all denominations of Christian Churches. It's not your theory. It's the foundation of the church. You don't have to doubt that. You shouldn't. Never mention it again. You cannot go against it."

I was in shock. As a pastor, I should not utter even

a word about disbelief. I shut the door behind me and stayed in my room.

Won Oak followed me and cried. "Young Min, please wake up. You are too honest if not stupid. Don't touch this delicate issue anymore. Please, you are a pastor now."

Won Oak cried. I sobbed too. We held each other and kissed. She searched my body. Her body was hot and wet. I pulled her closer and closer to me. I wanted to possess her, to save me and to save us. I felt again that she was my savior. We confirmed it with our bodies. We could not be separated anymore. As she said, I could not survive without her. Not even a short period of time. She snatched me, and I was happy to be stolen by her.

After that affair, she was changed dramatically. She wanted me to meet her parents. I was not ready but reluctantly agreed with a condition – only as a close friend. I told her not to tell them we would marry some-day or even considering engagement. Won Oak regarded my mother like her mother-in-law. She called my mom "mother" and prepared dinner at my home. My sister was not particularly happy about this, but she didn't make it an issue. My mom seemed happy about the possibility of Won Oak being her daughter-in-law. My mom knew Won Oak had saved my theology study and made me a pastor.

I prepared to study in the U.S., applying to various schools in New England. Won Oak was not applying for graduate study; she intended to accompany me. She visited my temporary place every weekend. She was determined to leave Korea with me. She wanted to tie me with string, so I would never get lost or wander off. She treated me as if I were a lost sheep and she the shep-herd. I didn't think about marriage seriously. I vaguely thought that I should be married when the time comes, but not this early. I was not financially ready to have a family yet. Some people believe marriage is no different from business. I believed marriage should be a business of the heart and soul. She seemed to believe marriage is a sort of partnership, as a co-owner of a company, with wedding vows as a kind of legal contract. To her, husband and wife are co-owners of a family. I said nothing, but I knew marriage was more than a binding. It was a combining of destinies between a man and a woman. I was not ready to marry Won Oak, but the circumstances developed beyond my control.

We maintained intimacy since that first night. One day my mother called me to let know that her pastor suggested we would be a good couple. I sensed that Won Oak urged her parents to contact my mom's pastor to arrange our engagement. I realized the time had come. I was not sure about our future, but I believed we would find ways to meet the challenges as a couple. We engaged the following month and got married two months after the engagement. We became husband and wife. We were ready to embark on our long journey toward the United States. We knew the waves were high, but I was sure we would not sink. We hugged and kissed in front of families and friends. She looked exceedingly happy.

We held each other tightly. Her body possessed an amazing healing power. It absorbed and melted my anxiety. I slept like a rock the rest of the night.

That day, we – the newlywed – left Korea for the U.S. It was hot and hazy. We visited both parents, knelt down, and bowed in the traditional way. Every mother would cry if her son left indefinitely. My mom was intensely emotional. She fled Communism with her husband, then lost him, now she is old and sick. She is no longer a strong-willed woman.

She wept and said, "Young Min, do what God wants of you. Study what you need, but don't forget that all should be used for Lord's work. Don't think too much. Every road leads to His world. Don't worry about me. I will soon move to the senior residential center. Take good care of yourself. If you are sick, you cannot serve God. Now go, my son. Don't look back."

My mom took Won Oak's hands and whispered, "Watch him carefully. When he falters, you hold him firmly. Make him a simple person. I rely on you."

She wiped the tears that had been streaming down in her cheeks. I wept too. I have not been a good son. I gave her too much trouble. Passengers lined up for the boarding area.

I held my mom's hands and said, "Mom, I will keep in mind what you said today."

And we parted. Mom to her place in Seoul, we to the departure gate. We had no clue when we could meet again. We entered the aircraft. It was Delta Air. We booked Delta because it was cheaper than the Korean Air. After many long and restless hours, we were finally on U.S. soil.

I started my graduate study at the State University of New York at Purchase. Unlike most of the Korean students, I didn't clamor for the Ivy Leagues. One reason was my academic grades. More importantly, I was not able to afford the high cost of private school. I liked the environment of small towns rather than a high traffic and noisy atmosphere. SUNY Purchase was perfect for me: less expensive, close to Manhattan, and it was in a sub-urban area. It was a relatively small college. The number of undergraduates was only about four thousand. The student-to-faculty ratio was 17 to 1. It was ideal for classroom discussion and debate. SUNY Purchase was in stark contrast to most colleges in Korea. Over there, teachers forced students to learn by heart. They didn't lead them to discussions.

I registered communications, psychology, English, and comparative religious studies. Since SUNY was not a seminary school, I was unable to take Bible study. The tuition was not outrageously expensive, but we needed income to support my education. My wife volunteered to find a job. She started work at a Korean-owned nail salon on weekdays and helped Westchester Korean Church on Sunday.

She didn't want me to have a part-time job saying, "Just concentrate on your studies. I will take care of the money matter. All I want is for you to become a broadly intelligent, big-scale preacher. Most of the Korean pastors are narrow; their only subject is mimicking 'Holy Spirit,' 'Jesus,' 'Eternal life,' and 'Amen.' They cannot persuade parishioners because they have no idea what people want nor how to deliver it. You have a great potential to become a brilliant pastor. I will support you all the way. "I truly appreciated her, but also felt sorry for her sacrifice. Eventually, I got a missionary job serving for the young adults at the same church. I gave sermon in English which provided me a good opportunity to improve my English. I always wanted to be a perfect bilingual preacher. My wife's job was not good for her health because she had to use chemicals to polish nails. It was also physically hard, with long hours. She came home late, and I prepared dinner. I did other domestic work too – laundry, food shopping, and cleaning. These chores never bothered me. I was happy to help her, and we formed a true bond between us. Her income and me being frugal were sufficient enough to maintain a modest living and pay for tuition. When my mother called and asked me if we were financially okay, I always answered,

"We are doing fine. Don't worry. Just take care of yourself."

One evening my wife announced in shy voice that she was pregnant. "Honey, I am pregnant. I was not sure for a few months. I went to a doctor yesterday and she confirmed it. I guess it happened before our wedding. The ultrasound said it would be a boy." It was a surprise because I was not ready to be a father and she had conceived the baby before our marriage. As a pastor it could be a problem if people knew. Won Oak pulled my hand to her stomach and I could feel the baby kicking.

We had a healthy baby boy in September 1978, and we named him Timothy. Our baby was cute, cried a lot, and made it impossible to sleep at night. We alternated waking up in the middle of the night to feed, cuddle, and change his diaper. We had added a family member, and that was extra work. As a father, I realized what my mother had gone through to raise me during the most difficult time. I felt sorry for making her worry.

My wife was happy to have a child in the U.S. Timothy was a born U.S. citizen. We applied for permanent residency as staff of the church. It wasn't that difficult in the early 1980's. It took us three years to receive our green cards. We began to work harder for the church. We were busy between study, work, and raising our son. My wife went back to work after four months, and I spent more hours taking care of the house. After graduation, I worked as a full-time assistant pastor for the church. I continued to read and write both in Korean and English. I contributed essays to one of the Korean community newspapers published in NYC. Lots of Korean immigrants subscribed to the paper, which at the time was the source of community news and information, all necessary for successful immigrant life. My essays helped me to be recognized by the local people. In the meantime, I spent a great portion of my time improving my English. I joined local English book clubs, read novels, and discussing what we had read. This helped to extend my connection with the so-called American people. I was the only non-native in the book club. I participated actively in the discussion, asked questions, and gave comments. People started to recognize me. They said they liked my perspective and encouraged me to keep on reading.

When I missed the book club, they asked me, "Why didn't you come last month? We missed your sharp comments." I felt like I was an important member of the club.

Chapter 5

He Snatched Me

1980, New Haven, Connecticut
Elena Reynolds

He was tall, handsome, and cool. His face was cleanly shaved, and he dressed conservatively – not jeans and plain top, but a designer shirt and brand name pants. His demeanor was calm, his choice of words was careful, and his smile was a bit reserved, but not shy. He looked articulate, controlled, wary, but gave me a good impression. I could not behave like a little girl in front of him. I had to match him. We met every other Saturday at Hartford art gallery. I recalled the moments we introduced each other.

"My name is Orlando Sierra," he said,

"Orlando what? I know Orlando is in Florida, not Sierra."

He smiled, "Orlando is my first name and Sierra is my last name." He said.

"I know the Sierra Nevada in California. I've never climbed there, but looked at the mountain from a distance." I said.

He smiled again and said, "Do you know there is a Sierra Nevada in Spain? The name came from there."

"How come you have such a funny name? Are you a Spaniard or Hispanic?" I said.

"I am a Cuban-American. I was born in Havana and fled when Castro took over Cuba. I was eight years old then." He said.

"Oh my God, I was born in Havana too. In 1959, the year of the Cuban Revolution. My parents left there when I was a baby, at age two. I don't remember anything. How could I?" He looked dumbfounded for a while. What a coincidence! He said to me, "Your name doesn't sound like a Cuban name. Are your parents really Cubans?"

"Yes, my grandfather was an English sailor, many decades ago. His ship met a severe storm and sank, my grandpa drifted toward Oriente and was rescued by locals. He met a Cuban girl and eventually they got married." I said.

"So your grandma was a Cuban. At least you have some Cuban blood. I am excited to meet you, a Cuban-American like me. I've kept a strong Cuban identity. My parents always remind me I am a Cuban. Cubans are smart, and I am very proud of my heritage." He said.

"I am not. I see myself as just an American, not a Cuban. I don't like to be called Cuban. My parents were born there, but they don't care much for their origin. Our family arrived Miami, lived there about five years, then left because they didn't like the culture. Our family liked to live as Americans, not Cubans in this country. If you want to meet a Cuban girl, you picked the wrong woman." He looked disappointed but regained his composure quickly.

"That's not an issue. Every Cuban is different. For

whatever reason, I have grown as a Cuban, but obviously, your case is different."

Americans treated Hispanics as second-class citizens. They looked down on all Spanish speaking people. For them, Latinos were Mexicans – illegal immigrants who crossed the border in the middle of night. There were reports of drug cartels and digging tunnels from the Mexican border to San Diego. The Cuban image was no different. Most Americans think Cubans are dark-faced, less educated, drunkard, and lazy. They saw some white Cubans, but they believed they didn't represent the real nationality. Of course, they had known many Cuban politicians – like Martinez of Florida or Tony Menendez of New Jersey. Generally speaking, the American's perception of Cubans is unfavorable if not entirely negative. Orlando Sierra had a different thought. He strongly believed Cubans were intelligent, courageous people and that he inherited that blood from his ancestors. He was ambitious. He wanted to mobilize Cuban brains to achieve his political dream. He got his law degree from NYU, worked for the UBS in Manhattan for a few years, and transferred to Stamford.

He was 31; I was 26. He was a successful corporate attorney. I was a failed artist and currently a teacher. His family had deep Cuban roots, while our family has almost forgotten them. His complexion was a bit dark, mine pure white. His father owned a construction company in New Jersey and was a close friend of Menendez, a rising star in NJ politics. My parents considered all politicians accomplished liars. His hobby was shooting photos like shooting an animal mercilessly with a gun. I took pictures with much anxiety. We were very different. My heart wanted to meet a delicate person like me, but my mind told me it was fine to associate with him.

I was in a state of confusion for some time and kept a distance from Orlando. As he courted me aggressively, I sought my parents' opinion. My mother seemed happy that I had found a promising Cuban man, but my father was cautious and said, "Sounds like he is an aggressive guy with greed. I cannot judge him until I meet him, but watch out until you are sure."

My mom expressed different views, "Cubans are happy-go-lucky people. They traditionally like music, dancing, and drinking rum. If he is sophisticated and brilliant, that's a plus. He will be a big shot someday.

I protested, "Mom, I really don't like a snob, a big shot. I want a regular, honest guy, not too ambitious. We agreed to wait and see how our relationship develops."

Orlando visited me at my school in the late afternoon and wanted to talk to me. We met for an early dinner. He explained to me why he wanted to marry me like a lawyer presented his case in front of the jury. "Elena, I come to visit you because I like you and I need you. I am a busy man who never wastes my time. I don't have many friends, only a few close friends. I hate small talk over coffee. I manage my time wisely. I believe we can make a good couple if we can reach an agreement. Marriage should be built on love and trust. Also, it is a kind of partnership. We should make up for each other's weaknesses and reinforce our strengths. I think you are a lovely woman. You are beautiful, elegant, well-educated and warm. Everybody loves you. You are that charming. Elena, I am fond of you. I love you dearly. Please think about me differently. I am a serious man. I want to meet your parents and introduce myself. I already told my parents. They are excited to have a Cuban-American daughter-in-law. Elena, I am in love with you. I will never hurt you. I will protect you. I will provide what you need. No doubt we can make a good family. A proud Cuban-American couple."

Orlando's presentation was over. He took a deep breath and looked at me like an attorney watched jurors. I didn't say anything at the moment. I needed time to think it over.

A few weeks later, my parents had dinner with him. He was polite, agreeable, and sincere. He didn't talk much and answered my parents' questions with courtesy. My mom asked about his Cuban days: Where he had lived, what kind of business his family had, how they managed to escape from Castro. He answered all of her questions with clarity based on what he had heard from his parents. He earnestly told my parents he wanted to visit Havana soon.

My father was trying to figure out what kind of guy he was and what kind of husband he would make if we got married. Orlando seemed prepared to face the moment and tried to assure them he would be a caring husband and a good father. He avoided elaborating on his ambitions. At the end of the evening, my mom seemed happy. My dad reserved his judgment. I guessed that a man might know a man better than a woman could.

The next day, my dad called me and said, "I am not totally sure of him. I think he's not a terrific choice, nor a bad one. Nothing's sure until you two live together. Your mom and I were the same. It's your decision, Elena. Only time will tell you the answer."

On that night, I was seriously thinking about marriage for the first time in my life. Too many questions came to me. What is a marriage? Is it a contract between a man and a woman? Orlando thinks that way. Local government issues a marriage license to the newly wed. Even gay couples receive the license. Why do people say "tie the knot"? Isn't it because a married couple has certain obligations and responsibilities? If marriage is a signed contract, can they cancel it and return the license? About half of married couple end up divorcing nowadays. Why should a bride and a groom vow before God, parents, and friends? What does the ring really mean? Do they give back the rings when they divorce? Is a marriage of convenience bad? How can a bride know that her husband-to-be loves her? What is true love? A successful marriage requires falling in love many times, always with the same person. I think I am kind of a weird girl. Isn't love a weird thing also?

I visited Edgar Allan Poe's cottage in the Bronx many years ago. He's quoted as saying, "We loved with a love that was more than love." Oh, how beautiful their love was. Can I find that kind of love in my lifetime? As my father said, it's hard to predict. Relationships are an experiment. Millions of men and women realize they've made bad decisions and separate every year. I hope I make the right decision. If it is proven wrong, I still have a choice. I decided to keep Elena Reynolds, my maiden name, after our marriage. I stopped thinking there. I turned off the light and went to bed. I slept soundly, like a baby.

It was a big wedding. Orlando already gave me a big diamond ring he had bought from Tiffany's when we became engaged. Our wedding was held at a private country club near Hartford. About four hundred guests were invited. His guests outnumbered mine three-to-one. Most of his guests were Cubans speaking Spanish. Menendez attended with a group of his supporters. One of my father's friends murmured "It's a Cuban party."

After we had delivered our wedding vows, we kissed as husband and wife in front of the witnesses. Then, we partied until midnight. Orlando suggested we have our honeymoon in Cancun and then visit Havana. My initial response was, "Why Havana? You speak Spanish well; I don't. And I have no memory of Cuba."

He said, "Havana has a five-star hotel. It's November here, but it's warm in Cuba. They have beautiful beaches, pure coastlines, and winding paths along the shore. They've preserved iconic Hemingway landmarks. And you know what, the food is delicious. Besides, I'd like to see how much Havana has changed since I left."

He explained to me that Cuban exiles, like his parents, were not allowed in the country, but young Cuban-Americans face no problems entering. We couldn't get visas in the U.S. but could receive Cuban visas in Mexico, that country having a diplomatic relationship with Cuba.

Finally, the thought of following Hemingway's footprints rekindled my interest in the Cuban capital. I wanted to see the places described in *The Old Man and the Sea*. My dream of becoming an artist was fading, but I didn't want to abandon it. I still wanted to be called Elena, the artist.

Havana Revisited

When we arrived at Cancun International Airport for our honeymoon, a man was waiting for us holding an 'Orlando Sierra' sign. I thought he was a chauffeur sent by the hotel. My guess was wrong. He and Orlando hugged affectionately and spoke in Spanish. I didn't understand what they were talking about, but they looked like more comrades than passenger-chauffeur.

Orlando's comrade didn't bring a limousine, which

I had expected; instead, he drove a mid-sized van. They discussed business in the car. He took us to a 4 – star hotel near El Centro, the downtown. I was disappointed but didn't complain. I was expecting a luxurious resort hotel by the water. He said his friend in Cancun booked the hotel. The room was spacious but wasn't a suite. I opened the window to look at the ocean. I could see the blue water, but it was far off, a good two-mile walk from the hotel.

I asked, "I thought you booked a waterfront resort. We can't walk to the beach."

He said, "I was thinking about that. I chose this one for two reasons: First, it's convenient. It's our honeymoon, but I also have some business to take care of here. The gated resort is inconvenient for my visitors. Second, the cost. A 5-star resort is ridiculously expensive – more than one thousand dollars a day. We need to save money to spend in Havana. I am very excited to visit there. It's been my dream ever since I left."

He might have noticed my disappointment but, he made no effort to console me. Instead, He pulled me into bed. I was not in the mood but didn't resist because we were married. While I was unpacking, someone called him. He told me he needed to meet the caller in the lobby before dinner. He went down with an envelope. I had no idea what business he had here and what was in the envelope. I had a strange feeling that he was hiding something from me. He came back about an hour later. I had plenty of time to think about Cancun.

I had been in Cancun during spring break when I was in college. Cancun was like an American city at the time. I heard English more than Spanish. It was flooded with American tourists including poor college kids like me. I came here with my girlfriends, and we stayed at inexpensive lodge under the friendly Caribbean sky.

At the time, it was the dead of winter in Connecticut. Snow piles were everywhere, and the wind was bone-chilling. As soon as the plane touched down, we took off our heavy jackets and changed into sleeveless tops.

The beach was calm and peaceful. We enjoyed the sound of the waves and let the sun burn our skin. The water was incredibly blue, and the sunset was awesome. We took the sunset cruise and drank tequila. Some of my friends got drunk. There were lots of activities too. We enjoyed scuba diving and snorkeling. I watched the cloudless skies. I saw seniors disembark from cruise ships. More cruise ships dropped off at Cozumel. They strolled busy shopping strips but didn't buy much. Maybe they didn't need those gifts. What they needed the most was their health.

I swam the warm water and looked for the vestige of winter, "Where is the winter? Come over. Are you hiding?"

I heard the wave's answer. "Looking for the winter? Go away. It's always summer here. Warm and friendly. If you get rid of greed, nature will embrace you." It was a friendly talk between the Caribbean Ocean and a literature lover.

Orlando went out again after dinner leaving behind his newly-wed wife. I was mad. I asked him, "What's going on Orlando? Are we here for our honeymoon or your dubious business?"

He looked surprised by my challenging question. "Dubious? Nothing illegal. I just want to help Cubans come to the U.S. Hundreds of thousand Cubans are coming every year. Miami is their favorite route, but some use Mexico. Cancun is a kind of liaison city. Lots of Americans get Cuban visas here since there's a diplomatic relationship between the two countries.

Cuban-Americans also use this city as a communication channel. My American organization gave me some work for my trip to Havana. By the way, we have to visit the Cuban Consulate tomorrow to get visas. I don't think you will have any problem because your last name is Reynolds, but my case is different. They may consider me one of the Cuban exiles. They treat them as traitors. And this is very important – we have to say we are not husband and wife. They will refuse to give us visas. I will pretend not to speak Spanish. I will ask for a translator. Please understand."

I was shocked, "Sounds like you are on some kind of secret mission. Why do we have to lie to them? Who gave you orders? Menendez? I don't like him at all. He seems like a corrupted politician to me."

He looked at me with a twisted face. He said, "He has a great future. He has a solid base in New Jersey. We need to bring more people from Cuba. Once they settle down, they will get asylum status, get green cards, and eventually will be U.S. citizens. Then they can vote."

I said, "I don't understand politics. But, I can tell you this – this is our honeymoon, not a business trip. You may disagree, but I didn't expect this." It was the first serious argument between us. It came much faster than I feared.

We visited the Cuban Consulate the following day. There was a long line. We had to wait three hours to have our interviews. A bald Cuban official looked at my U.S. passport carefully and asked, "Ms. Reynolds, what is your purpose for visiting Havana? Do you have any relatives there?"

I wanted to tell him I was born there, but said, "I am very interested in Cuban culture, especially the Hemingway trail. I am a high school English teacher. I need to teach the background of Hemingway's novels to my students."

I sensed he liked my answer. He said, "We, Cubans love the author. He is an idol. He is loved more than George Washington in our country. Welcome to Cuba." He stamped the visa onto my passport.

I waited for Orlando, who was being questioned in another room. He didn't come out for two hours. Finally, he came out but didn't look happy. "That guy denied my visa. He grilled me. He asked me all kinds of stupid questions: 'Why can't you speak Spanish? You are a Cuban exile. What mission do you have?' And many other suspicious questions. I have to come back tomorrow. Now I have to use the back channel."

I asked him, "What do you mean by back channel? What if you can't get a visa? I have no problem staying extra days here."

He said bluntly, "No problem. I just have to give him some money."

I was stunned, "You mean you have to bribe him. Is that how it works here?"

He replied, "Yes, it is. They are all corrupt. That's Communism. Nothing works without bribery in Cuba." He got the visa the next day. I didn't know how much he had paid or what channel he used. It just left me confused and disturbed. After we had got the visas, we made reservations for our flight to Havana.

As the plane approached Havana, he pulled the passenger window up and watched the panorama of the beach he had left decades ago. He seemed nostalgic, trying to recover his childhood memory of Havana. I had forgotten completely about Cuba, even though I was born here. When the aircraft lowered altitude and prepared for landing, he whispered in my ear, "Elena, look how beautiful our motherland is! Isn't it gorgeous? I've never seen as pretty harbor as Havana in my life. I am so excited to come back home."

I was mostly emotionless. His jubilation didn't resonate. Cuba was a forgotten country to me. As the plane touched down on the tarmac, he clapped his hands and embraced me. "Elena, we are here. We are in Havana. I will walk every corner of Havana and meet all my friends."

I wanted to say, "Meet friends? Stroll around Havana? Are we here for our honeymoon or business?" I didn't ask. Instead, I *told* him, "Orlando, we come here for our honeymoon, nothing else." He didn't answer.

Havana airport was small. The aircraft stopped close to the gate, but there was no gangway. Passengers walked to the gate for their passport check. The immigration official stopped him, peppered him how and where he got his Cuban visa. He seemed nervous but was permitted to enter after a long rigmarole. I looked around the airport. It was dim and narrow. It seemed eerie and deserted. There were no commercial advertisements. I peeked in on the duty-free shops. They were small and had only some cosmetics, rum, and cigars. My husband told me, "Well, Cuba is a socialist country. It's not the U.S. It's so different."

Someone opened and closed the airport door; it wasn't automatic. There was a throng of people including many children outside. I glimpsed their faces and found out most of them were black. This surprised me because the Cubans I met in the U.S. were mostly white. Orlando answered my unasked question. "White Cubans left the country, millions of them. Only African-Cubans remain. They came here as slaves hundreds of years ago."

As we came outside a chauffeur held a sign "Orlando." Orlando answered, and we began heading to our hotel in Old Town, Havana. It was not a big hotel and didn't look appealing from outside. Buildings around there were bleak and seemed like they had not been taken care of in decades. Orlando read my mind, "It's not the best hotel in town, but it's a historical one. This is Ambos Mundos, the Hemingway Hotel."

I saw Hemingway's picture in the lobby, and there was a plaque introduction of the great writer. Our room was spacious, but the surrounding area was quite noisy. It wasn't the kind of hotel for honeymooners, except for the name Hemingway. After check-in, my husband excused me for a meeting with the driver. He opened his luggage and pulled out a big envelope. I sat alone for at least an hour, wondering what he was doing with the strange Cuban. To me they all hid something, they were living in the darkness.

We had dinner at Ajiaco Café, Hemingway's favorite restaurant not far from his hotel. It didn't look like a fancy place. We had cocktails and Cuban dishes. I didn't know anything about Cuban cuisine. Orlando ordered my meal. There were numerous signs on the wall. Visitors from all over the world had written notes in their own languages. Despite the atmosphere, the food was delicious.

Someone called my husband while we were eating. I was surprised he had a local phone. He answered in Spanish and soon a young man came to see him. My husband excused himself to greet him. They talked for twenty minutes. I had no idea what they were talking about, but they seemed quite serious. In the meantime, I had another drink. I saw my husband gave him some American dollars. He seemed happy. They shook hands and left. That night I asked him, "Who was he and why did you give him money? Isn't it illegal to give U.S. dollars to locals?"

Orlando agreed, "If caught they go to jail. Castro hates the U.S. and is afraid of the CIA. We need money to bring Cubans to Miami. They have to pay the human traffickers. Cubans in the U.S. raised the money. I just passed the fund."

I was shocked. "If the government finds out, you would not be able to return to the States. You would go to jail. Why do you take that risk?"

He said, "Don't worry. We are smart, and they are all corrupt."

"Be careful, I don't want to leave you behind," I answered.

The next day he said he had three appointments with Cubans and suggested I join a city tour group. I was happy to be by myself and exploring Havana. The tour bus visited the Revolution Square first. There was a Jose Marti statue in the middle, a huge Fidel picture, and Che Guevara posters hanging on surrounding buildings. What amazed me most was the old American cars, made in the 1950s. Those Lincoln and Chevy Convertibles had been left here after the 1959 Revolution.

The guide said, "Cuban mechanics are the best in the world. They can put a Russian engine in those 60-year old American cars, and they are running well. Some are used as taxis, and some are private cars."

The tour bus showed us En El Floridita, the Hemingway Bar in Old Town. Once, he had had 25 cocktails there, getting so drunk that he could not move. His Cuban driver took him home. I saw a centuries-old Jewish synagogue at Old Town. The oldest synagogue in the western hemisphere is in St. Thomas, the biggest island of the U.S. Virgin Islands. It is believed Christopher Columbus was Jewish. After the Inquisition in southern Spain, Jews left there for fear of execution.

Many Jews joined Columbus and left for the New World. They settled in St. Thomas, the Dominican Republic, Panama and Cuba. Most of the Cuban Jews had left for the U.S. by now, but some remained. There are a few thousand in Cuba. The Castro brothers allowed them to live peacefully. They are all rich here.

Museo De La Revolucion, the Museum of Revolution, was another must-see. I saw a Lincoln statue there. Hemingway (affectionately nicknamed 'Papa') and Abraham Lincoln are the two Americans Cubans respect. All others Americans were enemies to them.

In the afternoon, I stopped by a local supermarket to buy water and fruits. It was a little after 5 o'clock. Shelves were empty, and prices were more expensive than in Connecticut. Credit cards were not accepted, only cash. All foreign currencies had to be changed to CUC, the Cuban currency. They closed at 6 O'clock, which I never understood. Orlando told me in the evening, "All Cubans carry ration cards. They buy all kinds of daily necessities, food, shoes, clothing, and they even use them for doctor's visits. Those prices are cheap. When they need more, they have to buy them at super or black markets, paying those much higher prices. I know you cannot understand, but that's how it works here."

I asked, "Do the Castro brothers use ration cards too?"

He smiled, "Theoretically yes, but I doubt it. Castro is the king. He is the law. Nobody can touch him. That's why educated Cubans left the country, and that's why we are trying to help them."

Orlando didn't have time to stay with me. Someone constantly visited him at the hotel. They exchanged papers and I sensed he gave them money. Orlando bought rums and cigars for his Cuban friends in the U.S. He said he needed to buy Havana Club and Romeo & Julieta.

Americans and Britons left Cuba a long time ago, but these English brand names are still very popular. He spent almost one thousand dollars.

When I asked, "Isn't it too much? Don't they ask you why?"

He smiled and said, "Why? They are happy to sell them. We may have some problems at customs. I want to put some of these in your bag." I worried but didn't protest.

I decided to explore Hemingway's footprints in Havana. Havana Hemingway House was much bigger than his Key West house. He lived in Key West for three years but lived here more than twenty years. He wrote *The Old Man and the Sea* and *For Whom the Bell Tolls* here. He bought his 18 – acre house with 1,800 dollars. There were 20 roosters, 60 cats, and many dogs. I saw a few dog graves. His dogs Black, Negrita, Linda, and Nero, were buried here. I was not allowed to enter his bedroom or study but saw his Royal typewriter. He typed his novels standing because of his bad knees.

His pool in Havana was much bigger than the one I saw at his Key West house. There, I saw *Pilar*, his boat, manufactured in Brooklyn and brought here. It was a good fishing boat. I imagined he enjoyed fishing in this boat and that this had given him the idea to create *The Old Man and the Sea*. The actual scene of the novel was Cojimar, about 20 miles from Havana. I saw a Hemingway statue.

Papa was beloved by all Cubans, then and now. He even befriended Fidel Castro. The U.S. government didn't like his close contact with Castro brothers. The CIA finally told him to leave Cuba. He was compelled to listen out of love for his country and returned to his Idaho ranch where he killed himself with a rifle. As an English teacher, looking at his house was special for me.

He was my idol. I liked his writing style; his sentences were short, but penetrating to readers' hearts. He always tried to find the best words to describe something. His Nobel prize-winning novel is only about 130 pages. I could not find any unnecessary words in it. I believe other writers would need at least 300 pages to say what Hemingway had said in that book. He was a wild man, but a very sensitive and deeply emotional man. He was selfish, arrogant, but also a brave man. He loved fishing, hunting, bull fighting, wine, and women. He was a man among men.

I looked at the rough water at Cojimar harbor, searching the fishing boat of the fisherman Santiago, and the boy who was so loyal to him. On the day, we left Havana; my husband was still meeting locals. He received a bunch of papers and seemed to be discussing strategies with the men around him. They looked like a gang of human smugglers. At the Havana airport, he said goodbye to his Cuban comrades and hugged them. He seemed satisfied that his mission was accomplished. He came here not for a honeymoon, but his secret business. I felt betrayed.

— Connection — connection — connection. Of course, I knew connections were an integral part of the society. We are social animals. We cannot survive without other people. We have to live together. It is true not only in politics. It applies to every sector of our society. My husband was an organizational genius. He understood where influence originated from, how it flew, and where it stopped. He was on the top rung of the Cuban political ladder, with Menendez as the center of power. They associated with the Jewish circle and expanded to the Tri-State political world.

As a corporate legal counsel and financial consultant, Orlando played a vital role in the Menendez inner circle.

He often attended political gatherings and wanted me to accompany him. I was not thrilled to go with him, but could not refuse every time. He introduced me as "Mrs. Elena Sierra", it didn't bother me, because I was his wife. As long as I was recognized as Elena Reynolds in the artistic community and at school, it was okay. His father's construction business needs a good government connection to get big projects. It was kind of give and take. He had donated campaign funds to candidates, and it usually paid off. It was strictly business.

One day my husband suggested sending my artistic photos to the Hartford gallery exhibition. I said, "I was rejected last time. I don't have new photo images. Why should I apply again knowing I would be refused?" He gave me an intriguing smile and said, "You never know. They have a new curator now. Maybe he has different criteria for selection." I reluctantly submitted my artwork and unexpectedly, they were accepted. I was pleased. I liked to believe that last time I was not accepted due to a biased curator. When I mentioned this to my husband at the dinner table, he smiled and told me, "It's all connections. The new director is a close friend of Menendez, and he nudged the curator to reconsider." This revelation startled me, but I was still happy. My school principal was happy, and my colleagues and students praised my work.

We had our first baby three years after our marriage. It was a girl. We named her Ashley. She was so beautiful and adorable that I spent all of my time with her. I got six months of maternity leave to take care of my daughter. My parents were so fond of her that they visited to see her every week. My mom said her granddaughter was a carbon copy of me when I was a baby. My in-laws were excited to have their first grandchild too. Ashley was like me. She was a stubborn, crying baby. She didn't stop crying once started, and I often couldn't go back to sleep. I knew from my own experience that she would grow to be a testy, intense girl. I felt like she was my other self and would be my best friend someday. I wanted to form a better relationship with Ashley than my mom, and I had shared.

Ashley grew to be mommy's girl rather than daddy's. She would not go to sleep without me. She fell asleep listening to my story telling. She liked my parents more than her father's and begged me to visit them on weekends. My parents would take her to the nearby park and beach until I picked her up after work. My parents and I brought her to Disney World when she reached five and went there again and again as she grew up. She wore Cinderella dresses at school and said, "My grandparents got me this."

Occasionally she visited her daddy's parents with us. Somehow, she didn't want to stay long. When she went to kindergarten, she liked art and always painted with a brush. One day she asked me quietly, "Mommy, why is my name Ashley Sierra? My friends laugh whenever they hear my name. I wish my name was Ashley Reynolds like yours.".

Surprised to hear this, I said, "Your name is Sierra because that's your daddy's name. Some people call me Mrs. Reynolds, some call me Mrs. Sierra. I keep my maiden name as an artist. It's common in artistic society."

Ashley said, "Then mommy, can I change my name to Ashley Reynolds as if I were an artist or a writer?"

I replied with caution, Yes, it's possible, honey. But don't say that in front of your daddy. He won't be happy."

Ashley whispered in my ear, "Don't worry, mom. I never do." She promised me. I embraced my lovely daughter and kissed her.

Chapter 6

I Am a Brooder

Houston, Texas, 1985
Young Min Park

When I was a kid, I watched hens hatching eggs. It was a wonder. I could not imagine how the birds bear eggs, and not one, but many. The eggs were warm. I picked them up carefully with my two hands and gave them to my mother. She was happy when she had many eggs and complained when she got few. Later on, I learned only female chickens could produce eggs, not roosters. Instead. Roosters cock-a-doodle-doo in their highest pitch. I often awoke to rooster crying in my childhood.

Hens brood to create eggs. They need time to deliver them. People who know me well say I am a brooder, and I agree. I produce something valuable only after working on it for a long time. People who don't know me often say I am pensive and sentimental. Some suspect I may be a psycho. They are absolutely wrong. They only look at the surface of deep water. I am a complicated man. I daydream a lot, but with purpose. I am not delusional, nor insane. I think I am a keen observer. I look at everything differently. I can see what other people cannot see. To me, it's great discovery which makes me thrill. I also possess analytical power. I can analyze complex things in a short amount of time. I am also a very emotional man. I often cry. Whenever I watch a sad movie, I weep and wipe the tears away with my hands. When I get really disturbed, I go to a beach park and stay there for a long while.

You may think I am a helpless, weak-minded man. You don't know me. I am a self-centered, focused man. I never waste my time and my resources. I always plan meticulously for something important to me. When I have to deliver a sermon, I brood about it for a week – making a draft, revising, and practicing. On Sunday morning, I am thoroughly prepared. My sermon is concise, powerful, and persuasive. My wife knows this, and so do the parishioners. I don't smile much and do not joke. I do not get along with many people, but people who know me really like me. They believe I am a man of integrity – a man of my word. I am a loyal guy. I try very hard not to betray anyone unless they betray me first.

Most people around me don't understand me deeply. Even my mother doesn't know me because she is blinded by her single-mindedness. She only cares about God, family, and business. Now she doesn't own a business. She only worships God and worries about me and my sister. My wife doesn't understand who her husband truly is. She might think she does, but I don't believe so. She is not deep enough to look into my heart. It looks calm, but there is a rogue wave somewhere in my heart. My mind occasionally turns into a hurricane when I meet a strong wind.

I have a few close friends here and in Korea. I have

known them for decades. When I feel lonely and isolated, I call or send messages to them. They are good listeners and don't divulge my secret to others. If they did, I wouldn't consider them my friends. I need at least one other person with which to vent out my frustrations and my inner feeling. I am waiting for someone who really understands me. I hope it's a woman rather than a man. I am pretty sure she is waiting for my call somewhere on this planet. I wish I could meet her not too late before I leave this beautiful world. I am saving my voice, my ardent passion for nature and art. I have dreamed of that moment since my childhood. Meantime, I have to do what I can as a pastor, husband, father, neighbor, and citizen.

> *Even if I knew that tomorrow the world would go to pieces, I would still plant my apple tree. All who call on God in true faith earnestly from the heart will certainly be heard and will receive what they have asked and desired. You are not only responsible for what you say but also what you do not say.*

> Martin Luther (1483-1546)

When Koreans say "religion" they usually mean Christianity, no other religion such as Buddhism or Hinduism. Those believers are "strange people," with whom Christians should not mingle. Christians should not ask questions about religion. Everything is in the Bible. That's God's Word. Just read it again and again and memorize it. Then, all your questions will be answered. Don't think too much. Just believe. Minister's sermon is God's message. Do not question, just take it. It's a good medicine.

I want to understand the tradition and rituals associated with Christianity. I am not rebellious. I just want to know the core belief of the religion. I want to learn how to answer questions if someone asks me. I want to help those people whose faith appears to be weak. These were the subjects I studied at graduate school. I wanted to know the history of world religions, not only Christian history, but also Islam, Judaism, Buddhism, and Hinduism. I was particularly interested in the Crusade, Inquisition, Hundred year's War, Martin Luther's Reform Movement, and the Turkish Ottoman Empire. I learned about them briefly in my theology class in Korea; it wasn't sufficient.

I was deeply concerned about the religious clashes happening now, at this time. Why do they hate each other so much and how can we reconcile them? I could not ask these questions to anyone. They would look at me with suspicious eyes and doubt my faith. They would say I have to believe without any condition – blindly. Everything is in the Bible.

I studied English literature and learned that most of the great writers had doubts about religion. Some never believed, some half-believed, and few went to church. Of course, some great thinkers and artists had accepted Christian faith in Medieval Europe, but modern novels rarely depict faith. When they did, novels mostly dealt with the struggle of faith or cultural clashes.

My study was an interdisciplinary approach. I never want to be a narrow-minded pastor. I did study sociology, psychology, and communications. Church is a social institution. It exists for people. Church helps cure social and moral issues. Church takes care of the invalid and the poor. Because of this, a Church has to employ economic theory to a certain extent. It is associated with every level of the society. After two years of hard work and my wife's sacrifices, I graduated with honors. It opened my eyes. I could see the religious world from a higher perspective.

At my graduation dinner, I said to my wife, "Thanks a lot. You deserve this degree. I think I can serve better with what I've learned. Church has a religious function as well as social responsibility. I will be a different pastor."

My wife seemed unconvinced and said, "Why do you want to be a different pastor? All the pastors are the same. They deliver God's Words written in the Bible. That's the safe way. If you deviate too far, you will be in trouble. People will question your faith no matter what your intention is. Honey, please be careful. Don't think too much. Be simple."

I knew what she meant, but I could not accept it. I didn't want to be a conventional preacher. My heart clamored to be a new kind of pastor, one suitable for today's religious environment. Why do people lie? Haven't you ever lied in your life? Are there good lies? Are some lies excusable? There are many natural liars. Politicians are habitual liars. They say, "American cars are the best in the world." even they don't really believe it. Imagine instead that they said, "American cars are worse than German or Japanese cars. They would be dead politically. They have to lie to win. A young man is courting a pretty girl and says, "I love you so much." She may not believe one hundred percent, but it sounds good. Used car salespersons are known as the best liars. "This car is inspected and test driven. You will have no problems for at least one year." Unless it is guaranteed in writing, buyers cannot make a claim when the car breaks down. Many American taxpayers lie too. They try to find every loophole to pay less. The IRS cannot track them all.

What about religious leaders? What if a Christian minister says Christianity is the only true religion? And an Imam says Islam is the one. Is one of them a liar? Pastors say that Jesus resurrected. Do they really believe that? Of course, they say that the Bible says Jesus resurrected three days after burial, and there were witnesses.

After graduation, I served four years as an assistant pastor at Westchester Korean Church. It was a good experience. I was an English Mission pastor and helped in the principal pastor's works. I made home visits to fellow members and comforted them, praying with them for a fast recovery. I prepared Sunday service and sometimes delivered Wednesday sermon. My wife was actively involved in all church activities. She got along with the wives of elders and deacons. She also occasionally taught Bible in the early morning service. She read Bible more than I and remembered key parts of chapters. She was an honor student from a Theology College after all.

Our church salary was not sufficient to support our three family members, and as a mother and missionary, she was not able to make time to earn extra income. At that time, I got a job offer from a Korean church in suburban Houston.

It was a medium-sized church about 40 miles from the Houston downtown. The offered salary was twice as much as what I earned in Westchester. More importantly, they hired me as the principal pastor. My wife was very happy. Finally, I was given an opportunity to prove myself. She believed she could help grow the church quickly. Her dream of being a pastor's wife was about to come true.

We were very excited when we visited the new church. The church shared its worship place with an American church. It was an old church, almost 150 years old. The main chapel can house 400 people. The church had a small theater, a decent size cafeteria, and many class-rooms for children's education. There was ample parking space. Across from the church was a small cemetery. The age of the congregation was young, and many had small children. There were many professionals working in the high – tech industry, hospitals, and oil refining companies. We sensed the atmosphere of the church was friendly, not contentious and rigorous as Korean urban churches in the Tri-State has been. The church had had an old, first generation, minister for the last twenty years, until his retirement. The recruiting committee was look-ing for a young and reform-minded pastor. They thought I was the right candidate. Before they made the final decision, I was given a chance to deliver a sermon, and they seemed really impressed. I could sense the warm, satisfying response immediately as I finished my speech. My wife approached me and murmured in my ear, "They seemed happy. I think we will get it."

We moved to Houston five years after coming to the U.S. Now we were Texans. I liked the new city and was ready to meet its new challenges. We rented a house near the church, which was paid by the church. My son Tim was four years old. The second baby, a girl named Sarah, was born in Houston. Tim was a naughty boy, didn't listen to his mom and fought with friends at the pre-kindergarten. As he grew up, he didn't like church. He always got up late on Sundays and forgot to carry his children's Bible. My wife scolded him sometimes, but he was uncontrollable. Instead, he liked to read comic books and watch wild movies.

My wife admonished him, "Do the right thing."

He protested, "Mom, I am doing the right things. Your right things are different from my right things. Don't push me so hard." She lost her words, not knowing how to respond to his repudiation. She wanted me to correct him, but I had a different thought. "Let him be himself. When he grows, he will find out who he is." My wife poured her love to new-born daughter. She was a smiling baby. She captured everybody's love and could often be found nestled in the arms of congregation members. This made her mom enormously happy, and she used the baby as a social tool to win the parishioner's attention.

Since I started work, the church grew noticeably every month. There were more incoming members than departing. Reputation traveled fast: I was regarded as a good pastor in the neighborhood, and lots of Koreans moved from other churches. My wife and I tried to strengthen the young members' education. Having a good Sunday school is one of the most crucial elements to the success of the immigrant church. The weekend school provided Bible class, Korean language and culture, art, and exercise class too. We began an English service. This was open to both Young adults and bilingual congregants. Some non-Koreans joined EM with their Korean friends, although the numbers were small. In the third year of my ministry, our church added about one hundred members. Church elders were very happy, and they all agreed that my wife's hard work contributed to the growth.

Some church members openly said, "We have the best pastor's wife. She is sweet, diligent, and she knows Bible. She gets along with women members so well that, whenever they have something to celebrate in their family, she is invited. She is the driving force of our church's thriving." I had to admit it too. I knew it all comes down to social networking.

Lawyers and journalists, writers and scholars, were not welcome in the church. Church should open its arms to anyone, but churches prefer doctors over lawyers. Doctors are mostly warm-hearted folk. Their job is to save lives and prevent people from getting sick.

One day at the Bible study, John Hong, one of the young college students, asked me an embarrassing question which drove me to an awkward situation. It evoked the dormant specter of my faith. John Hong was a law student at Texas State University. He was born in the U.S., and both of his parents were medical doctors. He didn't come to church every Sunday but occasionally came with his parents. I was teaching about Jesus's birth and his resurrection. I was very careful, always starting with "Bible said-"

John asked me in a defying voice, "Pastor Park, do you believe in the Resurrection of Jesus?". I hesitated for a moment and said, "Bible said clearly he resurrected. My job, as a minister, is delivering His Word to you."

He was not satisfied, "Pastor, you didn't answer my question. I asked whether *you,* personally, believe it or not."

He had pushed me into a corner. I said, "My view is not important. Bible tells everything. Christians have believed it for thousands of years. All Christians swear to it when they are baptized. Don't think too much. Just believe like other people."

He challenged me like a lawyer, "That's not the point. If you truly do not believe, you shouldn't talk about it. Now is a different time. We cannot accept everything in Bible blindly. Bible has to be reinterpreted according to the times. Look at the American churches. People are leaving. It's empty. Only Korean churches are thriving and build new churches."

John Hong didn't come to church after this confrontation. When my wife heard about this episode she praised me, "You gave him the best answer as a pastor. When other young members ask you same kind of question, just tell them to read Bible. That's the only answer."

That night, I couldn't sleep. John's challenge and my timid response made me restless. I knew my belief was not solid. My whole history testified to it. I know the church history tells many contradictory interpretations of Bible. I believed church had to be changed. Am I a modern Martin Luther? Am I courageous? Do I carry his Charisma? I felt shame. I may not be an honest minister. My wife is a better Christian because she says without any hesitation, "Yes, I strongly believe in Jesus' Resurrection and that we will be resurrected on Judgment Day." But, I am not. I am a coward.

The following Sunday, John's parents, approached me after service and apologized on behalf of their son. They said, "Sorry pastor. My son was not very respectable. We hope it didn't cause injury to you and our church. Young Koreans are not like us. We got through the Korean War and experienced poverty. The Christian missionaries came to Korea and rescued the poor, uneducated people. They sowed evangelical seeds and awoke the sleeping spirit in people. Without their sacrifices, our country could not grow to today's Korea. John and his generation cannot understand this, and we are sorry we didn't tell him the true story. We tried to convince him that he was wrong on the issue, but our advice was to no avail with him. He is already a grown man. He has strong opinions about religion. We believe you are a great pastor and the growth of our church proved it. Don't think about what happened and keep up the good work you've been doing."

I said to them, "No, don't worry. I think he raised a legitimate question. I just couldn't answer promptly. It's a fundamental issue of Christianity as you recognize.

Everything is in the Bible, but they don't read it and are not inclined to believe it. Science changed everything. It affects their thinking and lifestyle. I feel okay. Thank you for your concern."

Somehow the episode didn't stop there. Unfounded rumors were circulating that Pastor Park could not answer Jesus's Resurrection question at Bible study. Some members of our church believed it was spread by nearby Korean churches who had lost their church members. My wife was visibly upset. She contacted our church leaders to tell them that I gave John the best answer a pastor possibly can. "The Bible said clearly Jesus was resurrected. This is exactly what he said. There is no better answer than this.".

Most of the congregation didn't mind or forgot what had happened, but some disgruntled members continued to raise the issue. "Why did he hesitate? Does he truly believe in His Resurrection? What if he doesn't? Can we trust his faith?".

I didn't say much about this perplexing issue, keeping silent in the hope that it would die down soon. My wife was the fire extinguisher. She called women members to tell them whoever set out the rumor should be held accountable. Our church lost some members because of the episode. My wife became nervous. She watched me carefully and monitored my every move. She assured me my answer was perfect and not to dwell on it. But, this touched my old wounds.

I was trying to find the exit. I seriously considered taking Ph.D. courses to become a professor teaching comparative religion. A scholar can answer Bible questions with freedom. A pastor cannot say anything against Bible. But I could not utter a word to my wife. She will be mad. We have no other income source. I wanted to be a professor. I didn't want to be tied down by religious obligation. I thought I could take Ph.D. courses part time and keep my pastor job. First, I needed my wife's permission.

Whose church?

History may be servitude,
History may be freedom. See, now they vanish,
The faces and places, with the self which,
As it could, loved them,
To become renewed, transfigured, in another pattern.

— T.S. Eliot

I sat down with Professor James Morgan, the chairman of comparative religion studies of the University of Texas, in his office. I read his books and knew he was a reform-minded theology scholar. He looked in his 50s and was strong-built. On his desk was a picture of him playing football with his son.

He shook my hand and said, "Welcome to my office. You can ask me any questions. I am not a pastor, but a scholar. I am at liberty to discuss anything about religion."

I started to talk, "I am a pastor of a Korean church. My church grows as Houston adds to its Korean population. We are renting an American church now. Hopefully, we could have our own church in the future."

He said, "This growth from Asian populations is happening everywhere. Not only here in the U.S., in Europe too. As Harvey Cox said in his book *The Future of Faith*, Christianity has ceased to be a Western religion. The faith now is not European. The majority of the followers of

Jesus reside in the global South, where the movement is growing most rapidly. Most of them are mixed colored. Christianity today is culturally diverse, and its center of gravity lies in Latin America and the Asian Pacific region. It is growing in China. Religion follows the money and people. Religion exists for people. It is no secret that Korean churches are thriving. Everybody knows."

I said, "I think the question is 'for whom the church exists?'. 'Whose church?' is one of the fundamental issues. I read Daniel C. Maguire's book, and it answered some of my questions."

Professor Morgan agreed, "Absolutely, that's an important question. Religion should be a way of life. It has to be dispersed into our daily lives. Many people are Christians only in church. When they leave the church, they return to a non-Christian lifestyle. I believe many Americans and Europeans apply their belief to their lives. However, while Asians look very religious, they don't follow the teachings. I may be wrong. It's always dangerous to state religion in simple words. Religious matters are very complex and contentiously changing. People should be generous and tolerant, but they are hostile to those who have different views. The whole history of the church shows us this."

I asked him, "What's the difference between Faith and Belief?"

He answered, "It is about the same, though somewhat different. Initially, Faith meant a primary life orientation. But, the evolving clerical class now equates the two. Harvey Cox doesn't think the two are same. He says we could believe something to be true without it making much difference to us. It's hard to understand."

I said, "One of my young church members asked me whether I personally believe in Jesus' Resurrection. I answered that 'It is in the Bible. Don't question, just take it as it is.' He wasn't satisfied and said the Bible has to be reinterpreted according to the changing times. I believe science is changing young people's minds."

He said, "You gave him the best answer from a pastor's perspective. I do understand the young man's inquiry. You should be very careful. I've heard Asian congregations are very provocative and like to fight. Science and Christianity didn't get along for a while. The rise of natural science initiated the decline of Christianity. The Internet and social media further damaged the influence of the church. Look at church history. Galileo was the victim of the traditional Catholic Church. It is no small matter. The church's hostility toward science has alienated many young people. The church insists that it is not entirely accurate to picture Galileo as an innocent victim of the church's prejudice. Resurrection belief is a common question among the youth. Lots of people have doubts. But, they still go to church. Some believe it's not a big deal. There are many other elements in the Bible. I know many Christians are not happy with this argument. They believe if people only conveniently believe some parts of Bible, they cannot call themselves Christians. And if you believe only what is scientifically proven, it is not called faith, but science."

I continued to ask him, "Do you think the church will accept people who don't believe in the Second Coming? Can someone without this belief be a good pastor?"

He answered, "Eventually, but not soon. Again, the church exists for people. If people's minds change, the church has to be changed. It cannot stick to the theology of two thousand years ago. It has already started to accept gay couples, women pastors, and contraception. If the vast majority of the congregation doesn't believe in

His Second Coming, reform churches will start to accept this new outlook. The Bible cannot be read literally. It's like the U.S. Constitution. Progressive judges interpret it according to the times. The Bible is the constitution of the Christian belief. Be careful. You have to survive first. Many churches do not tolerate divergent views."

I said, "Thanks, Professor. One final question, what makes a healthy religion?"

He answered, "I believe religion should be a release from the isolation of egotism. A passion for the beauty of justice. An undefeated conviction that hope and joy can be at home in this universe."

We had talked for an hour, and it was getting dark. I told him I would seriously consider pursuing my theology study. I didn't forget to add, "If my wife permits."

He smiled and said, "Your wife is your boss. My wife is my boss too."

When I suggested perusing additional study to her, she was extremely upset. Her anger was beyond my anticipation.

She screamed, "What are you talking about? Enough is enough. Don't mention these stupid things anymore. There are pastors who don't believe in Resurrection. They just don't admit it. If they don't say, who will know? Nobody can read other peoples' minds. There are lots of mysteries in the Bible. Nobody raises questions. A pastor cannot be one hundred percent honest. Most of them are not. They read Bible and preach what Bible said. If you go for Ph.D., who's going to feed us? Me? No way. Do you want me to go back to the Korean nail salon? I can't. Our children don't want their mom to work there. I am as proud as you are. Don't be selfish. You only care about yourself. Think about your mother. She is praying every day for your successful ministry."

She cried. My daughter cried too. I couldn't say anything. I shut my door behind me. I put aside my Bible. There were many other books on the desk. I closed my eyes. I didn't want to read anything. I was exhausted. Tears streamed. Who wants tears? I don't believe tears are a sign of weakness. If you are without tears in a world of sorrow, it is a tragedy. All human beings have tears, and they should be shed. It is more than water. It is a deep well of emotions. All compassionate people weep sometimes. It is a pure water coming from the bottom of our hearts.

Broken but Beautiful

Bible – The Holy Scripture — The Word of God — Book of the books. The oldest and the most beloved book of our history. Even hotels keep this book for their travelers. I am in my study. It is not big, a modest size, upstairs, away from my wife. I am thinking about my mother. She doesn't read novels or history books, only Bible. It is the book of her whole life. She reads one chapter after another. Bible is her daily bread. It has been her teacher, her friend, and most importantly her guide. She copied the whole Bible twice. Whenever she closes Bible she sings this gospel song.

> *I'm pressing on the upward way,*
> *New heights I'm gaining every day;*
> *Still praying as I'm onward bound,*
> *"Lord, plant my feet on higher ground."*

It is 8 o'clock in the evening in Korea. She probably

just got done reading her Bible and is going to bed. She never plays musical instruments, never watches ball games, only prays. She always prays, in times of good or bad. She seeks answers only in her Bible and prayer.

My father read the Bible but spent far less time on it than my mother. He sometimes forgot to pray before meals and was scolded for this by his wife. He didn't miss the Bible study in the church. He met his friends there and discussed the Bible and about what was going on at church. He didn't know the Bible as well as my mom, but he had been a compassionate man nonetheless. He often gave money to the beggars at the underpass and donated to the charities. My sister was totally different. I never saw her read Bible. The closest she came to being religious was singing gospel songs at church. People applauded, and that was all she wanted. My wife reads the Bible every day. It is always on her nightstand. She seems to believe everything in the Bible. She also believes that the clearest view of everything that happens comes from Heaven. What about me? – What about me? I have to read this book. I hated this thick book. That's why I got D in Bible studies at Yonsei. Won Oak pushed and coached my Bible study. I barely graduated the Theology School. Over the course of my ministry, I had to read Bible. I accepted most parts of the Bible, but not every-thing – especially not His Second Coming. Some of my friends said, "You have to accept everything there. All or nothing. Never just a part. Even if you don't agree, just eat them. Your body will absorb."

My wife said, "I know you are not accepting every-thing in there. That's okay. Just don't tell that to others. When you deliver the sermon, quote what you are com-fortable with. Never mention something which makes you feel awkward. If you have any questions about Bible, ask me. I am sure I know Bible more than you."

I opened Bible and started to read. It is not my favorite book, but I have to read. I planned to read 20 pages a day. I read slowly and made notes and memorized important parts of each book. It became my routine, and I even enjoyed it for some time. Then, I got bored and tired. After my encounter with John Hong, I read the Resurrection and Second Coming parts again. I was not convinced. I tried just to take them. No question was allowed, as my wife said so many times. Just believe it. I wept. I went to the beach park with my leather-bound Bible. I sat on a bench. I started to read it again. I closed it. Suddenly it started to rain. I didn't have an umbrella. The rain intensified. Soon it was lightening. I was scared. I thought God would kill me. I couldn't keep the Bible dry. It was wet, crumpled and bloated. I felt guilty and wept. I rushed home.

My wife was looking for me. "Where have you been to? I called you for dinner. Oh, my God, you are all soaked, and your Bible is wet. How could this happen? You should keep your Bible dry. It is a Holy Book. You are a pastor." She gave me a new Bible the following day. She said, "Keep it safe. Love this Bible. Everything is in it. Just read. Do not question. You know, what I saw in you last night when you ran home? You were broken, but still beautiful. You looked so innocent. You were like a crying boy. Don't worry too much. God always protect the flawed, but good people."

Late 1980 was one of the darkest times in Houston history. An oil shock ripped the city. Houston is an oil city. It is recognized for its energy industry – oil and natural gas. Houston has NASA's Johnson Center, a world-renowned medical center, and many other industries, but the economic pipeline is from energy.

The city has numerous pipelines – oil, natural gas, and product lines. When the oil boom died down, Houston was devastated.

Thousands of Koreans left Houston and headed to Los Angeles or New York. Some moved to the north, Dallas-Ft. Worth area, but the number was small. Our church population dropped accordingly. It was conspicuous. Empty seats increased every Sunday. As the number of tithe givers decreased so did the total amount of each collection. The church financial team had to find ways to cut expenses. I volunteered that my salary is cut considerably. We even had to save electricity. The Houston summer is unbearably hot. During the summer it is common for temperatures to reach over 90 degrees. This makes the city "the most air-conditioned place on earth." Most of the public buildings are too cold for Koreans. They put on extra layers in the summer, while non-Koreans enjoy this cool indoor temperature. Our church set its thermometer at 75 degrees to reduce energy costs.

I had served for this church for five years now. It had grown steadily the last four years, but it went back to the old days quickly. Small Korean churches closed or were absorbed by bigger ones. It wasn't easy to live with our reduced salary. My son, Tim, needs extra activities. My daughter, Sarah, was taking piano lessons. This dampened my desire to seek a Ph.D. We barely maintained status-quo.

In September 1990 I received a call from the Westchester Korean Church. The principal pastor said he was retiring and suggested I apply as his successor. He hinted that he would recommend me for the job. The church had grown gradually since I left. Now it has over six hundred congregations, he said. They have two Korean services and one English each Sunday. They have an assistant pastor and two women missionaries. It is the biggest Korean church in the Westchester-Rockland County now. My wife was fervently happy to hear the news. She missed the New York culture and the atmosphere of Korean society. She immediately called the pastor's wife and asked their help to get the job. She had maintained a strong relationship with the Westchester pastor's wife. That's my wife. She never loosened her ties with influential friends. She would always send presents at Christmas. She was confident it would pay off this time. The search committee invited me for an interview and gave me an opportunity to deliver a sermon. I was glad to meet old church members, and they welcomed me.

My wife prayed. She shut the door, opened Bible, and prayed in a quiet voice. She believed God would answer her prayer. Whenever she faced difficult situations, she prayed pleadingly and eventually figured out how to make it through the circumstances. She also believed prayer was good for health. A specific amount of prayer per day could help prevent memory loss, mental decline, and even dementia or Alzheimer's. "Prayer has an amazing healing power. It's scientifically proven. It reduces the risk of death from heart attack and lessens anxiety and depression." She told women church members, and they echoed. My wife had prayed for one month for my new job. Finally, we got an answer. I was at the college library at the time.

"This is elder Chung of Westchester Korean Church. Is Pastor Park there?"

She knew her prayers had been answered from his pleasant voice. "Oh, elder Chung. He is at the library now. Do you have good news for us?"

"Yes, we are excited to tell you that he was chosen

as our next pastor. Whenever he's ready, you can move here. All our congregations are expecting to see him. We will send him an official letter."

I was doing research on the sermon for the coming Sunday. My wife came hurriedly to the library and pulled me out of the reference room. "Honey, we've got it. They called. You've got the job. We can go back to New York. My prayer was answered. God always answers my prayer." I was happy but worried. I knew New York was a tough environment, very diverse and contentious.

I called on a special elder's meeting to inform them of my leaving. They were stunned. It was not a good time for a change of pastor. Houston's economy was in trouble, the Korean community was shrinking, and so were the churches. I said sorry to them, and I really meant it. I gave them enough time to find my replacement and worked harder for the church. My wife was more concentrated on contacting Westchester women church members. Her mind was already in New York. Most of the Houston church people didn't notice, but she paid less attention to them now. She was looking forward to the future.

Six months later, they found a new pastor from Los Angeles who was about the same age as I had been when I assumed the responsibility five years ago. He graduated from a Theology school in Korea and continued his theology study in California for his master's degree. I said this at my farewell sermon.

"People meet and part during their lifetime. Sometimes the parting is short, sometimes a long while or even forever. People separate for good reasons and bad. Some separations are fate, separated by war or even death. It's painful. My departure is not pre-planned. It just happened. It may not be a big deal for this church because I confess to you, I have not been the ideal pastor you deserve. I worked hard, but I am not sure how many lambs I saved during my time here. Houston has declined financially but will come back. It's a resilient city. And our church will thrive again. The best days are yet to come. Dear, congregation. I am leaving, but my heart remains here. I love Houston, and I love you. And I received your love more than I gave. God will protect this church because you all are true Christians. May God bless you. Amen."

Some people wept. Women members hugged my wife and me. They formed two lines and paid their farewells to us.

One young woman church member told me in a quiet voice, "Pastor, you are an honest, honorable man. You gave us unfiltered messages with unpolluted voice. I was touched by your sermon, and it nurtured my soul. You may not be a great pastor, but you are a great messenger of truth. You are not the kind of pastor we know. May God protect you." She looked at me and wept.

I embraced her and said, "Thank you. I perfectly understand what you are saying. You knew me by heart." The morning we left Houston, it was foggy. Gradually, the sun lifted the fog and revealed clear afternoon skies. Our family headed for New York. My wife seemed happier than I.

Chapter 7

A River Between Us

1988, West Port, Connecticut
Elena Reynolds

I am almost forty years old now. I am a teacher. My beautiful daughter, Ashley, is a teenager. She is my only child. My husband wanted to have a son, but I avoided having another baby. I will tell you why later. As a school teacher, I had lots of time to travel. We work only half of the year. I have traveled almost 30 countries during the last 15 years. I joined tour groups, mostly by myself. A few times, I traveled with my husband. He has been busy all our married life. For Orlando, traveling is boring. He enjoys meeting people, shaking hands, discussing politics, and social networking. I like nature. He prefers the human forest. I care about people. He cares about money and power. He would attend various parties almost every weekend and spent his time at conferences, group talks, and participating conventions. He wanted me to go with him, but most of the time I declined. I was sick and tired of saying, "Hello, good to see you. Oh, you look wonderful!" We had been a good couple only a few years out of our entire marriage. I found many differences, flowing like a wide river between us. The gulf was too wide to be bridged and too deep to cross. As an artist and a writer, I can imagine there is a river in our body – a river of emotion. Some people have a deep river, some a shallow one. Some hearts flow with a pure river of emotion; some are polluted. Like a real river, each person has distinct elements and characteristics in his or her water. I have seen many different rivers throughout my years of traveling.

The Nile is the longest river in the world. It is the major north-flowing river in northeastern Africa. The Yangtze is the longest river in Asia. Its source begins in Tibetan glaciers and flows only through China. The Mississippi is another long river, flowing 2,350 miles through the center of the continental U.S. to the Gulf of Mexico. Human minds are as unique as these rivers. Some people think hard on something; some refuse to think seriously at all. Some rivers discharge enormous volumes of water. The Amazon is the largest river, by discharge, in the world. Some people contain a great amount of emotion and discharge it like a great fall. Some rivers are deep, while some shallow. Certain parts of the Amazon, Yangtze, and Hudson rivers are very deep, while some small rivers, like the Jordan, are permanently shallow. Some people have deep emotion, while some are thin skinned.

Most of the world's rivers flow from north to south, but the Nile and Alaska river flow south to north. In the same way, some people like to think in reverse and go against established sentiments. Some waters are clear, some muddy. The Siberia rivers carry cold, clear water The Ganges in India is severely polluted. The Suwanee River, which flows from southern Georgia to Florida, is very muddy. Some people have clear and pure hearts. Others have minds full of secrets and conspiracies. Usually, the upstream water is clean and cold. The Ganges originates from the snowy mountains of the Himalaya, and the Amazon water comes from the snow-melted water of the Andes. While the Amazon is still clean, the Ganges quickly becomes dirty. People's minds are the same; they are born pure, but often become dirty as they go through difficult times. Some try to purify it, some never mind.

All rivers flow to the ocean. The Mississippi flows to the Gulf of Mexico, the Danube to the Mediterranean, the Amazon to the Atlantic, and the Hudson to the New York harbor. I am not sure where people's minds and hearts flow, perhaps they are absorbed in someone else's heart. Some countries control the flow of a river wisely; building dams, digging canals, and piling up levees. People are the same; some control their emotions well, some let it burst, and it causes tremendous injury to others. Now I will tell you what happened to our rivers and how we managed them. We both originated from Cuba, but at some point took divergent paths. Each heart went its own way without harmony between the two. It's sad but helpless.

Let me go back to several years ago. My husband seemed to have rediscovered his Cuban roots after our Havana trip. He told me repeatedly how proud he was to be born in Cuban and wanted me to feel the same. This bothered me a lot. I was born in Cuba but had left at age two. Why should I be a Cuban?

I challenged him, "Don't put a Cuban label on me. I am an American, not a Cuban."

Nevertheless, he always introduced me at parties by saying, "My wife was born in Cuba like me. She is a proud

Cuban. She understands Cubans, and she loves Spanish-speaking people." He represented me the wrong way intentionally. I knew why he did it. He needed to mobilize Cuban voters in order to expand his base to the other Hispanics. Eventually, he would link them to the Jewish community to exercise maximum political influence.

Cubans in the United States had a national organization at the time. Menendez was one of the pillars of the structure and Orlando was his right – hand man. His dream was to be elected to state senate and climb the political ladder. I got a sense that he used my pure white face and intelligence for his ambition.

One night, after we returned from a party, I protested, "Orlando, don't use me anymore. I am not a puppet or showcase. I hate politicians. They are all liars and hypocrites. I don't want to look at their faces. The leaves of a cedar tree are more graceful than their greedy expressions. I don't want to hear their voices. The rumpling sounds of reeds provoke better sensations than their husky voices. I really don't want to gaze into their eyes. The curious eyes of ducks are more beautiful than their cloudy glares. I have to take care of Ashley. She needs a mom. Okay? I am done."

He was angry, "You degraded Cubans. If they heard you, they would kill me. I am politically dead. I told you from the beginning we are partners. My success is your success, so is my failure. If I become State Senator, you will be a senator's wife. I cannot be president of this country because I was not born here, but I can be a governor or Senator of the United States. Isn't that a worthy goal? Politics is networking, and I need your support."

I was laughing, "You dream big, but I really don't care. I don't want to be a politician's wife. I want to be a writer and an artist. I will publish my first collection of short stories next year. I have to concentrate on the project."

He said, "You know what Elena? Who will publish a no-name author's book? You need connections, and I can be a great help."

It sounded like a good barter, but I rejected, "I know somebody who can help me. If that doesn't work, I can choose a self-publishing company."

He didn't back down, "Politics is the most sophisticated game. It's the game of games. If I win, I win big. I can help you to achieve your dream as a writer. Politics stands on top of everything."

I didn't surrender, "I am telling you in plain and simple English. I will be my own. I am not your partner anymore."

He was really mad. He threw his suitcase at me and rushed to his room. I didn't blink an eye. I calmly picked his suitcase up and put it on the table. I didn't sleep with him that night. This incidence changed the whole chemistry of our marriage. I visited my parents a few days later to tell them what had happened.

My father's face hardened. He said, "This was what I feared from the beginning. Don't rush your judgment. Take a deep breath and cool down. Every marriage has peaks and valleys. Take your time. Love Ashley and be a good teacher. You have to be respected in your school from fellow teachers and students. That's your permanent job."

My mother seemed very disappointed about what was going on. She said to me, "Why don't you try to understand him? You can help him fulfill his ambition. You lose nothing. He still loves you and Ashley. Unless he has another woman, you cannot put the blame on him for his political ambition."

That was my mom's usual attitude, and I disdained her approach. She has a strong Cuban mentality like

Orlando. My father is more American than his wife. His name is Reynolds, not Hernandez, Cruz, or Martinez. His first name is John, not Juan. My uncle's name is Peter, not Pedro. They have English blood while my mom has lots of Spanish-Cuban blood. That made the difference. My mom envies authority; my dad regards integrity and dignity higher than anything else. My parents are starkly different, but they don't fight, because neither of my parents is as greedy as Orlando. My river and his river started to flow into divergent waterways. I was not sure the two waters could ever meet again. Water is natural; it cannot be manipulated easily. People want to control everything – even human minds. I refused to be altered. My mind and heart are more important than his lust for power.

Tensions between us escalated. I got out of his way and shut the door behind me. I didn't want to see him. My surprising move further angered him and hurt his pride deeply. His eyes turned cold, his lips tight, and his mouth shut. It was a disturbing development and had enormous consequences for our marriage. Ignoring to each other did not bode well for reconciliation. This came at a time when his building of a political empire began to be fulfilled. He wanted us not to cut ties, but rather reduce our conflict and maintain some limited cooperation. It seemed that he needed time to recalculate our relationship.

My husband's family was caught by surprise. They suspected we were not getting along well but didn't antic-ipate it had gotten this bad. They called my mother, who was a Cuban like them, to facilitate dialogue and calm our tensions, but I wouldn't listen to her. Her effort was useless because I didn't appreciate her interference. Somehow, I believed she was not on my side.

I shouted at her, "Mom, get out of my way. I don't like your Cuban way of thinking. Your involvement will only accelerate our animosity."

She was shocked. She shut the door abruptly and went into her house. We didn't see each other for a month afterward. We were mom and daughter but lived in different worlds.

My husband came home for a while. He ate with his friends, and I didn't prepare his dinners. Ashley and I went out to eat or heated leftovers and ate in a different room. He went to work early in the morning before my daughter, and I went to school. We lived under the same roof, but we were separated.

One day he told me, "I am moving to the NYC office. It helps my networking. Most of the big shots are in the city. Occasionally, I might sleep at my company's apartment in the city."

Big shot? Not sleeping at home? That was okay with me. Actually, I liked it. I hoped he would live there permanently, but I could not suggest this. The following week, he texted me saying we should attend the birthday party of Tony Menendez together.

"He invited couples, it would be very awkward for me to be there alone," He said.

I replied "I am sorry. I cannot be there with you that night. Ashley 's school concert comes on that day. I promised her I would attend. At least one parent should be there."

He replied back right away, "Things have not been going well recently between us – Intentionally or unintentionally. I am running out of patience. You are not helping me. I feel like we are living in a different world."

I said to myself. We are living in a different country. You live in Cuba, and I live in the U.S. You live in the political world. I live in nature.

There was another issue dividing us. He wanted Ashley to study Spanish as a second language, but Ashley wanted to learn French. I was on her side.

He said, "Over three hundred million people speak Spanish. Look at Latin America, they all speak Spanish. Brazilians speak Portuguese, but they understand Spanish. French is spoken only in France and a few other tiny countries."

Ashley didn't agree, "Most of the bright students in my school want to study French. They consider Spanish as a second – class citizen's language. French is still influential in the cultural world. I want to learn French, and I want to travel to Paris soon."

I agreed with Ashley. Spanish is widely spoken and learning Spanish may help in building important connections, but it's Ashley's choice. We can express our opinions, but cannot force her. My husband looked awfully disappointed. Emotions soured among Orlando, Ashley, and I. We were a family at odds.

The year Ashley entered high school, we joined a tour group advertised by The New York Times and visited Berlin, Dresden, Weimar, and many other German cities. These cities were in former East Germany. My husband had not been coming home lately. I assumed he was not interested in traveling with us, so I didn't bother to ask him. I sent a message that we will be traveling through Germany and would not be home for about two weeks.

Our trip was primarily a history tour. Berlin is surrounded by many canals. We visited Dresden too. It was the capital of the German state of Saxony. On that night in Dresden, our tour group slept at a three-star hotel near the city center. We saw the Volga River the next morning. We walked along the river bank for about an hour. There we found the river was separating and flowing into different tributaries at certain points.

Ashley asked me, "Mom, where is the source of the Volga?"

"It originates from the Valdai Hills, which is northeast of Moscow. It flows mostly in Russia but comes down to German cities like Dresden. Look at the water. It flows really slowly, even slower than our walk. Some parts of the river are pretty deep, but here it looks shallow." I answered.

Ashley continued, "Mom, look, the river separates here, each tributary flowing their own way. Why is that?"

I smiled and said, "Because they don't like each other. Small streams flow into a river; they get along well for a certain period of time, then they get sick and tired of each other, they fight and then go their own way. That's why there are so many tributaries in the big river. The Volga has two big branches, Karma on the right and Oka on the left. Look at them. They don't even look at each other. They hate one another."

Ashley smiled, "Mom, are you talking about your marriage? I guess you guys got married because of love but became sick of each other. Now, dad is not even coming home. I think you don't mind that at all."

We smiled. I said, "It's partially true. Human being and nature cannot be the same, but I think the situation is similar. If they don't trust and like each other, they have to be separated. They can enjoy freedom without the awful stress of living together."

Ashley studied my face and added, "Mom, where is the mouth of Volga? I think all rivers flow into the ocean."

I said, "Yes, all waters meet in the ocean. They feel comfortable in the big, wide ocean. It's so big that they have no idea where they came from."

Ashley teased me, "So you and dad won't recognize

each other when you meet there. It's like we meet again in heaven after we die."

I said, "Ashley, I don't believe in eternal life. I am not a believer. I don't think your dad has the Christian faith either. His faith is in money and influence. That's his religion. I cannot change him because he doesn't want to be changed. That's why we fought, and we flew different ways. We may meet in the ocean, but we won't get along."

Ashley murmured, "Mom, you are too much. You are very kind and warm to your friends and students, but tough to the ones you don't like."

"That's who I am, Ashley. I hate someone who attempts to use me to satisfy their greed. That's your dad. I think we are approaching the breaking point." I said.

It was eight in the morning. We hurried back to the hotel, ate breakfast, and joined the tour group. We had a busy schedule that day. In Weimar, we saw the statues of Goethe and Bach.

The guide said, "Bach had twenty kids. He had to work really hard to feed them."

We were all surprised and asked him, "Twenty kids? Did he remember their names? From one wife or more than one?"

She answered, "From two wives. He got confused about their order of birth. But, his wives clearly remembered the order."

We all laughed. We also toured Weimar theater and the Goethe museum. When the tour was about to end, it was already dark. The tour guide was in her late 70s.

She said this to us, "I was born and raised here. When I was a small girl, Germany was defeated by Allied forces. American troops came to this city. It was the first time I saw black people. I never knew there were dark-skinned people in the world. They threw chocolates to us, and we ate. During the Soviet occupation, we had to learn and speak Russian. Many Germans were killed trying to escape from the East. After Germany had become united, my husband visited New York to perform music at Hunter College. It was a big and diverse city. Now my grandson is studying in Boston. Without your help, we could not enjoy our freedom and prosperity. I really thank you." She was sobbing.

We held her hands and applauded her. It was an emotional moment. This was the beauty of traveling. We travel to understand other people, their culture, and their history.

Chapter 8

Who Am I?

Westchester, NY. 1993
Young Min Park

I am a bird watcher. I spend hours looking at tall trees from my study. There are hundreds, or maybe thousands of birds. There are small birds, probably sparrows. They like having their early morning conference. They flock to the tops of the trees, sit on branches and leaves, and discuss matters very important to them. It's like the direct democracy of old Greece. They don't elect their representatives. They are participating by themselves and decide their own business. It's so noisy. They cannot reach an agreement and are often arguing fiercely. Today, they had a heated debate for about thirty minutes before adjourning. The birds then flew to their nests peacefully in droves. They didn't throw insults or push one another. They took rest, feed themselves during the daytime, and meet again in the evening at the same tree. They debate again until nightfall came and went to sleep. I found them very interesting and learned a lot from them.

Am I a bird? If I am a bird, what kind of a bird am I? I graduated from Yonsei University, but I don't think I am an eagle. I am not large and powerfully built as eagles are. I don't have long and broad wings and cannot fly high in the sky for long whiles. They are ranked at the top of the food chain and build their nests in tall trees deep in the mountains. I am a delicate, medium-height man and not muscular at all.

Am I a pelican? Probably not. I saw a pelican habitat at Low Country in South Carolina many years ago. It was a big nest and was so beautiful. There were hundreds of pelicans in a big pond. I saw some alligators there too. Pelicans are large water birds. They have long necks and large throat pouches. I first thought they looked like white swans. They are gregarious birds, traveling in flocks, hunting cooperatively, and breeding colonially. I think my wife has a pelican personality. She likes people and always maintains a cordial relationship.

Am I a Mockingbird? I am quiet and occasionally cry in the night like the mockingbird, but I cannot sing as mockingbirds do. The bird mimics the songs of other birds and the sounds of insects, often loudly and in rapid succession. It is an innocent bird. They never hurt crops. Harper Lee characterized Tom Robinson as a mockingbird – an innocent slave who was found guilty by a prejudiced white jury – in her masterpiece, *To Kill a Mockingbird*.

Am I a nightingale? It is a small bird best known for its powerful and beautiful song. The songs of the nightingale have been depicted as one of the prettiest sounds in nature, inspiring songs, fairy tales, and a great deal of poems. This bird sings mostly at night. I have never known a woman who resembles a nightingale, but someday I might come across one.

I might be a hummingbird. Hummingbirds had their name because of the humming sound created by their beating wings, which flap at high frequencies, audible to humans. They hover in mid-air using high rapid wing-flapping rates – typically around fifty times per second. They conserve energy when food is scarce, and meet only when foraging at night. They migrate south-ward in fall to spend the winter in the Caribbean islands. I am a quiet man, unsociable, lonely as a hummingbird. I am a low-key, down-to-earth man. I sing in a low voice. People might think I am a wavering man, but they underestimate me. I am very focused and determined. I am trying not to bother people as would pigeons or ducks, who spoil beaches and verandas. I like to be char-acterized as a humble person who sings in a quiet but persuasive voice. I am a hummingbird.

The Westchester Korean community is much smaller than the ones in Queens or New Jersey. There are hun-dreds of churches in Queens and on Long Island. Some of them are real big, they have thousands of members and have their own church buildings. Westchester is different. The number of Korean residents is not much more than ten thousand, and this is not increasing. There are not many Korean small businesses in Westchester, so Koreans go to Queens or New Jersey for grocery shopping and beauty salons. Professional and small business owners are in about equal numbers here. There are about ten Korean churches in the county. Our church is the biggest, and the rest are medium or small in size. Some have less than one hundred congregates, barely enough to support themselves. Real small churches have no means to pay for a pastor's salary. Some pastors have to have another job in order to feed their family.

Our church has grown steadily after I assumed the

pastor's responsibility. We had almost seven hundred parishioners and owned our own church building. It's not a big church, but we have a pretty big chapel and some small rooms for young adults and children. The parking lot is small, one of our deacons has to direct cars to find spots on Sundays. We have two services for Koreans and one English Mission on Sunday. I lead all three services every Sunday. Our church has a meeting every Saturday to discuss important church matters. Six standing elders from the Korean side and two so-called American elders are supposed to participate, but non-Koreans often don't show up. There is obviously a communication problem which dampers the non-Korean member's enthusiasm for participation. Our church is virtually run by Koreans.Elder Huh is the oldest; he is one of the founding members, and he exercises a great influence. The rest are in their 50's mostly, while a few are in their 60's.

Some of you might ask me," Don't you choose people you like as elders?" I heard this question often, and I knew that was the case in most of the Korean immigrant churches, but I refused to be involved. My wife was very concerned about this issue because she knew I needed majority support to implement my philosophy and ministry ideas. I didn't touch the financial matters either. I told the elder in charge of church finance not to report to me the amount of weekly collection and how it is spent. I didn't ask the church to support my family sufficiently. Church elders recommended I drive a better car, but I insisted my Sonata is more than enough. My wife drove her own car. I suspected church members talked to my wife about our family's finance without my knowledge, but I didn't pay much attention. I knew money was tight for our family and that was alright.

On the tenth year of my coming back to the church,

senior elder Huh proposed to add an education center to the main church building.

He said, "Without a good education facility, our church cannot grow. Parents will go to a big church in Queens, and it's happening now. It is a difficult task, but we need to look at the future. We have to sacrifice now to save our House of God."

Elders, deacons, and parishioners were divided. We all hoped to have an annex and to grow our church, but how can we raise the enormous construction cost? It was estimated to be about one million dollars. Church members looked at my face and demanded my position over this perplexing issue. I asked my wife because she gauges the wind of the church. She was a decisive woman, but she couldn't make up her mind. If we don't handle this issue prudently, our church will be swept into a ruckus.

She said, "As a pastor of this church, you should decide which way we need to go."

I said, "I am against the massive project. If we go for it, I have to ask for donations in my sermon. I know lots of Korean pastors do, but I don't want to. One pastor in New Jersey delivered a donation sermon for seven straight weeks, and this drove their church people crazy. I know our classrooms are crowded, but we can manage. I am not sure how much our church can grow. Our congregations are getting older; soon they will retire to the warm weather and the second generation will abandon their parents' church. I am not confident. Won Oak, I want to contact people and persuade them to give up this idea."

She didn't respond. She keenly knew how explosive this complex issue was.

It was Saturday. It was raining. We heard thunder from our conference room. The heightened tension overwhelmed the room. All eight elders, six from the Korean side and two from English-Mission were there. I was sitting in the center.

I opened the conference, "Thanks for being here tonight. This is the crucial moment of our church. We have talked about this issue for months and reached the point to draw a conclusion. Each one of you has a chance to address your opinion and then we will vote. Let us accept whatever decision we make. That's the fundamental principle of Democracy, and we should follow the rule. The worst thing we need is division and animosity among our church members. It causes pain to all of us, and I believe that's not what God wants. Lord is watching us from Above now." I tread warily amid tensions and controversy. I said, "Elder Huh, would you please tell your opinion first?".

He cleared his voice and said, "As you know, I have served for this church the last twenty years. I started from a deacon, became an elder; my son was married in this church, and my grand-kids were baptized here. It's God's church, and I feel like it's my second home. Our church started from scratch and grew this big. Three pastors, including current pastor Park, have served. Now I see our church is too small to accommodate growing numbers, especially for our children. They don't have rooms to learn God's Words and no rooms for Korean programs either. We desperately need more space. As I said numerously before, without a good education center, our church cannot grow. We will lose congregations to the big churches in Queens and New Jersey. They are one bridge away. We all know it's not easy, but we have to do something. Look at the church history. All grand holy places were built on people's sacrifices. I know some of us will complain or move to other church, but when it's done everybody will be happy."

Three other elders expressed similar opinions in succession. Tom Curtis, English Mission elder, was the first opposed to building the education center. "I don't know the Korean community well. Westchester is a buffer zone between Queens, Bergen County, and Connecticut. I've heard and seen that the Korean residents here are mostly seniors approaching retirement. There is no guarantee our church will keep growing and be able to pay for the debt incurred. If we don't make the payment, we will be accountable for the mortgage. Honestly, I cannot take the legal responsibility. My wife would kill me. If you make the decision to build another building, I have to resign. It's too heavy of a burden on my shoulders."

Elders looked at others face. I noticed some tightened their expressions. After two hours of tense debate, we cast our votes. It was a tie, four "Yea" and four "Nay." I had the deciding vote.

I said, "I don't want to give a big burden to any member of our church. I do understand how elder Huh and others love this church and that we should make sacrifices for the next generation. But, too much is too much. We don't have to invite a bondage burden. I don't see the growth of the Korean community in Westchester. We should not pass down our debt to our children. Yes, it is a difficult decision. Let's take a safe path. I know it is crowded, but we can find ways to manage and provide a good education to our children. Let us close our debate here and move forward. Please don't take this personally. It's a collective decision, not an individual one. Thank you." We shook hands. Elder Huh looked unhappy. Two American elders seemed relieved. The thunder stopped outside. It was ten o'clock at night. Suddenly, I felt thirsty. I opened the office fridge. There was no water. I closed the door behind me and walked to my car. Elder Huh and three other Korean elders were talking in the dining room. I glanced at them.

I heard someone said, "Pastor Park lacks Holy Spirit."

The argument was uncomfortably known to all church members. People were divided into two groups. One for elder Huh and the other for me. People watched curiously as it developed. It sparked controversy and soon went out of control. All Korean churches fight when they grow. I hoped it was only growing pains, but It was much worse than that. My specter was invoked once again.

Elder Huh has lived through many controversies, so he was used to it now. He even seemed to be enjoying it. He accused me of not trusting God. He called influential church people, insisting that I was against the education center because I lacked Holy Spirit and God's will. He attempted to control me. I didn't want to be controlled. My wife pleaded with his wife to stop attacking me, but she didn't prevail. I was caught in a maelstrom again. My wife and I grew frustrated with the whole situation. Some urged me to fight back. I hesitated because this was not a "civil war" and if I did, he would be more vicious. My wife suggested I address this issue in my Sunday sermon from the pulpit, but I balked. I had no intention to be engaged in a war of words with him. I hoped my innocence and honesty would make the difference.

I received a letter from my mother. Since I left Korea, I haven't visited to see her. She came here twice, once in Houston and a few years ago here in New York. She didn't stay long. She missed her church, the one she has attended since my parents left North Korea and settled in Seoul.

She said, "Your church is good. All churches are

owned by Jesus Christ, but somehow I feel more comfortable with my church in Seoul. I am a living history of that church. It started from the ashes of war and had grown into one of the biggest and most glorious churches in the country. I know everybody there, their family roots, and their siblings." And then she left the U.S.

My wife has maintained close contact with my mom. She told her what was going on in our church and sought her advice. I called her only a few times a year. I was not a good son.

"Dear Pastor, I am just back from Friday service. You are my only son, but I call you a "pastor." I always wanted to. We have one pastor much younger than you, in his 20's, but I call him a "pastor" too because he is giving us God's words. Ministry is always difficult. A church should be Christ's home run by people. We are all created by God, but we are all different. There are all kinds of people in the church. And all churches have to grow through the ordeals. It's God's test. You have to win their respect. Respect is not given. It is earned. You have to win with resilience, patience, and love. Love is the answer. Love can melt hatred. My dear son, open your heart, embrace your church people, even those who don't like you. If you embrace them with God's love they will be changed. Pastor, don't worry about me. God protects me. Your sister is okay too. She had her third child last month. A beautiful baby girl. Now I have five grandchildren. I pray every day for all of you. Your mom. From Seoul."

"Dear mother. You are Kwonsa Nim (a senior woman deacon), but I am calling you "Mother!" because you were my mother before you became a deacon. I have not been a good son. I know how you and my father endured

the hardships after you fled Communism. I still vividly remember the days you worked so hard to support us: set a fire during the harsh winter to warm your cold hands, stayed all day at the store and came home after dark. I didn't answer your wish. You told me a pastor's life is never easy and I am experiencing difficulties now. I am trying to find the answer in my prayer. Won Oak and I pray every day. I agree that love is the answer. I truly love my parishioners. Hopefully, everything will settle down soon. I am tired. I need peace. I like to walk the beaches without worrying too much about church. Mom, I love you. Stay well. Your son."

My wife once again took off her gloves to save me. She's been my savior twice before, and she was determined to rescue me from this trouble. She knew this was a much tougher challenge. She tried to diffuse the tensions between the two sides. She could not talk to the elders and deacons directly. Instead, she visited their homes to talk to their wives. She was good in one-on-one dialogue.

She said to elder Huh's wife, "Pastor is a good, sincere man. He is one of us. He hates internal conflict. His approach is risk-free and more comprehensive. He truly understands your husband's intention, but he believes this is not the right time. Please tell him to think differently." Won Oak cried. Tears rolled down her face.

The elder's wife felt sorry for her and said, "My husband is a stubborn man. I cannot persuade him. He is over seventy years old. Too old to be dramatically changed from whom he is."

My wife visited other elders' home too. "We have to face reality. The picture is not so rosy. Korean population in our county is not young, but getting older. Who's going to pay the huge mortgage? Our children?

No way. We cannot pass down the burden. It's a kind of sin. God doesn't want that. Please tell your husband not to be too ambitious."

Some church members urged me to fight back against the unruly elders. They said, "An inaction is no good. Silence is no answer. You should defend yourself. Be aggressive. Tell us your genuine opinion in your sermon."

After a long pause, I decided to address the conflicting problem in my Sunday speech. I added this part at the end of my preaching.

"Dear church members. I am a flawed, imperfect man. I don't think I am one of the greatest pastors in our community. But, I strongly believe in my integrity as a man and a pastor. I wanted to be a different pastor from the very beginning. These are the types of pastor I didn't want to be. First, I hate a power game at the church. If someone loves power plays, he should go to politics. Church is not the place. Unfortunately, I have heard many not so pleasant stories in Korean churches. When a church becomes bigger, there is usually someone who doesn't agree with the church and starts the war, dividing the church. We are not big enough to be divided, and we shouldn't be. That's not God's wish. Second, I don't want to be deeply involved in church finances. I didn't become a pastor to make money. If I did, I would be a businessman instead. I am more than happy and very thankful that you support my family and me. I am not a greedy man. We have to be financially prudent. We have to live within our means. We cannot hold our children accountable for future debt. I believe individual freedom and judgment. Each one of us is God's son and daughter. You and I, a baby, a student, and an elder. We have to respect and love each other. Church builds on mutual trust and love. I feel humble to serve for you. I am privileged working with you for God's kingdom. I don't want to be a burden. My conscience is very important to me. Dear church members, let us be one. We cannot be two. Our church cannot grow if we are divided. We can only grow when we love each other. The answer is love. Love in God."

People kept silent and quietly left the church. I hoped my sermon would help in bringing harmony between members. My wife believed the same thing. Unexpectedly, something cynical had happened. Elder Huh and his group distorted my sermon and spread words that I was ready to leave the church. It was a vicious attack on me. Most church members who heard the sermon disagreed, but Huh and his followers inflamed the controversy. For the first time in my life, I felt disdain for the ones who disrespected me. I was angry. I regretted being a pastor in Korean church. Meanwhile, the English Mission people expressed their ardent support for me. But, they are minorities. Their voice was not heard.

My wife has been very energetic since her college days. That's her trademark. But, never-ending controversy drained her vigor and vitality. She ate less, exercised infrequently, often woke up in the middle of the night and read Bible. She was in her mid-40's. I thought she might be approaching menopause and that it affected her rhythm. However, she could not slow down her church work. She still led early-morning Bible study twice a week – on Tuesdays and Thursdays. I was vehemently against the early-morning prayer. I have known almost every Korean church in Korea and here have been adopting the practice. They believed that it inspires their spiritual power and helps them in leading their daily life normally. I have different thoughts. "Why bother with their sleep? Why do they need to pray and study Bible in the darkness? Why can't they wait till daytime or evening? What's the difference between an hour's prayer from ten minutes' prayer? The longer, the better? What if are they involved in an accident?"

When I started my ministry in Houston, I insisted this ritual stop and people reluctantly agreed. The young, progressive-minded members didn't want to shorten their sleep. It was a different story in New York. Most of the early-morning worshippers were seniors. They have been attending early-morning service all their lives, and they usually sleep early and wake up early. Their life cycle is opposite that of the young. I suggested it be discontinued but lost the argument. Instead, we agreed to meet only two mornings a week. My wife, who is a missionary, volunteered to lead it because she knew I didn't want to get up in the wee morning hours. About twenty people come to the prayer gatherings. There had been a few incidents last several years: One senior woman was hit by a car, and one senior man fell and broke his ankle.

It was rainy and dark. Won Oak got up at five o'clock. I was deep in my sleep. She was careful not to stir me, quietly slipping out and starting her car.

I received a call at about six from the church, "Pastor, is your wife home? She didn't come yet. We didn't start early-morning service."

I immediately looked at my bed. She wasn't there, and her Bible was not there either. I said, "She left already. What has happened to her? I will be there right away."

I started to worry about her immediately. It was an ominous sign. When I arrived at the church, there were about twenty people there. They were singing gospel songs and reading Bible. Won Oak hadn't shown up, and it was already seven in the morning. We all thought something bad must have happened to her. I started to call nearby hospitals to check. I called Westchester Medical Center Emergency Room first. There, I learned they had an Asian woman patient who was severely injured in a car accident. A deacon and I rushed to the hospital. The emergency room was crowded, and the staff was very busy.

I asked nervously, "Is my wife here? She is an Asian."

The hospital secretary looked at me indifferently and said, "What's your wife's name? Ambulances brought an accident victim in this morning, and the doctors rushed her to the operating room. It was a dire situation. Can I have your ID?".

"Her name is Won Oak Park. I'm her husband." I showed my driver's license and she made a copy. I asked, "Is she okay?"

She answered, "We have no updates. She is still in the operating room. She's been there for two hours already. They said they had no idea how long it would take. She was bleeding all over. It looked like a drunk driver hit her car. The driver was injured too."

I waited there nervously for three hours. The deacon brought coffee and bagels, and we shared them in the waiting room. At about ten, the surgeon came out to the waiting room looking for me.

He said, "The surgery went well. She had suffered a severe head injury, and there was some internal bleeding. We did what was needed. She is unconscious now. The right side of her body was hit hard and likely paralyzed. I cannot say what's going to happen next. I don't believe it's life-threatening, though. We have to wait and see. I'm hoping for the best. She's been moved to the ICU."

I was too unsteady to ask him questions. The only words resonated was "not life threatening." It meant she was not going to die. She will stay with me. I still have a chance to help her, to make up for my neglect. I took a deep breath and prayed for her recovery.

My wife recovered her consciousness, but stayed two more weeks in the hospital and had a second surgery. When I first looked at her, I doubted my eyes. She didn't look like my wife. As the doctor said, the right side of her body was crushed. Her right eye, shoulder, knee, and leg were damaged considerably. The doctor said she was lucky to survive. She needs rehab for at least six months, and even this doesn't guarantee her full recovery.

Sarah, Tim, and I had to take care of her. We did all the housework, even cooking. Female church members visited her and brought food for us. It was enough for our family. She was kept in bed and slept extra hours under the influence of painkillers. She looked devastated. I took her to rehab twice a week after she came home. She didn't talk as much as before.

Drinking and driving is dangerous. This is what the police report said. As Won Oak entered Saw Mill Parkway, a pickup truck swerved and crossed the lane. She panicked, turned to the left, and hit the guard rail. She could not get out of her car and lost consciousness. Another oncoming car couldn't stop in time and hit Won Oak's Camry again. A passing motorist witnessed the accident and called 911. Police arrived at the scene within minutes, and an ambulance was called.

The driver of the swerving truck was driving under the influence of alcohol. The blood test said his alcohol level was twice the legal limit. He was also bleeding and taken to the same hospital. Police reported the other driver's name was David Haley, a convicted drunk driver. His car was not insured, and his license was suspended at the time of the accident. He was arrested for numerous charges, DUI, driving without a license, and even aggravated assault.

Being hit by an uninsured car caused enormous problems. Who's going to pay the exorbitant cost of the hospital charges and doctor's fee? Because the other car had no insurance, we could not claim for medical expenses and the compensation for my wife's injuries. We consulted car accident lawyers but heard we had no one to claim. After much effort, my wife's medical cost was eventually paid by our car insurance company. We were twice unlucky. She was hit hard and hit by the wrong car. My wife is a good Christian. She prayed for the poor driver and his family.

My wife's tragic accident silenced the education center controversy temporarily. Everyone believed it was not the right time to argue about that issue. After some time, when the issue began to resurface, Won Oak consulted me. She said, "Calm down and reach out to everyone. Embrace Elder Huh and consult church matters with him. He doesn't want to be isolated. He's been an outspoken critic of you because he felt nobody listens to him. He is a stubborn, senior man. He believes he still can control our church. Let him be himself."

Chapter 9

You Never Loved Me

1995, West Port, Connecticut
Elena Reynolds

"Do you love me, Orlando?"
"Yes, I do."
"Do you love me, Elena?"
"I do."
That's why we got married.

We promised. We swore before God. Time has passed since we took those vows. Almost fifteen years. We no longer say, "I love you." Maybe we did, but not now. What had happened between us with time? The answer is very complex. The entrance was wide. The exit was narrow. There were many witnesses when we got married, no witnesses when we separated. We just stopped seeing each other. I felt more comfortable when he was not around me. I believed he felt the same. We were happier being alone. We had reached the breaking point. We crossed a river with no hope of return. I feel sorry, but I would not cry.

You might ask me, "Why did you marry him?"

That's a good question. I wish I could give you a good answer. I don't have that answer. I say now that it was a mistake – a big mistake. I should have been more careful, but I was too young to know what marriage should be. I was not driven by ardent love. I just thought he would make me happy. Looking back, I now realize that we never loved one another truly.

You will ask me, "Why did you have his baby?" I had Ashley from him. She is my darling, and she is exactly like me. She won't leave me. I am her mom, and she is my daughter. We cannot be separated. Never, ever. After Ashley, I conceived his second child. I aborted the baby because I didn't love him anymore. Do I want to marry again in the future? I am dreaming of finding real love, but I have no answer at the moment. I might. If I meet someone I genuinely love. But I will be very careful not to make another mistake. One misfortune is enough. Not again. Maybe he is waiting for me somewhere in this world. Or perhaps, he is looking for me every day.

One Saturday, while Orlando was home, he called Ashley to his study and asked her, "Ashley, we are starting a voter registration drive for minorities. Could you join us?"

My daughter was quite surprised to hear this, "Dad, who are we? I've never done anything like that."

He said, "It is a Cuban American youth group. The group is starting a voter registration campaign for this year's election. The goal is ten thousand. I think it can shift the result one way or the other. Of course, we want the Democratic candidates to win."

Ashley was not pleased to be asked to participate so suddenly, "Dad, I am not Cuban. I am not interested in politics. I don't want to join."

He said, "It's not a political act. It's a civic activity. As you know, voting is every citizen's right and duty. But, only about fifty percent participate in the elections. People have to register to vote. Lots of minorities do not register, so they cannot vote. We need their votes to get our candidates elected."

Ashley flatly rejected, "Dad, I am not going to be a part of that. Never. I don't want to knock on someone's door to get their signature or roam around on the street. Please find someone else."

Orlando was irritated, "I need you. I am supervising the drive. If you participate, I can proudly tell my staffs. That can save me face."

Ashley continued to doggedly oppose, "Don't force me. You cannot change my mind."

Orlando screamed, "Why are your mom and you actively working against me? What's the matter with you? Why do you team up?"

Ashley shrieked back, "It's not teamwork. We just don't agree with what you are doing. We hate politics, and you love politics, and that causes tension between us."

Orlando threw something at Ashley. She cried and burst out of his room. I was stunned. I hugged her and hurried her into my room. His face reddened. He drove back to the city and didn't come home for several weeks.

We went out to eat and discussed what was going on in our family. I told Ashley, "Your dad is a political animal. His family fled Castro's regime. They are Cuban exiles. I heard his uncle was killed by the Revolution army in 1959. His parents and all his Cuban friends harbor vengeance against the Castro brothers, Fidel and Raul, and hope their government collapse. I knew he was interested in politics, but I didn't know the intensity before we revisited Cuba. He secretly met some of his relatives and gave them money. Your dad is kind of clandestine, always hiding something from me. He is working with Menendez and wants to move to New Jersey to run for state senator. That's why he is so involved in politics."

Ashley asked me, "Mom, why did you marry him? I don't think you guys are getting along."

"I cannot give you a good answer. I just didn't know him. I didn't read his mind. I thought it would work out. Your grandma pushed me. She is as Cuban as your dad."

Ashley said, "Mom, does he support us financially? Or we do live on your paycheck?"

"He doesn't give me much. He only pays the mortgage and taxes on this house. I take care of the rest." I said.

She added, "Who's going to pay my college tuition? That's not far off. It's next year."

"I hope he does. I am not sure how long our marriage will last. If he fails, I will do it. Hopefully, you can receive a full scholarship." I said.

Ashley replied, "I will try mom, but you know me I am not super smart. I can apply to a relatively easy school to get a good scholarship."

"Let's see what happens. If we separate or divorce, I will ask him to support your college tuition. He should do it." I said with a sigh. We ate sushi, had dessert, and came home.

Our relationship worsened since his fight with Ashley. One day he came home in order to pack his suits and other necessary stuff. I didn't stop him. He no longer asked me to attend political activities such as fundraisers. One day, I heard he frequently came to these political events with an unknown woman. I didn't bother to ask him who she was.

In the meantime, something unpleasant was reported

in the Bergen Record – a local newspaper. Menendez and some of his donors were under investigation for alleged corruption charges. To my surprise, Orlando's father was implicated, and all records of his company were seized by New Jersey's attorney general's office. It was a blow to his family. I heard later on that Orlando formed a defense team to fight against the charges. It usually takes years to reach a verdict. I can easily imagine that put tremendous pressure on their family. Since hearing the news, Orlando had virtually cut ties with us. I had not seen him for weeks. One day, I got a letter from a law office. He wanted legal separation from me, saying our marriage has been so damaged that it was beyond reconciliation. I gave the letter to my attorney. I had heard lots of nasty fights surrounding contested divorce procedures. It takes years to resolve conflicting issues, and it often costs tens of thousands of dollars. Because he was a lawyer, it doesn't cost him much – but it was different for me. My lawyer suggested a quick settlement. I told him to draft a proposal to end our marriage as soon as possible. My lawyer said it still could take several months. To make matters worse, the Hartford gallery sent me a letter saying they would no longer exhibit my photos. It was unexpected because there were only five pictures displayed there. It was no big deal, but I wanted to know what had changed the curator's mind.

She didn't give me an explanation, but one staff member told me, "Someone contacted the museum director and told them not to display your works." I knew who he was. It was him, Orlando Sierra. He played a dirty trick to embarrass me. I felt mad initially but regained my calm. I did not consider myself a great photographer anymore. I was more interested in writing.

My lawyer said Orlando wanted an uncontested, quick divorce, citing the following grounds: my negligence, teaming up with my daughter to disengage him, and degrading his Cuban heritage. For these reasons, he demanded I should agree to an immediate divorce. I was outraged by his unfounded claims and disrespect to Ashley and me. I, after consultation with my lawyer, countered his argument: it was he who disregarded my heritage, he who exercised both verbal and physical violence to Ashley and me, he has been engaged in illicit relationships with another woman, and he abandoned his family. We demanded, for these reasons, that he pay a half million dollars of alimony, as well as pay off the mortgage on our house, support Ashley's college education until graduation, and stop harassing us immediately.

It took several months of back and forth. Sometimes, I sensed a mysterious person stalking me. This was a nasty fight – a real nightmare. The rumor mill said Orlando now lived with a Latino, white woman in his Manhattan apartment, but I didn't send a spy to confirm it. He had left my mind a long time ago. I just wanted a fast and reasonable settlement. After proposal and counter proposal, we reached an agreement. He pays ten years of the mortgage, I will be the sole owner of my current house, he supports Ashley's college tuition and no additional alimony. I knew he had a considerable amount of money in the stock market, but I didn't ask for more. Money was no motivation for our divorce. We both signed the papers and sent them to the Family Court. It was done. No crying, no bitterness, no yelling, and no court battle. It could have been worse. I have seen many long and ugly divorces.

We didn't shake hands. We looked at each other with cold eyes and didn't initiate conversation. No thanks, no sorry. We just closed one chapter of our lives. The day we parted for the last time, the wind was blowing hard. It was a Northwest gust from New England. He turned his back and walked to his car without giving me a glance. The strong wind pushed his back as if saying to him, "Don't look back. Go fast. Don't come back. Leave her alone." That was it. I had to give a sigh of relief. Ashley and I smiled happily. I told my parents what had happened. My father was glad to hear it. My mother didn't say anything. I kept more distance from my mother. Ashley didn't like her grandmother either. A few days later, I hired cleaners to empty his room and throw away all his leftover belongings. Then, I hired a painter to repaint the whole house. I needed fresh air and a new start. I wanted to forget all the unpleasant memories I had of him.

Chapter 10

An Injured Bird

1997, Westchester, New York
Young Min Park

It was a cloudless October afternoon. My wife was lying in her room, looking at the trees through the windows. The birds were happy, twittering noisily and teasing at each other. They were small ones, chasing one another from one tree to another. It's their game. Our house was not far from the woods. There were tall trees around, and all sorts of birds came and went. Occasionally, some big birds flew in and chased the small ones away. Won Oak loves birds. When we were studying theology in Korea, she disappeared from time to time to watch birds in the forest. There were plenty of high trees around the school buildings.

Years ago, we traveled to Washington, D.C. and visited the Smithsonian Air and Space Museum. There, we learned that the Wright brothers were inspired to invent the first plane by watching birds flying high in the sky. It was 1903 at a beach in North Carolina. Orville and Wilbur Wright played with other boys at the beach. At that moment, big birds were flying against the blue sky with their wings beating powerfully. They stopped playing, struck with awe, and then fell into deep thought. They asked themselves, "How can the birds fly but we can't?" They spent many months designing a flying machine and finally piloted the first powered airplane, 20 feet above a wind-swept beach in North Carolina. It was airborne for 12 seconds and covered 120 feet. It all came from sharp observation and curiosity. I always tell my young parishioners, "Think big. Ask questions. Imagine. All great discoveries and inventions come from imaginations."

My wife and I believe bird watching can help soar our trajectory. A few years ago, I was frightened by a birds' attack. There are two small trees at our entrance. Whenever we tried to open the door, the birds appeared suddenly and scared us. They flew like warbirds, so close to our face that we felt real danger. We didn't know what was going on for some time, finally figuring out that they built a nest at one of the trees and were trying to protect it. I made a grave mistake. I knocked down their nest to safeguard our family. For a week, whenever I unlocked the door, the birds attacked me. I was not severely injured, but they hit my back, and I suffered a few minor injuries. I never removed a bird's nest again after that incident. I learned the hard way. A few months ago, I found a bird on our doorstep. It looked injured, could not fly or even move. The bird episode crossed my mind, "What should I do with this poor bird?" I decided to leave it there. A few hours later the bird was gone. I assumed the bird recovered strength and flew to the woods.

I am with my wife now. She is going through wear and tear. She is weakened physically and mentally. She was an injured bird and could not fly as free as before or sing with other birds as before. She cannot walk, drive, or talk to women church members without pain. Her wings were broken. She was a wounded bird.

I felt pity for her. I said, "You are looking at the birds. I know you want to fly. It will take some time. You will be able to fly again. Even higher and farther."

She stopped weeping and said, "I know. God will give me stronger wings. I can pick more prey and deliver that to the church people. Pray for my fast recovery."

I held her hands gently and prayed, "Lord, thank you for saving her life. Her body is fragile, but I believe you can lift her spirit again. She is the mother of our church. She saved me many times. Lord, please help me to help my dear wife."

She fell asleep. I looked at her face. It was covered in bruises and cuts. Won Oak was not the same wife I had seen the last twenty years. She looked exhausted and so different. I shut the door quietly behind me.

Her injury was too extensive and deep to be healed in a few months. Her broken body was not responding well to normal life. She lost her appetite, suffered sleeping disorders, and her mind was full of negative thoughts. She was angry at herself and our son Tim. Only Sarah was allowed to stay close to her and so took care of her needs. My wife often complained that her life was not worth living anymore. We worried about not only her physical health and but also possible depression. She sometimes closed her door and refrained either Tim or me from entering. She was falling deep into isolation and despair. Her recovery slowed down. I wanted to take her to the psychotherapist, but she refused. Before, she was gregarious and fond of associating with female church members but was now telling them not to come to see her. She didn't want to show her damaged body to them. She was too proud to expose her weakness.

I noticed that Won Oak began to drink wine. She thought a glass of red wine was good for her heart. I remember she told me that her father drank too much. She used to say, "When my father came home drunk, I shut my door and wouldn't come out until morning." Her uncle drank too. She said, "Drinking is embedded in our family's blood." I recommended drinking tea instead of wine, but she didn't listen, "It helps me to sleep, reduces tension, and relaxes me. I am my father's daughter." I warned her even moderate alcohol consumption is associated with developing cancer, violence, and injuries from falls.

"It's hard science." I reminded her.

I took her to a Korean physical therapist twice a week. They helped remedy her physical impairment and disabilities through the promotion of mobility and functional ability. That enhanced and maintained her physical fitness and overall health. Our church choir director recommended musical therapy. My wife loves music, especially gospel songs. Sarah played a tape recorder full of the songs Won Oak liked the most. She sang along in a low voice and wept. The music director said moderate weeping is actually good for her health because it washed away anxieties. He believed in the healing power of music. She drank less and less. Her family's drinking problem told her to stop drinking, and she did.

She began to walk slowly in the third month after the accident. Sarah held her hands and walked around the block for twenty minutes at a time. As she gained strength, Sarah took her longer distances. She started light exercise, including stationary biking at home. We purchased exercise equipment for our family. Around the fourth month, her mobility had improved considerably. My wife's injury enhanced the relationship between Sarah and her mom.

I heard my wife saying to Sarah, "Thank you, Sarah. You are the best daughter. You are a better daughter than I was at your age."

Sarah said, "What are you talking about? You are my mom, and you are sick now. Who else can help you?" Sarah looked around and said to her mother, "Mom, I have no idea what Tim is doing. He is not coming home on time. He doesn't go to church. He doesn't read Bible. And I heard he said to his friends that Bible is a made-up story. How can a pastor's son say that?"

My wife was so shocked that she pretended she hadn't heard for a time. Eventually, she responded, "Is Bible a fiction? Is he insane? Of course, Bible is based on truth. Even if he has some doubts, he shouldn't say that at school or church. His dad is a pastor."

On that evening, my wife called me with concern on her face and told me the story. It made me worry. If anybody in our church heard him, it would definitely cause a big controversy. My wife's unfortunate injury silenced the fury for the time being. I felt the flame would soon rekindle to haunt me.

I told to my wife, "I will tell him not to say that again. Don't worry. I will calm him down."

Won Oak did not seem satisfied, "Can you teach him? He is as stubborn and odd as you are. He is a father's son, while Sarah is a mother's daughter." She added, "We need peace at home and church. Maybe the latter is more important. It's consequential."

My son, Tim, is 18 years old. He is taller than me. I am 5'10", he is a strong-built 6 feet. He had been a top student at Westchester High School and was accepted by Dartmouth College. He was very excited, and we are happy for him. Tim wants to study business at Dartmouth and get an MBA. He got scholarships, but still we have to pay twenty thousand dollars a year. As a pastor's family, we have little savings. My mother called us a few weeks ago and said she would give us her savings.

She said, "I don't have much money, but I will give whatever I have to my grandson. I think your grandpa will agree."

Tim sent a grateful thank you letter to her, explaining that he would use the money as an investment to make more in the future.

I asked, "Oh, you want to be a rich guy. A millionaire."

He said, "A millionaire? It's nothing in today's economy. I want to make hundreds of millions, if not billions."

"So you want to be super rich, not just rich. Why do you want to make so much money?" I said.

He looked at me and said, "For you, Dad. And for mom. You will probably need my support. If I am not rich, how can I help you?"

I was perplexed, "How do you know I will be poor?"

Tim paused a few minutes and replied, "It's my instinct. Nobody will help you but I. Dad, I know you well – your integrity, your strength, and your weakness as a man and as a pastor. Don't worry. I will be on your side. You can rely on me when in need. I think Sarah will be okay. She is such a nice girl. She will meet a great guy. Mom is unstable after the accident, but she is a strong woman, she will manage by herself."

I don't know what to say to my son. I was pleased that he knew me quite well and appreciated his deep concern for my future. I changed the subject. He was on the high school golf team. He couldn't afford that much time to practice months ago, but now he enjoys the game after his acceptance to Dartmouth. "So how was your game today? Any eagles? Or at least some birdies?"

He said, "Golf is a hard game. No eagle. A couple of birdies, but I screwed up four holes. Two doubles and two triples. I don't think I am a good golfer. Golf is my hobby, not my profession."

I said, "That's okay. It is a very sophisticated game. It requires patience, strategy, composure, confidence. I like the game, but my score is always bad. I cannot control my emotion."

He said, "Me too. People might think I am a calm person, but I can be a volatile guy. I am your son, dad. I got your personality. Mom says I am exactly like you. Good or bad. I hope more good than bad. It cannot be all good. Nobody's perfect."

It was not a perfect moment, but I was compelled to discuss his thought about the Holy Bible. I said to him, "Tim, do you read Bible? Someone said you were missing Bible study often. Is that true? If yes, why? You are a pastor's son, if you don't attend Bible studies, people will say something bad about us."

He seemed uncomfortable being asked, "Dad, I don't want to go to Bible study. I don't believe. I am not interested at all. I would rather read history books and biographies at that time."

It was not unanticipated, but I was astounded by his bluntness. I said, "What are you talking about? The Bible is the greatest book that has ever been written. It was read over thousands of years by uncountable numbers of people. In it, God Himself speaks to men. It is a book of divine instruction. And also, Bible rebukes our sin. It gives daily inspiration for our every need. Besides, it is not simply one book. It is the book of books. It is an entire library of books covering the whole range of literature. It includes history, poetry, drama, biography, and even science."

He said, "Science? Divine instruction? I am sorry to say this. I think it is against modern science and the whole story is based on divine lies. Yes, it is true that Bible is the most read book in the history, but I can never understand why. I just believe any book written two thousand years ago is outdated and has to be revised to meet our times."

I said, "Divine lie? That's a dangerous description. You should not utter the words. Don't you believe in Genesis?"

Tim laughed and said, "It's a great car. Proudly made in Korea. I wish I had a Genesis. Sorry, dad. I don't believe in Genesis. First parts of Genesis were beautifully written. 'God created the heaven and earth—God called the light Day, and the darkness he called Night. God called the dry land Earth, and gathering together of the waters called them Sea—He made the Stars.' But, I don't believe He made male and female."

Tim said he was not sure about Creation theory. I cannot blame him. It is an endless debate. Bible said God created the world, but scientists disagree. I was thinking of my wife. She wanted me to persuade Tim to believe Bible. I said, "The Bible alone truly answers the greatest questions that men of all ages have asked: Where have I come from? How can I know the truth? Bible reveals the truth about God, explains the origin of man, points out the only way to salvation and eternal life, and explains the problem of sin and suffering. All answers are in the Bible. Read it every day. A chapter a day. Bible is a telescope and a microscope. You can see the whole universe and find out all of the marvelous details of the spiritual world.

Tim seemed unconvinced. He said, "There are too

many miracles in the Bible. I first thought Bible is a good book, but there are so many incredible tales in it."

I said, "Only God creates those miracles. We humans can't. That's why we believe in Him. He is Above us. He has super powers."

Tim didn't back down, "Dad, how can scientifically trained people believe those miracles? And they say it's truth, not even legend. I cannot believe Jesus made wine from water, raised lepers from death, feed thousands of people with a few pieces of bread, and opened the blind man's eyes with dirt. It's too much for me." Tim continued, "I like his teaching. Jesus is the greatest teacher. I especially admire, 'Love your enemies, bless them that curse you, do good to them that hate you and pray for them which spitefully use you and persecute you. And love your neighbor.' His Words made us humble. They help us forgive people and deepen our love."

I couldn't continue to talk about Bible deep into the evening. He may be one of those young men who doesn't believe the whole thing in the Bible. I guess he thinks Bible is a great book, but couldn't accept everything in there. If I were not a pastor, I would not push him to read and memorize.

I said to my son, "Thanks for your time. I think we had a good talk. We have some disagreement, but it's not the end of the world. We need more talk later on."

Tim replied, "Thank you, dad. Everybody says you are an honorable man and I am very proud of you. I feel lucky to have you. Most of the Korean parents have no communication with their children. I know what's going on in our church. Some elders don't like you. They might make more trouble in the future. I will be careful expressing my opinion. I will contact my peer group to sway the opinion. I love you, dad." We hugged. Father and son confirmed their respect and deep love to each other that night. What I found out that night was that he loved me and he was deeply concerned about my wellness. I thought he was a naughty boy, careless of his family. I was glad to learn that he really cared about us and was trying to help. I knew I should not fall into miserable situations only to be rescued, but you never know.

I heard my wife coughing. Sarah was beside her. Sarah kept busy taking care of her. She even slept beside her bed when her mom couldn't move. I knew my wife wanted to know how my discussion with Tim was going. I told my wife we had a good conversation. She smiled but seemed doubtful. My wife was right. Tim made another big mistake, and it haunted us.

An assistant pastor's job is delicate. He shouldn't be either too rebellious or too obedient to the principal pastor. When I was in that position, I just did my job. I didn't try to curry favor from the principal pastor or give him too many suggestions. I did my daily routine faithfully. Since the principal pastor was my senior in theology school, he liked and trusted me. I had no problem with key church members, and I won their respect. I recently heard what had happened at a certain Korean church. One Sunday, the chief pastor suddenly announced that the first assistant pastor was leaving the church as of that day. No reason was given. No advance notice. He was just fired. Rumors circulated not only in the church but in the whole community. The young pastor was a bright, ambitious, and capable. He gave excellent sermons when he substituted for his boss. He was loved by all levels of the congregation. The principal pastor was precarious about his job security and tried to find excuses to get rid of his subordinate. One day, he heard from one of the influential elders that his assistant pastor was trying to start his own church in the neighborhood. It infuriated him and he dismissed him overnight. Months after he was fired, he actually opened a new church about three miles away from this first church.

Our church also had an assistant pastor. He was hired by my predecessor. I knew he was a clever man and pliable to powerful church members. He was five years younger than I and got his theology education in Seoul. He said his father was an elder and his maternal grandfather was a pastor. When our church was swirled in controversy, elder Huh approached him and attempted to make him "his man." My wife knew this and advised me to be wary of him. She knew I hated the division and power game.

Elder Huh had two sons. The first son was a bank manager of a Korean bank in Manhattan and the second son a college student. Youth group Bible study was given by Curtis, the English mission elder. He taught Bible every Sunday after service. About twenty high school and college students participated. Huh's sons always attended youth group. Sarah was also a regular member, and Tim had been attending on and off. He was absent more often than present. This was the place where Sarah heard her brother question the truth of the Bible. Elder Curtis didn't take it seriously; he was challenged many times from other students. He said he welcomed the questions and addressed the whole truth of the Bible. Tim said he was thankful for his answer and told him that he would read Bible more carefully.

Huh's son had twisted what had happened and brought it to the attention of his father, "Pastor Park's son, Tim, said he did not believe what's in the Bible. He thinks Bible is a fiction."

Elder Huh was happy to hear this. This was the kind

of story he was looking for. He spread the story to his fellow elders and to assistant pastor Kim. They amplified it and circulated it among all of the youth group members. Tim was furious to hear this. He figured out the source of the rumor and challenged Tom Huh.

"Tom, I thought you were a gentleman. It was true that I raised the question, but Curtis said it was a legitimate one. How can you distort it viciously and attack me?"

Tom was in a fret. He hurriedly escaped the confrontation. My wife was disturbed by the whole episode. As an injured pastor's wife, this is the last thing she wanted to hear.

She called her church friends, "Someone distorted my son's question. I am injured and still not well. Please do not make this an issue. It might be my fault because I didn't teach my son the right thing. He regrets that. Soon he will go to college. Let us bury this nonsense and move forward. Tim promised me to raise money for the youth group summer retreat."

Most women were concerned over my wife's health and dismissed it. But Huh's wife, Pastor Kim's wife, and their friends refused to extinguish the firestorm. They believed they had grasped a good chance to embarrass me. It made me mad.

I called Pastor Kim into my office and said, "We cannot demand our sons be the same as us. They are young, rash and challenging. They could ask questions with which we don't agree. That's their privilege. We shouldn't curtail their imagination. I have a son, and you have a son. Don't use the episode to your advantage. You have to earn the respect of church people. Respect is not given easily. You will be the main pastor someday. Maybe sooner than you think. Look ahead, don't just watch your feet. I wish you to be changed."

He didn't say anything. No apology. No regret. He didn't hide that he was Huh's subordinate. I got a strong impression that he was not an honorable man. He is an opportunist. The kind of people I dislike. I hated church politicians. I did not believe he would be a good pastor in the future. I don't believe he is a man of conscience. I told him, "I am not going anywhere. You should be a man of honor before being a pastor." I banged the door behind his back.

The Joy of Love

Elder Curtis invited me to a dinner two weeks after Tim's controversy. He lived in Rockland County, about 30 minutes from our church. Curtis is an engineer. He has worked for a big machinery company for the past thirty years. He was a born Christian. His father was a deacon, and his mother was a pastor's daughter. He was approaching retirement age. He worked fewer hours at his career and managed to find more time for church work. His family attended a Presbyterian church not far from his house. As new immigrants were coming to the neighborhood, he saw the community changing rapidly. Day laborers were standing at the corner of the main roads, and white retirees moved to warmer weather. One day, he attended his granddaughter's school concert. He was surprised to find out that almost half of the students were minorities. Congregations of his church have decreased steadily; every Sunday he heard someone had retired and moved to Florida. The church pews were half filled, then quarter filled, and finally less than twenty people attended. His church could not be maintained financially. It barely supported their pastor thanks only to the donation of a recently deceased member.

Michelle Curtis, Elder Curtis' granddaughter, had a Korean friend at school. Katie Kim was one of the best students in the middle school. Her parents had a beauty supply store in a mixed neighborhood. Kim's family attended Westchester Korean Church, and the two girls went to the church for Sunday service. One Sunday, Curtis went to the church to pick Michelle up and met Young Min. He was impressed by his calm demeanor and decided to move to the ethnically diverse immigrant church. As our Korean church's English mission added members, we needed an elder. I asked Curtis, and he agreed. This was three years ago.

The English mission started small but was growing gradually and a year ago, reached forty members. Elder Curtis and I met after service every other Sunday to discuss church matters. As our church was swirled by controversy, and there was a division between the English and Korean congregations, we didn't feel comfortable sitting together at the church. There were too many watchful eyes.

During one of our secret meetings, he welcomed me and said, "Thanks for coming. My wife went to visit her parents in Florida. Her mother is sick. She has been ill for a few years. I hear she is very weak. My wife stays with her mom 2-3 months a year. By the way, how is your mother in Korea?"

I replied, "She is fine, goes to church every morning, every Wednesday evening, and of course never misses Sunday service. She worries about me."

He responded, "Incredible! You know what I learned from Korean church? You are too religious and rigorous. It's like Do or Die. Faith is not a matter of life or death.

Everybody should enjoy the freedom of belief. Why do Korean churches have early morning services? Don't they sleep at all?"

I said, "I agree with you. There are lots of Korean churchgoers like my mom. Especially the old generation. I believe they are controlled by religion, not enjoying their freedom of faith. I don't think we should have a Bible study in the early morning and I proposed not to have one, but they questioned my faith. My wife was leading it twice a week until she was hurt by that serious car accident. I always ask them to loosen up, but they don't listen to me. They've built a thick wall. I cannot break it. My mom is the same. She doesn't listen. She virtually lives at the church. Church is her home."

Our discussion moved to other church matters. I said, "Thanks for leading junior Bible class. I know Tim asked you stupid questions. I didn't expect him to be religious, but I guess he went too far. He shouldn't question the integrity of Bible. People who don't like me use Tim's questions as a weapon to attack me."

He said, "No, it's a legitimate doubt. I had the same question when I was his age. The Bible was not written by Jesus himself. Someone wrote His Words based on what he had heard and learned. I think legends and folklore supplied some of the material. Young minds should have lots of questions; that's their privilege. Tim raised the inevitable issue. He is not the first one. Many students have asked me similar questions. If someone distorted that to attack you, they were not good Christians. This is another thing I hardly understand about Korean churches. Some people think of a church as a battlefield. I don't understand why they insult others. They don't enjoy the Joy of Love. Church should be a place of forgiveness, tolerance, and love of God."

I said, "I believe the church has to be changed to reflect the new era. We are living in the social media times. Science occupies people's mind. Our families are broken. Even our church has divorcees, lots of single moms, and drug addicts. We have to embrace them."

Curtis agreed, "Absolutely. We need to accept gay people and unmarried straight couples too. It should be a global church. We should pursue diversity. The church should greet families with empathy and comfort. The church has made the mistake of alienating some people who want to be closer to the church by using Bible passages against these people. The Catholic churches are going in the right direction, as do some reformed Protestant churches. Modern churches need another reform movement like that of Martin Luther – especially Korean churches. Maybe you should be the trailblazer. Somebody has to break the glass ceiling. The church doctrine is not a weight to be carried. It is a good piece of bread which can help people live. I wish you would be one of the first pastors to go in that direction."

I was shocked. I felt my face redden. I knew I was not brave. I have been a weak believer. I was nervous.

Curtis noticed my uneasiness. "Pastor Park, I know some people criticize you and are even trying to expel you from the church. They don't know you. Their minds are clouded by self-righteousness. They are not trying to understand each other. They don't know how to love. They only know how to hate and destroy others. They are not Christians. They are street gangs. They should leave this church, not you. I heard they are questioning your belief in the Resurrection and His Second Coming. There's already discussion among scholars in theology. Jesus's Resurrection is a mystery. The Bible says there were witnesses, but scientific-minded people hardly

155

believe it. His Second Coming is even harder to believe. Will Jesus come to the world from Heaven and awaken the dead? Who would believe this? If it happens, who would feed them? The planet would be overcrowded and explode. I think more people will deny this and someday the church has to accept that. Remember, the church denied gays, abortion, contraception, and even the role of women. Now it is widely accepted. Only a few ultra-conservative churches refuse to recognize these rights. Church will be changed as the times change. A church is a social institution. Churches exists for people. If a majority of people do not believe in His Resurrection and Second Coming, the Church will interpret the Bible differently. Those who don't believe will not be shamed or pressured. I know it's a different story for pastors. I think many pastors have doubts. They just don't admit them. They always quote the Bible. 'The Bible says this' and 'the Bible says that.' I believe some day, not decades from now; some reformed-minded pastors will say they do not believe in resurrection and the second coming. They might feel uncomfortable for some time, but eventually, they will prevail. Pastor Park, you are thinking too much. Please do not worry. Everybody knows you are honest. Your sermons move peoples' hearts because they come from your deep emotion. I know what you are facing now. You are at the crossroad. Bad people are trying to kill you. Be strong. Someone will rescue you. I invited you here tonight to give you these words. You looked very tired. You need a break. You need to have a vacation. Go to some quiet place and forget everything."

It was already dark. I looked into his face with awe. I am 5' 10", he is 6', but he looked so much taller than me. He is only ten years older than me, but I felt like a baby in front of him that evening. I said, "Thank you, Elder

Curtis. You know everything about me, and I cannot hide it. I know who I am. And that haunts me."

Curtis hugged me and said, "Don't think too much. Nothing is more important than your happiness. I will pray for you. Every day."

When I came home, my wife asked me where I had been off to. I said that I had visited Curtis. She said, "He is a fine man. He will never hurt you. He cannot help you much either. Americans are a minority in our church. Elder Huh's group consider them enemies. They are a Do or Die type of people. Be careful. Don't be caught in the trap."

I hugged her and said, "I know the dangers. I have to avoid the nets like a fish. I need a vacation. I am thinking of taking a trip to the Amazon with Tim. It would be his graduation present and also a celebration of his acceptance to Dartmouth. We should be proud of him. He has been a headache for you, but I believe he loves our family and will help us in the future."

My wife said, "Okay. You two can have a vacation. Cool off your head and recharge your energy. Tough times are waiting for us."

Chapter 11

Meeting of Waters

Quito, Ecuador
Elena Reynolds

"12 Day Kaleidoscope of Ecuador, through the Andes
Mountains & Amazon."

I was fascinated by this ad. I was looking for an escape
from the brutal cold. I called the travel agency and
asked a thousand questions. The price was right, a
bit less than three thousand dollars, including airfare.
12 days would be about right too, not too short and not
too long. The itinerary was well organized; two days in
Quito, two days in the deep Andes, one day in Cuenca,
two days at the Amazon Basin, and finally three more
days in Manaus, Brazil, which is the heart of the Amazon.

When I mentioned my travel plan to Ashley, she
immediately jumped in, "Mom, I am joining too. Don't
leave me alone. I like remote areas. I hate big cities.
Those places are full of lies. I want to meet natives. My
sociology teacher even suggested traveling. He usually
gives us extra credit when we submit a good travel essay."

What she said was what I was thinking. I couldn't agree more with her. I also believe big cities are full of hypocrisies and deceit. They lie to win. That's the game of politics and business. The natives don't have to lie because their lives are so simple. Nature feeds them. They just cultivate the land. They have plenty of sun and rain. I wanted to meet those innocent people. I called the tour company again and booked the trip for the two of us.

When our flight landed in Quito, Ashley complained, "Mom, it's hard to breathe. How about you?".

I said, "I told you, Ashley. We are at a higher altitude, close to 2,500 meters above the sea level. Don't rush. Slow down and drink a lot of water. Don't worry; you will be okay. People have lived here forever at this height. Your heart will adjust soon."

There were several people in baggage claim already. I saw two Asian men there. They looked like a father and son. We checked into Mercure Hotel, not far from downtown. It was a busy tourist hotel. Our room was not spacious, but it was convenient. I knew from travel experience that most of the big city hotel rooms are small. That night, we joined the welcoming session – a kind of get-together where we would meet each other and learn our tour schedule. It was a good – sized tour group, 21 people in total. People came from all over, a senior woman from Kentucky, three from Pennsylvania, two from Virginia, a couple from Toronto, two from Florida, two from California, and several from many other states. The age range was diverse too. Most of them looked like retirees, but some were in their 50s and 40s, as well as two young people. The young ones were Ashley and an Asian guy. We introduced ourselves; where we came from and our brief travel experiences. Nobody asked about our professions. That was too private to ask, as we had just met. We had drinks, I, a glass of white wine, Ashley, a diet coke. Other travelers drank wine or beer. The tour guide gave us badges and luggage tags. Dinner was up to us. Ashley and I went to the hotel cafeteria and ate lightly. The tour guide advised us to get up at 6, eat breakfast at 7, and be at the city tour by 8 a.m. the next morning.

Our group first went to discover Quito's colonial quarter, the largest and best preserved in South America, designated a UNESCO World Heritage Site. Here, I heard the Asian man, introduced as Young, asking lots of questions to the guide. He always carried a small notebook and jotted down what he had learned. He looked as serious as a student, trying not to miss anything that his teacher said. I vaguely thought he must be a journalist or a scholar.

We entered the church. It wasn't huge compared to the ones I had seen in Europe. The church was built by President Sergio Moreno, and there was a statue of him in the middle of the square. There were lots of hawkers selling shawls – two for five dollars. I bought two from a young woman who carried a beautiful baby on her back, although I wasn't sure about the quality. I wanted to ask her where her husband was but didn't. I imagined he was working somewhere else. At 11 a.m., we went to President's Square to watch the changing of the royal guard ceremony. I had seen them in London and Ottawa, Canada, but this was unique. Rafael Correa, the president of Ecuador, presided over the ceremony, with his wife, from a high balcony – waving to the crowd. The military band played the national anthem, and the crowd sang. To my disappointment, I could not hear the actual ceremony because of the hawkers incessant yelling.

Ecuador has used the US dollar as their currency since 1999. Their economy is booming, and prices are stabilized. Because the dollar works there, we could buy a bunch of fruit for five dollars on the street. People seemed not well educated, but they looked innocent. They never pushed tourists to buy anything. The natives were short, sturdy, and strong.

Our last stop of the day was to the Equator. It was half an hour drive from downtown Quito. Quito, the Ecuadorian capital, came from the word 'Equator.' This, of course, is an imagined line drawn around the Earth equally distant from both poles. It divides the earth into the northern and southern hemispheres and constitutes the parallel of latitude 0. The sun passes over the Equator twice a year, on March 21st and September 23rd. Here the length of day, sunrise to sunset, is almost constant across the whole year. Each day is 14 minutes longer than the night. There were a tower and yellow line marking the exact location of the equator. It passes from here to Colombia, Brazil, crosses the Atlantic Ocean, and goes on to Africa. It passes through Gabon, Congo, Uganda, Kenya, crosses the Indian Ocean, and meets again in Indonesia. The natives discovered this three thousand years ago, and its name spread to Europe. French and German astrologists came here to study. There are many statutes of the astrologists along with sculptures of hummingbirds.

I took many pictures with Ashley as well as our group picture. I stood with one leg in the northern and the other in the southern hemispheres. Ashley and I walked the yellow line, the Equator. Here I saw Young again asking many questions and taking notes. He copied words from informational boards and looked at the statues very carefully. I have never seen such a serious traveler before.

We were right under the Equator, but it was windy and cool. We were still at a high altitude, 2,483 meters above sea level. It wasn't easy to breathe. I saw Ashley was talking to Young's son, introduced as Tim. He looked like a sincere and agreeable young man.

Our tour group had dinner together that night. We happened to sit at the same table as Tim and Young. Young didn't talk much, looking a bit shy and eating quietly. He drank a glass of local beer, and I ordered a glass of white wine. I learned that he was originally from Korea, although he lives in Westchester now. I didn't ask about his job, and he didn't want to know mine either. Our first encounter as travel mate was courteous, and we kept a certain distance.

That night, Ashley told me about them. Tim was a high school senior and had been accepted by Dartmouth in an early action program. They lived about 30 miles from us. Tim's mother didn't come because of an injury sustained in a car accident. Ashley said that Tim's dad contributes essays to a Korean ethnic paper and that he had received a Master's degree in communication from the State University of New York. I didn't ask any further questions. Young was an unusual, serious traveler, but it seemed to fit him. As a teacher, I always read related books before and after a trip, but I was not as serious as him. I liked to enjoy the moment, and not be agonized as to what to write next.

Riobamba, Ecuador

Young Min Park

Riobamba was at a high altitude. I could feel it as soon

as we got off the bus. We couldn't see the river. The guide told us that it flowed far from here and was considered a small river. Our hotel looked like an old colonial Spanish mansion was built hundreds of years ago. Everything there was old: the small lobby, typewriters, old pictures, an old fireplace, old Fisher sewing machines, lots of antiques, and even old phones. The room was small too, barely big enough for two of us. The bathroom was so tiny that we could hardly move inside. It was inconvenient, but it wasn't a big deal because we stayed only one night.

The food, on the other hand, was delicious. They served soups, trout dishes, and good desert. Tim and Ashley sat together, and Elena and I joined again. For the first time in our travel, I had a chance to talk to her. She looked in her mid-forties, was pretty, and I learned she was an English teacher in Connecticut. I also learned that she was born in Cuba, but left there at age two. She said she couldn't speak Spanish and didn't consider herself a Cuban-American. She also said her grandfather was an English sailor and that's why her name is Reynolds. I knew some Britons lived in Cuba and that they ruled Cuba for a short period.

As our travel continued, the tour members got to know each other naturally. I admired Helen King, a woman from Kentucky. She was 88 years old but in excellent shape. She has 26 grandkids. She was gracious, a true Christian, and very caring. I lost my insect-repelling bracelet twice. She found them for me. Another time, we misplaced our room key and again she found it. She didn't go rainforest hiking or rafting but joined light excursions. Patricia from Philadelphia was very tall, 6'1' the tallest woman I've ever met. She is a serious traveler who likes to travel to remote countries like Costa Rica, Bolivia, Sicily, Estonia, Serbia, and Tibet. She said she once tried having a roommate to save money, but she no longer does that in order to maintain her privacy. Whenever Patricia, the big American girl, walked, all the short natives looked up to her. She was a nice woman, caring about other people. Linda, from Palm Beach, was another interesting woman. She had traveled 82 countries, about half of the countries in the world. She was a retired English teacher. She taught English in many Latin American countries and had lots of students there. I noticed Joe from Virginia approached her and they befriended quickly and slept together. People said they both were divorcees, no reason not to be close. It was a bit odd to me, but I know it happens a lot these days.

Jim, from Arkansas, and Bill, from Pennsylvania, were very friendly to me. Jim approached me as I took notes. He was a radio broadcaster. He knew I was a serious traveler. We had good discussions about the local newspaper and the broadcasting business. He said his wife passed away three years ago. There were some arrogant people in our group too. It was no surprise. There are always people who don't want to try to understand others.

One person drew my attention more than the other. It was Elena. She was not shy, but not aggressive either. She was active, never missed difficult excursions, and asked interesting questions to local people. Whenever I asked questions, some stupid ones too, she listened carefully. She seemed appreciative of my intense curiosity of nature and its flora and fauna. I noticed Ashley was trying to be close to Tim and he didn't discourage her. Sometimes they disappeared alone for an hour or more.

The Guayaquil-Quito railway was built in 1897. About 4,000 Jamaicans, 200 Barbados, and 240 Puerto Ricans were brought in for the construction. Among them, 2,500 died from fatigue, malaria, or yellow fever. Natives believed the devil took them. There is a huge rock on top of the mountain that looks like the nose of a devil. The Quito-Guayaquil train was still running, but not many passengers used it after the Pan-American Highway opened in 1962. The railway is too narrow and doesn't run at night. Only tourism trains run these days. It was a 2-hour ride. A small river – it actually looked like a stream – runs along the rail. The view was breathtaking. People looked outside and shouted for joy. I climbed to the railway museum at the station. It says the rail carried riches of the Ecuadorian coast to the Sierra and connected the rural villages. It also said condors, the big birds, left when the rail was built. The noise of dynamite explosions chased the birds away, and they never came back. What fascinated passengers most was the natives' dancing. Men in red shawls and white pants, women in red skirts and white blouses danced beautifully. One by one, tourists joined. Tall Patricia danced with a short man, and everybody laughed. Ashley danced with another native man and eventually pulled Tim in. I had never seen my son dance. He did okay. Many other people danced with natives, and this went on for at least 30 minutes. I hoped Elena would dance, but she didn't. I am a terrible dancer.

After the train ride, we had lunch near the Aluasi Train station. We all were talking about the dancing. We agreed Patricia's dancing was the funniest and Linda's was the best. Elena asked me, "Why didn't you dance?"

I felt my face flushed. Tim told her, "My dad is too shy to dance in front of many people. He is a terrible dancer."

Elena smiled and said, "That's okay. I am not a good dancer either. But, I dance when I meet a good partner." I didn't ask her what she meant.

San Isidro Lodge, Hummingbird Park

Elena Reynolds

It's February 14th, Valentine's Day. Ashley said, 'Happy Valentine's, mom."

I said, "Happy Valentine's to you. I have nobody as you know. Do you have someone?" My daughter replied, "Mom, you know I don't have a boyfriend. Maybe in the near future."

I looked at her face to figure out what she meant. She smiled unabashedly. I guessed she was referring to Tim in our tour group.

We visited the hummingbird habitat at San Isidro, a rainforest in the not-so-high Andes. It was drizzling. Most of us didn't take an umbrella. We wore hooded rain gear instead because carrying an umbrella was too burdensome for hiking. The tour guide told us interesting stories about hummingbirds. Hummingbirds live only in Canada, the United States, and South America. There are about 170 different species in Ecuador and 17 different ones in this valley alone. Hummingbirds are mostly small, often finger-sized, and they fly low. They drink a kind of nectar from red flowers growing in the wet valley. These birds sing in not-so-high a pitch, and sometimes they just listen. A giant hummingbird is about 6 inches. They vibrate their bodies 2-3 times a second. Thumb-size smaller birds vibrate 80 times a second. I saw many birds flying in the woods. I saw clear water was flowing from the deep mountain, so pure that I could see the bottom of the deep stream. There were numerous poisonous mushrooms there. Tim and Ashley walked in the front with the guide and Young Min, and I followed. I heard him asking many questions to the guide. The guide seemed curious of his nonstop questioning.

He said, "I can see you are very much interested in hummingbirds. Do you have any particular reason?"

I was surprised to hear his answer, "Yea, I think I am like a hummingbird."

I couldn't stop from asking him, "Young, why do you think you are a hummingbird?"

He hesitated for a moment and said, "Those birds live in deep, rainy, dark valleys. They don't have many friends, only some monkeys. The bird is a good listener. They are listening to what we are talking about right now. It is a rare kind of bird, not found everywhere. Somehow I like this bird, and I think it reflects me."

His answer surprised me. I said, "They looks like sad, unsocial birds. But watch out, there are lots of enemies in this valley: poison ivy, poisonous mushrooms, and wild animals. And it rains all year. Don't you like the sunshine? Why do you compare yourself with these sad birds? You should be happier. I consider myself more of a condor, a powerful bird flying high. It's the national bird of Ecuador." I didn't pursue anymore. I just felt Young was a bit of a pathetic person. I wanted to explore his inner world but didn't ask further.

The sunlight speaks. And it's voice is a bird:
It glitters half-guessed half seen half-heard
Above the flower bed. Over the lawn ...
A flashing dip and it is gone.
And all it lends to the eye is this —
A sunbeam giving the air a kiss.

The Hummingbird – by Harry Kemp

On that evening, Ashley told me something about Young. He was born and raised in Korea. He has been living in the U.S. for twenty years. He aspires to be a writer, plans to publish his first collection of short stories in English this year, and is very good at public speaking. Ashley added, "I asked Tim what his profession was, but he avoided answering. I guess they didn't want to talk about that." I sensed that he wasn't happy about his job.

On that night, Tim and Ashley sat at the same table for dinner. Young was eating with Jim and Bill, and I was sitting with Helen and Patricia. I admired Helen. She looked gracious. I couldn't find anger or arrogance in her face. She asked me, "Honey, do you go to church?"

I said, "I was baptized, but have not been going to church every week."

Helen answered, "Oh, you accepted Jesus. Someone will make you go back to church."

I was a bit surprised, "Someone? Someone who? My mom goes to church, but I don't listen to her."

Helen said, "Not your mom. It may be a man. An imperfect man. You don't like people who believe they are perfect. I think you like a flawed man. And you seem to have found one here."

I was intrigued and asked, "Who do you think he is, Helen?"

She looked at me attentively and said, "It's Young. A quiet, thoughtful man. Tim's father."

I was stunned, "How can you say that?".

Helen smiled and responded, "It's my instinct. When people get old, they develop good instincts."

Helen is much older than my mother. My mother cannot read her daughter's mind, but this senior woman might be able to. Young was sitting across from me. He was eating quietly. I took a glimpse at him. He looked lonely. I noticed that he had had more than two glasses of wine. When dinner was over, Tim grabbed his arm and led him to their room. He looked very sad that night, and I was sorry to bear witness to that sadness. That night I saw Tim in the lobby. I asked him, "Is your dad okay? He didn't look good today."

Tim answered, "He is in a bad mood now, but he will

be okay tomorrow. We will be in the Amazon Basin, and he will ask tons of questions again. He is a student. He wants to be a student and a professor someday."

I said only, "I hope everyone in our group feels okay. We have a diverse group, but everyone is punctual and cooperating well. I hope your dad is okay. I got sick once from food poisoning during a Havana trip years ago. Tim. You take care of him."

Tim said, "Of course, I will. He is my dad. Like you are Ashley's mom."

At the moment, Ashley came down from our room. She said, "We are going to look at the gift shop here and then play ping pong. I will be back in an hour. Mom, you take a shower first. Hot water here is not hot water." They looked happy and that made me happy.

Amazon Basin, Ecuador

Young Min Park

On the bus toward the Amazon Basin, Daniel, our tour guide, asked a few questions to the travelers. Daniel was young, but he had a pretty good knowledge about the Amazon. I guessed he did a lot of research. He asked, "Do you know what Amazon means?"

No one answered immediately, so I said, "It means brave. Amazon is English. It's Amazonas in Spanish. It originally came from Greek mythology. When Spanish people came to the Amazon, they were hit by Indian arrows. They believed women fired the shots. Actually, they were men. In native culture, women take care of the kids, cultivate the land, and do domestic works. Men fought wars and did the hunting and fishing. However, the invaders believed Indian women were brave enough to shoot, so they called them Amazonas."

Daniel said, "Perfect. Where did you get that story?"

I answered, "I read books."

Tim looked proud, and Ashley echoed, "Wow, you should be our tour guide." Elena gave me a smile.

Our hotel was located right on the Napo River, one of the many tributaries of the Amazon. Our room was spacious: it had four beds, a big toilet, and an overlooking veranda. But, it didn't have a telephone, refrigerator, TV. It was hot and humid. A high ceiling fan was the only thing we could depend on. Later on, I learned Wi-Fi was available, but not free, and the service was unreliable. I preferred not to have access to it. I had no urgent business to the world I had left. I felt like nobody wanted to know where I was or what I was doing. Tim was connecting to his mother and sister constantly.

Our group had two river excursions; hiking the rainforest and visiting an animal rescue center. Amazon Basin hiking was not so hard. There were two courses, a 2-mile hike, and a 1-mile easy walking. Tim, Elena, Ashley, and I took the challenging one with some of the others. We all wore rubber boots to protect ourselves from ants and other insects. It made the climb more difficult, but we had no choice. The forest was not so dense. There was a suspension bridge and a swing crossing the valley. We could see the view of Napo River at the top of the mountain, but it wasn't as spectacular as I had imagined.

In the afternoon, we visited the animal rescue center by canoe. There we met Nanna, a Danish woman guide. She was young, energetic, very knowledgeable about animal behavior, and her English was excellent. Here we met Trumpie. It's a bird's name. It was a kind of trumpeter bird which looks like a swan. I am telling you what

Nanna told us that day. It is a loyal bird, an assistant guide to Nanna. She would always walk in front of the group – from the beginning to the end. When the tour ended, she dropped her head and said goodbye. I was fond of this bird, and I admired her loyalty and patience. I have never seen such a faithful bird in my life. I wished I had a friend like this bird. Nana told us an interesting story about a naughty monkey. For whatever reasons, he hates Nanna – a beautiful, white blonde. Whenever she approaches the cage, he would grab a stone and threw it at her. Fortunately, she was not hurt thanks to the nets. She said the monkey doesn't like anything about her; her hair color, her voice, her smell, or any aspect of her appearance. It was hard to understand.

We saw lots of parrots there. Nanna said some parrots speak Spanish and a few speak simple English. Animals here were sent by individuals or organizations. They were traumatized once, and now they are either sick or badly behaved. I asked, "How do you know they are traumatized?"

Nanna said, "They don't eat, don't sleep normally, and behave strangely." We learned a lot about Amazon animals – even the ones kept in cages. When they recover health, they are sent to the Amazon jungle again.

That night we had our farewell dinner at a restaurant in the hotel. Elena, Helen, Joe, Bill, and I sat at the same table. We were talking about Trumpie. Helen asked me, "Do you have a loyal friend like that bird?"

I said, "No, I only have bad monkeys who are trying to hurt me." I was surprised I said that. I shouldn't say anything about what was going on in New York.

Helen looked at both Elena and me and said, "Young Min, you have a Trumpie here. Elena is your Trumpie. You and Elena were made special by the Lord. She will guide and save you from trouble."

We were shocked. Elena said, "Helen, I don't know what you are talking about. We barely know each other. We just met here as travelers. Helen smiled and said, "Time will tell you. Elena, you have to protect Young. You two are fated to be friends. I already figured out what kind of individual he is. Young doesn't like chitchat. His heart is very deep. Some might think he is insecure. He has a tendency to save up his points. When he finally speaks up, his points come out almost like a Gatling gun. He is an excellent communicator. He is book smart, but not street smart. He hates to fight. Elena, you can fight. You are fearless. You are decisive. Young needs your protection."

We couldn't say anything. Her aura of civility, kindness, and faith overwhelmed us. It was like a divine order. We just looked at Helen's face. Her gracious and wrinkled old face was smiling. I ordered a bottle of white wine and shared it with Helen and Elena. I said, "Let's cheer for Helen's health and good luck to us."

Helen looked very happy. Elena was all smiles. It was the happiest moment of the trip. All of us hugged and said goodbye to Helen. Only seven of us were set to continue our travels to the Amazon in Brazil. The rest were going home. Helen, an 88-year senior woman, didn't extend her trip. She said, "You guys have a good trip. I am heading home. One week of Ecuador travel is enough for me."

I held her hands and said, "I will miss you. I will pray for you. I am so grateful that I met you here."

She hugged me and whispered in my ear, "Young Min, be simple. Contact Elena when you go home. I will pray for you." I showed tears to her. She has been the most inspiring senior citizen I ever met in my whole life.

Manaus, Brazil

Elena Reynolds

It was hot and humid again. We were at sea level and close to the equator. When we arrived at Manaus airport, late in the morning, the sun was right overhead. It was a busy, tropical airport. Ana Figueroa, our tour guide, was waiting for us. She greeted us, "Welcome to Manaus. You are in the heart of Amazonas."

I looked around and smiled, "Where is the Amazon? I only see the human jungle."

Ana smiled, and said, "It's not far. You will see the real jungle. The tour starts after lunch. We are, altogether 12 people. Five arrived from Miami earlier. It's a good size. Enough for two canoes."

My mind was already in the jungle with the natives. I was anxious to see the real Amazon, not simply the Amazon Basin of Ecuador. The hotel was in a busy area, a typical tourist hot-spot. The lobby was crowded, people in light clothes were coming and going. I expected most of them were tourists like us, but they seemed otherwise. I realized Manaus was the capital of the state of Amazonas – a duty-free zone. More business people come here than tourists. Perhaps, they still are looking for El Dorado, an imaginary gold mine far off in the Amazon.

After lunch, Ana called us together and gave us our tour schedule. "We go on the city tour this afternoon. And we will pass the city center. We are going to the commercial zone. The price is good. You can buy electronic items and other gifts with no duty. I don't think you will buy boats and construction materials here. Then we go to local markets of Amazonas. I don't expect you to purchase bunches of fruits, vegetables, or fish, but just to have an idea what comes from the jungle. Be careful of pick-pockets. Don't carry your passport and any other important items. Put them in the safe. Carry only one credit card and some cash. They accept U.S. dollar here. We will have a welcoming dinner at hotel restaurant tonight. Tomorrow we go to the jungle and never come back. You live there with indigenous people. Can you? I saw a young lady's worrying face. Are you Ashley? Don't worry. We will come back after two full days excursion. We will take the river cruise to see the Meeting of Waters when we come back from the jungle. That's the highlight of Manaus tour. You can never see the fantastic scene in any other place in the world. It's so amazing. Only Amazonas River can make it. Pouring tropical showers are coming at any time. An umbrella is useless. You will be soaked to the skin. I heard from many people it was the best experience they had in Amazon. It dries fast. Any questions?" I looked at Young Min. He didn't say anything. If he doesn't ask any questions, usually nobody does.

Manaus has a two-million people, but there are no high rises downtown. The city was spread out. The Brazilian government designated this city as a free-trade zone. All major industries over the world set up factories here. I saw many Korean company signs, Samsung, LG, and Hyundai-Kia. My TV is from Samsung, and my washing machine is from LG. I have never visited Korea, but somehow I felt Korea would be a friendly country to me. Now that Young and Tim are here, they gave me a chance to understand Koreans better.

I liked wandering around the farmers' market. I could feel their undefiled faces, simple expressions, and natural products, brought from their farms. I tasted many local fruits at the farmer's market on the road in Ecuador.

Here, Young and I were looking at many fish and vegetables. He pointed to a peculiar fish asked me what they
were. I had no idea, "Young, I am not a good house-
wife. I don't cook that much. Let's ask to Ana." We both
smiled. We learned a lot about Amazon produce and
fish. I picked up some mangoes and papaya and gave
a few to Tim. At about 5 p.m., our tour group finished
the schedule.

Young suggested, "We have about an hour until
dinner. Why don't we visit a historical museum here? I
want to see one I read about in an Amazon book." We
went hurriedly to the municipal museum. There, we saw
a very interesting Indian ritual and a shrunken human
head. We read the English explanation, which said it
was a real human head. The natives cut off a captive's
head and desiccated it. It has been a centuries-old ritual,
which still happens in deep Amazon villages. Ashley
frowned and asked Young, "Is it still permitted? It's so
cruel and savage."

Young answered, "Maybe the law doesn't reach to
them. They shun civilization. And, you know what, Mexican drug cartels cut off heads and throw them on the
highway. Usually, thirteen heads at a time."

Ashley was shocked, "Why thirteen? Does the number
mean something?"

I heard Young answer, "I think that's the cartel's ominous number. We are still living in a cruel world. Some
people enjoy dirty fighting. We have to avoid it, but it's
not easy sometimes."

I saw his face darken as he said this. I guessed he was
referring to something which he could not forget. Tim
glanced at him with a bleak face. I couldn't figure out
what Young was going through. I suddenly remembered
what Helen had said the other day, "Save him. He is a

good man. Make contact when you go home."

Acajatuba Jungle Lodge

Young Min Park

At the Negro River, the water was dark – even darker than the Gulf of Mexico. I could see nothing in the water. Everything was hidden in the darkness. The only thing I could see was floating on top of the river – some tree branches and plastic bottles. I ambiguously thought fish were jumping while sea leaves danced with the current. Villages dotted the river, and smoke billowed from the huts. I saw some floating houses and canoes anchored at a marina.

The jungle lodge was 32 miles from Manaus. It took us more than an hour to get there. It was the real Amazon river, not a basin or tributary. It was much wider than any river I had ever seen. It looked like an ocean. Soon Tim, Ashley, and Elena joined. We took pictures. Ashley yelled, "Mom, do you want to take a picture with Tim's dad? Why not? It's just a picture." Elena looked at me. I hesitated.

Tim stepped in, "My dad doesn't like pictures. Ashley, don't try. Dad, would you take a shot for the three of us?"

I said, "Sure. Beautiful. You all look gorgeous." I hoped Elena didn't ask me why I declined to take a photo with her and she didn't.

We arrived at the Acajatuba, a remote village on the river bank. We saw small boats and canoes, but no cars. Canoes functioned as a water taxi, the only means of transportation here. This place was completely isolated from the outside world. I wished to live in this primitive world, and this dream came true, even though it was only a short while. Hotel rooms looked like they were sitting on the treetops. They were always at least one floor above the water. Ashley pointed to marks on the tree and asked me what they were. "It's the watermark. Water reaches this high during the wet season. That's why rooms are sitting so high. I believe people here are really scared in the rainy months."

Ashley said, "It looks beautiful. I think I would be thrilled to live here during the wet season. We can catch fish with our bare hands. Don't you think so, Tim?"

Tim responded, "Sure. Maybe you can catch them. I doubt my dad can. He is not that fast." I agreed with him. As soon as we approached the front office, we heard parrots singing and saw monkeys jumping in the trees. A bunch of natives welcomed us with a dance. They brought fruit cocktails. It was a such a romantic place. I wanted to stay here at least a week. The tour guide told us the Amazon jungle lodges cater to all sorts of travelers' expectations. We can walk the rainforests, can do bountiful fishing, go on long walks to the chattering of monkeys, and enjoy the vibrating silence of jungle nights. We can even meet some of the indigenous peoples.

After checking in, our group took motorized canoes and crossed the Negro River. It was much wider and deeper than the Napo River. We were guided by Thomas, a German-Brazilian guide. Millions of German-origin Brazilians live in the country, mostly in the south of Sao Paulo. He stopped our canoes in the deep river, "Look over there! You will see pink Amazon dolphins. The Amazon river dolphins are not as big as sea dolphins, but they are beautiful."

Soon we saw a school of dolphins jumping out of the black water. The Brazilian government forbids adventurers from catching or killing them. We saw some cruise ships there. The guide said, "Those ships sail along the upper river toward Bethel, which is the mouth to the north Atlantic Ocean. It takes at least a week to get there."

We went rainforest hiking for two hours. We had to wear rubber boots for protection, just as we did in Ecuador. This rainforest was much deeper and was thick with trees and plants. Some plants were used for medicine. The guide said major drug companies sent research staffs here to collect them and plant them at their farms. The trail was stiffer, denser, and there were some wild animals. There were no suspension bridges or swings.

We were caught in a sudden downpour and soaked to the skin. It was a passing shower and not a cold rain. We screamed and tried squeezing water out of our clothes, but we were happy. It dried quickly as we continued walking. I looked at Ashley and Tim. They looked peaceful in the jungle. We all wandered unspoiled jungle like Indians. We returned to nature and enjoyed it. The guide said, "This downpour is nothing. You may have longer and severer rain tomorrow when we go caiman hunting. It rains more at night here in the Amazon. That's a present from heaven. You cannot experience this in any other place. Look at the deep water. The Amazon River is the largest river by volume in the world. This place is blessed, and you are blessed to be here."

We all agreed. Nobody said anything. It was a unique moment. When we arrived at the hotel, the guide told us, "Wash your clothes at the sink and spread them at outside. They will dry quickly. You are in the Amazon. Forget civilization for a while. Behave like natives. Do what nature tells you. You can be friends and love each other."

I looked at Elena. She smiled at me. It was a brilliant

smile. She looked very happy, and she was pretty with that smile on her face. She was as pure as the Amazon River. We met again at dinner. I was relaxed. Tim poured me a glass of wine. I offered one to Elena. She offered me another glass. We drank more than three glasses. She asked me, "Why do you like white wine?"

I answered, "Because it looks pure." Pure-pure-pure. I used this word many times on this trip. Yes, I like pure people. Elena wanted to be as pure as the Amazon water. But—but, my mind is clouded with worries. It is like a cloud forest in the Andes valleys.

On that night, Tim told me, "Dad, I think Ashley took a picture of you and her mom."

I said, "Why did she do that? I didn't want it."

Tim responded, "Dad, don't worry. It's just a picture. She won't show it to any other people. Even her mom didn't know." I was just happy to be here in the deep part of Amazon with Tim and Ashley, and Elena. I wanted to forget everything. The church, my future, even my wife.

Acajatuba Jungle Lodge, Manaus

Elena Reynolds

Today is our last day in the jungle. My heart tells me to stay longer, but I cannot live here forever. To be honest, I couldn't even make it a month. I have to go back home.

The tour guide briefed us on today's schedule, "First, we go to see local rubber trees and watch how they extract juice to make solid rubber. When Spaniards came to the Amazon, they saw children playing with bouncing white balls. They asked kids where they got it from. They learned it was from certain kinds of trees, which turned out to be rubber trees. That was the beginning of the rubber industry. Around 1900, Ford Motor Company started production of the T-Mobile. They needed millions of tires. Spanish conquerors sent Indians to the rainforest to catch rubber juices. All natural rubber comes from these trees. Many of you might think it is some kind of fruit; it's not. It's like maple syrup. Early in the morning, people peel rubber trees and catch the flowing liquid. It stops coming late in the morning. Then, locals boiled the juice in big kettles to solidify it. It's then called rubber. Rubber trees need a certain distance and different angle from each other. Facing trees don't produce juice. Amazon had tens of millions, maybe more, who knew the exact numbers, but they couldn't meet the demands. Someone stole rubber trees from here and planted them in Malaysia and other warm countries. That's the beginning of the end for the Amazon rubber industry. With the decline of traffic, the Manaus Opera House lost its fame. Europeans left here in droves, and Amazon was dead for a while. We will visit a primitive form of rubber kettles soon. The natives will explain the whole process."

I heard Young asking a question, "You said facing rubber trees don't produce juices. What if people moved the tree to a different angle?"

Thomas, the guide, smiled, "That's a good question. I heard people already tried, but it didn't work. The trees recognized each other and continued to hate. Everything has to be naturally fit. A little different soil and forced relocation couldn't satisfy them. Trees are like people. They have to like each other. Otherwise, they cannot get along." I saw Young was nodding. Even trees have to like one another to bear fruit. How about a man and a woman? I learned a big lesson in the Amazon jungle.

Attraction is a rule of the jungle.

The native rubber man was old and lean. His all-wrinkled face and gray hair told us the history of the rubber business. He said, "I am almost 85 years old. I roamed rainforest to take rubber liquid. My father taught me how to boil and make products. And suddenly rubber days were gone. I heard they planted millions of trees in the tropical South Asian countries and they produced better rubbers. What you see now is the old tradition." Then he showed all the processes with his skilled hands.

We purchased some wares made of rubber as souvenirs. I saw Young had bought a couple of items. I knew he got them not because he liked them in themselves, but out of respect for their tradition.

There was a public school not far from the rubber huts. It was at the bank of the river. Canoes were anchored nearby. There was only one classroom. It didn't have windows. A young female teacher told us about the school. "I am the only teacher here. I teach from kindergarten to sixth grade. We have 20 students. They come here from all over by canoe. This school doesn't have windows because it's too hot. When the storm comes, we close with wood panels. This school is subsidized by the Amazonas state government, but money is short for months at a time. A number of foreign charity organizations help us. The kids are beautiful. They are better educated than their parents. Many leave here to Manaus or other cities once they can read and write."

As a teacher, I was interested greatly by this primitive school. There were not enough desks or school supplies. My biggest question was how one teacher could teach all subjects and at all levels. It was beyond my understanding. The tour company prepared some school supplies for them. If I had known, I would have prepared some myself. I asked the guide whether we could donate some money. He said, "They are supposed not to accept it. If the government knew they would say something, but I don't think they care. They are not helping this school anyway." I looked at Young, and we reached a tacit agreement. We donated one hundred dollars. I guessed it was a pretty hefty sum for them. Other tourists chipped in some too. I just hoped they would spend it properly.

At 5 p.m. that evening, our tour guide summoned all us, "We are going caiman hunting tonight. It's quite challenging, but not very dangerous. Because we get there by canoe, in the pitch darkness, it could be somewhat dangerous. Only flashlights. The local guide knows the water and exact spot where caimans are. They hide in the swamp. Our canoes will approach there silently. They are afraid of lights and will be confused. Our guys will catch them, and you are going to eat them. Just kidding. Don't be scared. He will catch and release them. It is so dark that some of you may feel scared. There will be bumps in the current. One time our canoe lost power, and we were drifted for an hour. Another danger is a severe thunderstorm. As I said, we have storms at night. When the temperature drops, the storm approaches. It could last about half an hour. Water suddenly swells, and the wind pushes canoe to the corner. You will be completely soaked and may feel chilly. It's your choice. I would recommend elderly and sick people to stay at the hotel. You certainly have some risks, and we are not insured. I can assure you, though; this will be one of the highlights of your Amazon trip. You will never forget the moments. Anybody who wants to join must sign this form. Basically, it says you take your own risk, and we are not liable."

Some of us were scared. Four people gave up. Ashley,

Young, Tim, and I signed the form. Three other young travelers followed. The guide said, 'Okay, seven people signed. There will be ten altogether including me and two local guides. We meet at seven, here. It's dark. If you have rain gear, wear it. It might not be good enough but will help. Don't bring any important items. Just bring your body and courage. Nature doesn't check your passport, and it doesn't want your money. We don't wait for you. If you don't show up, we consider you are giving up." He looked stern and unwavering. I looked at Young. He signaled he was ready.

We, four of us had an early dinner and met at seven. We felt like we were pirates or smugglers. We were in an adventurous mood. Everything went exactly as the guide told us. Darkness covered the whole river. We couldn't see an inch ahead. Two flashlights guided us through the water. The local guides knew the current. It took more than 30 minutes to reach the spot. The local guides killed the engine and rowed by paddle. They couldn't locate the hiding place of the caiman at first. They searched another spot. They failed again and looked frustrated. Thomas told them to go farther and finally they signaled that they had found a likely spot. They pushed aside bushes and shed the flashlight across the water. Then they exclaimed that they had indeed found them. We were deadly silent, not a single one of us stirring. One guide extended his bare hands and, caught two caimans. The other guide caught three. They opened the caimans' mouths and put something in them. Then they tied them shut and showed the reptiles to all of us. They weren't big, about the size of fish I had seen at the market. The guy peeled the skin off one of the caimans and said, "Actually, this is delicious. We broiled them in the oven and ate. There are some alligators in this water. We cannot catch them in the night. It's too dangerous."

When we were about to turn around, we heard thunder. Soon we could see lightening. Thomas screamed, "We have to escape. It's dangerous. We have only several minutes. There are two caves nearby. We have to run. Guys, anchor the canoes to the trees. Hurry up. No time to hesitate." We were shocked. We hurriedly took off our life vests and followed the guides. The caves were 5 minutes uphill. Already the storm was hitting us. A severe storm brought torrential rain. Rain gear was useless. We rushed to the two small caves. Tim and Ashley took the big one, and Young and I entered the small one with two others. The sky was angry. It roared and poured solid sheets of water from the sky. We heard trees falling and birds screaming in the dark sky. We were completely soaked. I felt soaked down to my underwear. I looked at Young.

He gazed back at me with worried eyes and asked, "Elena, are you okay? No chill? I am okay. I enjoy this moment."

I answered, "I am okay, but a bit chilly. I am enjoying this moment too. I dreamed about it. My childhood dream came true." I touched Young's hands. He answered. He embraced me. I pulled myself closer to him. Our wet bodies touched one another. I felt warm. I smiled. He smiled. I was happy. He looked happy.

The thunderstorm stopped after half an hour. Thomas screamed, "We have to wait at least 20 more minutes here. There are fallen trees, and our canoes might be damaged. The river current is wild, but it will calm soon. Use your caution. This hill is slippery after a storm. We will guide you."

I saw Ashley and Tim. Their faces were red with excitement. They held each other tightly. I guessed they might have kissed in the darkness of the cave. They looked very happy. I hope they continue to meet and love each other. They met in the Amazon, the land of extremes, a pure land. I had been anxious to climb down from the high Andes. It was hard to breathe there. I was dying to leave that hot and humid, Ecuadorian coastal town. But not this Amazon jungle. It has everything I had dreamed of for a long time. Wilderness, adventures, challenges, purity, and love. Love for nature. Love for someone who loves nature dearly. But, we are not living in *Alice in Wonderland*. We live in the real world. People in that cold northern land are waiting for us. For me, my students, Ashley, her school, Tim, his studies and his mother and sister. For Young, I am not sure what was waiting for him, maybe a great anxiety and sorrow. We left the jungle the next morning. We had to. We were not born and raised here. We cannot possess this land. We came here temporarily. We can only dream of staying here forever. It was hard to say "Goodbye, Amazon jungle." Tears came down my eyes. I looked back at the dark Negro River.

Manaus, Brazil

Young Min Park

We are back from the jungle into a big city. From the rainforest to the human forest. From the innocent place to the greedy world. From primitiveness to civilization. It was hot and humid, typical tropical weather, not far from the equator. It was the last day of our Amazon tour and the final leg of our 12-day trip. Before we took the Amazonas river cruise, Thomas briefed us, "We are going to the point called Meeting of Waters. This natural phenomenon is caused by the confluence of the Negro River's dark water and the Solimoes River's muddy brown water. The two rivers flow thousands of miles from the high mountains of the Andes. Finally, they meet here and form the Amazonas River. Strangely, the two rivers run side by side for 3.7 miles without mixing. They refuse to get along. They hate each other. You will clearly see the distinct line between the two waterways. The Negro and Solimoes rivers originate from different points. Negro water is black because its upper water was pure, but fallen tree leaves caught mud. Solimoes has lots of waterfalls; its current is much faster, and it doesn't have as many fallen leaves as the Negro. Each river represents a different tribe. They have fought for centuries; they killed the other tribe, hang their heads, took their women. They were real enemies. This is not a scientific reason of the waters not mixing, but the natives still believe it. The real reason for this happening is not clear. It is likely that the main factors are the difference in the speed of the current, the volume of water, the different density of the two rivers, and also the difference of temperature and acidity may affect the mixing process. The Negro River flows slow, approximately 2 km per hour at 82 degrees F, while the Solimoes flows at 4-6 km at 72 degrees F. The two rivers mix eventually and flow to the mouth of the Atlantic Ocean. They cannot live together hating each other forever. People divorce, waters separate, but they merge eventually. They always meet in the ocean. I am telling you this because we will go on the river cruise as a big group, more than one hundred people together. People come from all over to watch this phenomenon."

I looked over the water. Everything was floating here: Floating marina, floating hotel, floating gas stations, and people selling necessities in their boats. I saw high watermarks at the dock; the water reached that high in the wet season. That's why they made docks and marinas with cut trees, to adjust to the water level. About 40 minutes passed. Then, suddenly people screamed, "See the waters. They don't mix. It's so amazing. Incredible. How could it happen?" Elena was with me. We saw clear river lines between the two waters. They flew separately, one muddy and the other black. The cruise boat approached the line. People were busy to taking pictures. Tim, Ashley, and Elena took shots. They didn't invite me in, and I didn't volunteer.

Elena said, "Those two rivers are like a man and a woman. If they don't like each other, they turn their back. Like-minded waters mix naturally. It's exactly like people."

I said, "But, they flow into the sea. Nature forces them. Nature cannot force people. People are stubborn. People die. Water never dies. They live forever. They evaporate and turn into water again. They resurrect. It's not like people."

Elena watched my face carefully before saying, "Don't you believe in Jesus's Resurrection?"

I was shocked by her unexpected question. I hesitated for a few minutes. And painfully said, "I don't."

Elena responded without any hesitation, "I don't believe it either."

The cruise stopped at a tropical island. We were given an off hour's excursion time. Tim and Ashley disappeared into the woods. They wanted to enjoy the last day by themselves. Elena and I wandered the hot, strange island. It was very different from rainforest. We saw redwoods, fallen trees, very high water marks, and lotus flowers. We saw the native children holding big snakes and soliciting money, but I avoided them. I've hated snakes from my childhood. They always attacked me in my dreams, and it traumatized me.

Elena said, "I think you are the lotus in the muddy water. You would be in danger whenever a flood comes in the rainy season. You need to learn how to survive." I looked at her intently but didn't say anything. She might already imagine what I might face when I go home. She held my hands and said, "I still remember what Helen told me in Quito. 'Protect Young. Save him.'" If you need me, I will be available. We are on the same page."

I said, "Thank you, Elena." I couldn't continue with words. I just hugged her and looked up to the cloudless sky.

When we returned from the river cruise, Thomas told us, "We will have our farewell dinner tonight at a fancy restaurant in Manaus. This is the place where the rich and famous rubber tappers and their women dined and danced. They have live music. You can enjoy dancing with locals or with each other. You could bring your best dress tonight if you had one. It is air-conditioned there. You can have two glasses of wine tonight. If someone doesn't drink, you can pass it to your family or friends. We meet at 7 pm in the lobby."

When I entered my room, Tim said, "Mom said she didn't feel well. She asked me how we were doing. I answered that we were fine and anxious to see her. I think mom misses us a lot."

I said, "Tell her I miss her too." I was surprised to say that. I haven't thought about her much. I wanted to forget everything and everybody over there.

Manaus, Brazil

Elena Reynolds

What should I wear? Should I dress plainly or sexy? I was

thinking this over for some time. Ashley took her shower first and was dressed up already. She is my daughter but looked so pretty. I had brought a nice dress and blouse but wasn't sure if it was proper to put them on in this tropical weather. Ashley said, "Mom, hurry up. Wear your best. The place is cool, and our bus is air-conditioned. We will dance, mom." I decided to wear my best.

It was a fancy restaurant. It was richly decorated. The band was playing Latin music. The food was excellent. There were more than 60 customers and some of them danced even before dinner. I watched one Spanish woman dancing. She looked so natural. Her whole body, even her fingers followed the rhythm. Everybody admired her swing. I had two glasses of white wine, and Young had three, one from Tim. He looked red but didn't show much emotion. He was wearing a jacket and looked handsome. His air was completely different tonight. As soon as dinner was finished, the dance floor was filled with people. Ashley took Tim's hands, and they got mixed up with the others. I watched Young. He seemed not to be in the mood. Someone approached me and extended his hand.

He spoke to me in broken English, "I am from Argentina. Are you an American? You look so beautiful. Can I dance with you?"

I looked at Young. He smiled. I didn't refuse. He was a good dancer. He led me smoothly. I shot a glimpse at Young while dancing. He was deep in thought. I couldn't resist watching him. I excused the man and pulled Young to the floor. We danced to the slow music. I spoke to his ear, "Young, don't think too much. Don't dwell in the past. Live today. Tomorrow is another day. We were fated to meet here in the Amazon. Don't forget me when you go home." He nodded, "I found you here. You look so beautiful tonight. The prettiest woman I ever met. This is the happiest moment in my life. My dream came true. Maybe a little too late. Only time has the answer."

I said, " Never 'too late.' This is only the beginning. The Amazon made us come together." I felt a flash of light. Ashley was smiling. I knew she had taken a picture of us. Tim looked happy with my daughter. He whispered into Ashley's ear. I don't know what he said, but Ashley looked very happy. I guessed that Tim might have said that he loved my daughter. At 9 p.m., we all got up. Some of our tour group was leaving tonight. I leave early tomorrow morning for Tampa and the transfer flight to New York. I heard Young has a 10 a.m. flight to Miami and then transfer to New York. It was our last night of our trip. I am sure Tim and Ashley will meet again, but I am not sure Young and I will ever see each other again. It was a big question. He said only time would answer. I saw Ashley and Tim held each other and said goodbye in the hotel lobby. I looked at Young. I saw tears welling in his eyes. I approached him and wiped his tears. I said "Good night. Have a safe trip home. I will miss you."

He said in a low voice, "Me, too."

I turned around to look at him. He was looking at me. We waved our hands. I heard a bird singing somewhere in the darkness. It was a hummingbird.

Chapter 12

Leave me Alone

Westchester, New York
Young Min Park

Why do people fight in the church? For power? For money? For what? Is there enough at stake for bloody fighting? The answer is not simple. When you ask what's going on at Korean churches, each side will tell you a long story. You will grow tired of their war stories. The end result of internal dispute is obvious: they split the congregation and form another church; then, fight again to grab more people to their side. This is the sad history of the Korean immigrant churches. It happens so often that when Korean churchgoers meet they ask, "Is your church quiet? How many people are coming for the service? Do parishioners like your pastor? Is your pastor getting along well with elders?" These are strange questions, but it is a commonplace.

I hate any fight in the church, and I was determined not to let it happen in our church. To my great disappointment, I am in the center of it. We have an army of rebels. Huh is the commander. Pastor Kim is his lieutenant. Three more elders are his warriors, and he has several deacon soldiers. Huh is in his early 70s. He is bald, but physically in good shape. He moves with the agility of a young man. He is energetic and has an insatiable appetite for fighting. I heard he was a Marine in Korea and fought in the Vietnam War. I also heard he was divorced from his first wife. He remarried with his current wife about twenty years ago. He owned a liquor store in White Plains, and his business was investigated for large cash deposits many years ago. He paid the penalty for tax evasion and escaped criminal charges. He knows how to fight. He has used all kinds of dirty tricks to dig out my past. I learned he got my academic record from the theology school and checked my graduation certificate. He looked into my family background and my days in Houston. There, he found that I awkwardly answered a young man's question about Jesus' Resurrection. He even checked my marriage record. He and his comrades made a complete list of my background and distributed it to the church members.

I was dumbfounded at his blatant hostility and contemptible behavior. My wife was furious. She had heard about church strife, but this was beyond her imagination. I asked her, "What should we do? Fight or quit?"

She answered, "Quit? Never surrender. We should fight. We have people who support us. Huh is a disgusting man. He should be defeated."

But, how? For what? What's the trophy? I couldn't sleep at night. Nightmares woke me up every night. My wife's recovery slowed because of the never – ending controversy. Again, I wanted to quit the ministry and find another job. I was ready to open a small convenience store if I don't have any other choice. Suddenly, I recalled what my son, told me months ago. He is studying business to make a lot of money and support our family. He might have foreseen this magnitude of trouble. Won Oak is a fighter, but she is a wounded warrior. She is not as vigorous as before. I am a reluctant fighter. I can argue in court, but only for something worthwhile. This is so dirty that I feel shameful to be drawn into it.

So, what are my options? I contacted some neutral, supportive elders and deacons to ask their opinions. They all expressed outrage over Huh's behavior. One member said, "He believes he is a good Christian, but he is the opposite. He wants to destroy our church. That's what he did to another church before he moved to this church. We should stop him this time. We can appeal to the authorities for a restraining order. He used illegal methods to discredit you."

I was in pain. Court order? That should be the last resort. Can anybody change his mind? I said, "Let's pray for our church and for him. God knows what's going on. God will save our church – His house of worship."

Weeks passed. There was not any sign of easing tensions. I was in a dilemma. Should I fight like a soldier? What do they want? Is there any middle ground where we can meet? I wanted to hear from them. I tried to look at the conflict from their point of view. What did I do wrong? The matter of fact is that internal dispute is detrimental to the church. I decided to use a third-party person to find a solution. I asked Elder Min, who is not an active elder, but widely respected, to talk to them. He reported a few days later, "They are not saying clearly what they want. They didn't give me any bottom line. They accuse you of this and that. You lack faith, do not want our church to grow, do not respect old church members, and so on. I guess Huh wants you to leave and put Pastor Kim in your place. He believes he can totally control Kim." I told him, "How come they are so stubborn? I think they don't know how to communicate with people who have different opinions. They are not listeners. They just talk and leave. They closed their minds. They don't realize lingering conflicts use up resources — time, energy, and the reputation of the church." I told Elder Min that elder Huh's opinion would be respected, and I would let assistant pastor Kim deliver sermon once a month.

Min said the next day, "They laughed, looked not satisfied. I got a feeling they believed they could push you out. They said they had enough evidence to embarrass you."

I said, "What evidence do they have? I didn't embezzle church funds. I am not involved in any scandal. My wife has worked hard for this church. She was severely injured doing church work. What else do they want?" I thanked Min's effort and prayed for the church with him. As long as they have a winner-take-all mentality, there was no room for compromise. They didn't know how to save face, how to preserve dignity, and I don't think they have any desire to save our church.

My mother called the next day. I guess she heard what was going on from my wife. "Pastor, I know how you feel. There are always people who think they are good Christians but actually are not. I have seen so many of them in my life. Don't fight with them. Take the high road and pray for them. When we deal with desperate people, we can look for the spiritual lessons embedded in our difficulties — lessons that can help us rely on God, who causes all things, to work together for our good and His glory, as Bible says. I believe God gives you the faith that you can bring good out of any situation. Love your enemies."

I said, "Thank you, mother, but they are so mean. They have become zealous, combative, and even tried to find ways to destroy me. I cannot ignore them or treat them like gadflies. I don't know what to do. I maybe have to quit the ministry. I can't stand it."

My mother wept, "Son, don't give up. You have an honest heart, and they don't. Honesty is the best policy and the only policy. It takes time. Bad people seem to win at first, but a good person ultimately prevails. I will pray for you this Sunday at church."

I saw several cars which had license plates frames like "Hallelujah. Praise the Lord". I didn't know to whom the cars belonged. I heard Elder Huh bought a bunch of frames and gave them to "his people." They believe they are good Christians and want to advertise it. My wife said she heard one church member murmured, "They are hypocrites. They are the ones who make all the trouble."

I don't say I am a pastor unless someone asks me. I never wore the college badge. I hated wearing my high school uniform. I didn't say where I had lived in Korea. Over the years, Koreans ask lots of personal questions like, "What is your fathers' job? Where do you live? What kind of car do you own? Where is your birthplace? What college are you from? What newspaper do you subscribe to?" Why should I answer any of these uninvited questions? I am not a secretive man, but that's my privacy. I like to believe they are true Christians, but they have to prove themselves by their deeds, not just words.

I seldom heard my wife cry. She is not as emotional as I. She is strong. She didn't cry out even when her body was tattered in the car accident. I was shocked by the fierceness of her crying now. She told me what she had heard from one of her church friends. "They dug out our past. They got our college transcripts. They know you got a D in your Bible study, and that you attempted to move to an English major. They uncovered our relationship at school. It was so disgusting. They even found out that I was pregnant before our marriage, that we rushed the wedding. They found out that Tim was born before our marriage had reached nine months. They say it's unchristian. They are bullying us. I never knew they were that vicious. How can I hold up my face in front of female church members?"

I said, "Why on earth are they so persistent to destroy us? Who provided our information to them? Yonsei shouldn't do that without our consent. Somebody broke their policy. How can they know the date of our marriage and the nature of our relationship? Why does this happen? Where is the dignity?" I was really mad. I was determined to find out the whole story. I asked my sister in Seoul to look into the matter. Two weeks later she told us what she had learned. It was more astonishing than we had thought. Assistant Pastor Kim's brother worked as a staff at the University. He looked at our transcripts and interviewed our old classmates. One of the male students, my wife knows him well because he liked her, but was rejected by her, was involved. He knew about our intimacy twenty years ago. It looks like he told Kim's brother the whole story. Won Oak said the guy was jealous of our relationship and showed some hostility to her then.

My sister is a fighter. She complained vehemently to the school administration and the school reprimanded the clerk. Kim's brother denied the allegations, but an internal investigation uncovered solid evidence. The school apologized to us for its recklessness and informed us Kim's brother had been fired from his job. Now we have evidence to prove their dishonesty. We haven't decided yet whether to use this information against them or not. It was not our intention to directly engage in this dirty war. My wife seemed very much shaken by the revelation that our premarital affair had been exposed. It was blown to her as a pastor's wife. She knew she was the one who lured me. She never imagined it would haunt her after twenty years.

The on-going conflict hit our church hard. Some of our church members were tired of this silly nonsense and moved to another church. The silent members who disdained church fighting left first and other members followed. By the second year of the conflict, more than a quarter of the Koreans stopped coming to the service. Americans and youth members stayed. They didn't want to know what was happening and kept their distance from the seniors.

Huh's people accused me of the decline of the church. They said, "People left because they realized the pastor's faith was not strong. He refused to build an education annex. Pastor Park should be blamed for all the problems, and he should step down. There is no other solution. The ship is sinking. We have to replace the captain." They never admitted their fault. They have no conscience to recognize their mistakes. They were the ones who made the big hole in the bottom of the ship. They believed they could escape from the sinking vessel and only my family would be drowned.

I sobbed, "Please leave me alone. Looked at your face in the mirror. Not just once in the morning, many times throughout the day. Is it clean? Don't you need to shave? Show your face to your wife? She may notice a scar on your face that you don't know. Show your face to your children. They may find your disgrace. You may think you are perfectly okay, but nobody is flawless. Show your face to your church friends. They may find conspiracy in your face. Don't be complacent. We are all sinners. The difference is clear. I know my sin. You don't know who you are. Look at your face over and over. Wash your face many times a day. Wash your hands with soap. Clean your mind. Purify your heart."

Chapter 13

I Found Him

2002, Milford, Connecticut
Elena Reynolds

After my divorce, I moved from the Bridgeport school district to Milford. Milford is a coastal city in southwestern New Haven County, located between Bridgeport and New Haven. There are three high schools, Joseph A. Foran, Jonathan Law, and The Academy. I was assigned to Jonathan Law. I have taught seventeen years now. I accumulated enough credit to move to a better district. Milford is an upscale city; residents pay huge school taxes, and the school district pays their teachers twenty thousand dollars a year more than Bridgeport. And, the students are smarter. The graduation ratio is one of the highest in the state with many students going on to Ivy League colleges every year. I was considering selling our house and moving close to the new school, but because Orlando pays the mortgages I didn't pursue it.

Now, I am in the second year at this school. When I started a new semester in the new school, the townspeople were celebrating their annual Oyster Festival. It serves as a combination of a typical town fair with a culinary celebration of the town's location on historically shell-fish-rich Long Island Sound. To celebrate this festival, I told my students to read a book about one of the area's well-known historical figures. "I want you to read *The River of Doubt* by Candice Millard. It's a biography of Theodore Roosevelt, the 26th president of our country. It outlines his heroic mapping expedition to the Amazon. Has anyone traveled to the Amazon?" I asked. Nobody raised their hand. "I traveled to Alaska last summer and the Amazon this winter. Both are lands of extremes. Alaska is always cold, and the Amazon is always hot. It's close to the equator. The Amazon is beautiful, pure nature. I cannot tell you much of it now."

One student asked me a question, "Ms. Reynolds, did you meet the aborigine? Do they live deep in the jungle and river basin? Do they still avoid civilization?"

I answered, "We met some natives, but they are not aborigine as you think of them. The Brazilian government protects them now."

Another student asked, "Did you go there individually or with a tour group? I want to go there too. Did you meet any interesting people there?"

I said, "My daughter and I joined a tour group. It was a small group, only eleven of us. What do you mean by interesting people?"

The student said, "Oh, I just thought that people who travel to the Amazon would be adventurers."

I said, "It was a good, diverse group. I met one interesting person." I didn't say who that person was. I was thinking about Young. He seemed to have a complicated, but investigative mind. I learned a lot from his questions, his insightful observation, and his perspectives. He was not born in the U.S., but he is well versed in English literature and knows the U.S. and world history more than I. He is a very intelligent man, but somehow he looked sad and unstable. He was as mysterious as the Amazon River.

Many months have passed since the Amazon trip. Ashley is in eleventh grade now. She has to choose which college she should apply to soon. I asked to her at dinner, "So what do you want to study? Which school do you want to go? Dartmouth like the guy you met in the Amazon? He is pretty smart, and he looked like a good guy – bright, energetic, and social. Unlike his dad."

Ashley said, "He really is a good guy. I wish I could go to Dartmouth, but I know I am not that smart. But, I can get into the University of Connecticut like you, mom. I'd like to be a teacher too. Not a high school teacher, an elementary school teacher. I like kids. I want to be either a kindergarten, first or second-grade teacher. Fifth or six graders are hard. They don't listen to their teachers. I may apply for education study at U Conn."

"Teaching is a good job. Especially for women. Your future husband will like a teacher as his wife. Teachers work only half of the year. Of course, a teacher has to be prepared to teach, but they can afford the time to take care of their family. And the benefits are excellent. Some of my colleagues' husbands are real professionals: one is a judge, two are bankers, three are doctors, one is a lawyer, and one a college professor."

Ashley said, "Tim is studying business at Dartmouth and wants to go for his MBA there. I heard Dartmouth's MBA is one of the best in the country. He wants to make lots of money to support his parents, especially his dad. His dad is a pastor, but he doesn't enjoy his job according to Tim."

I said, "Is he really? He didn't look like a pastor. Not at all. I thought he was a writer or a journalist. By the way, are you in contact with Tim? I imagine he is pretty busy studying.

Ashley replied, "We exchange emails, mom. We met a few times and will meet again soon. They live only thirty minutes from us. He occasionally comes home from school and passing our town on the way. I see him on his way home. He will be sophomore soon, and he has a car. A junk, but a car is a car. Mom, can you teach me how to drive? I want to apply for my junior permit. Mom, will you buy me a car or will you buy a new car and give your old car to me? It is good enough for a novice driver like me."

I said, "I am afraid of you driving. Only a few months ago, a young woman driver from here was killed in an accident."

"Mom, you don't trust me? I have a good temperament. I am patient, careful, and able to control my emotion." She said.

"I know you, Ashley. You are not like me. I am a highly emotional person; you are not. That is good for you. A teacher has to be warm, mild-tempered."

"Mom, what do you think about Tim? He said I was a beautiful, agreeable, and intelligent girl. I like him. Can I go out on a date with him if he wants?"

"It's your choice. I think he has good manners. Obviously, he is bright, ambitious, not greedy, and most importantly, he respects other people. I saw you guys walking together and talking a lot in the Amazon. I spied you holding hands. It looked very natural."

Ashley said, "I enticed him to grab my hand. We sneaked into woods. Mom, remember we were caught in the thunderstorm? I was scared to death. But we were happy. We really liked nature. He said his dad is a nature lover. He writes poems in Korean and short stories in English."

I said, "I knew he was an insatiable reader. He is very articulate, and he knows what he is talking about. He is a well-organized man."

Ashley looked at my face and said, "Mom, sounds like you are interested in him. But, he is a married man. I heard his wife was severely injured in a car accident last year. But, you could go to his church. Tim told me they have an English service too. About forty people come to the service. If you want, I can get his contact information through Tim."

I didn't answer. I was not sure. I want to see him and participate in his service, but I had never been a true believer in my whole life. I hadn't read the Bible in many years. Suddenly, I remembered his sad face when we said goodbye at the hotel lobby. I still harbor the memory in my heart. What Helen said constantly echoed within me. "Elena, contact him when you go home. He needs you."

I hadn't attempted to contact him. Why should I? I was not sure whether he wanted to see me or not. My mother brought me to Catholic church when I was a kid, but I was so bored I fell asleep during the service. She said she was embarrassed by my behavior. After that, she didn't bring me to church. My father is a non-believer. He only goes to church twice a year, Easter and Christmas, not because he is Christian, but because my mom pushes him.

Two months later, Ashley asked me whether she could bring Tim to me, "Mom, can I invite him to dinner? He eats anything – pizza, pasta, Chinese or whatever. You don't have to cook. He is a real nice guy. Down-to-earth."

I was a bit surprised, "That's fine. We can go out to eat. Ask him what he wants to eat. There's a good

Japanese restaurant here. Are you guys already close enough to invite for dinner? That's so fast, even in today's environment." I smiled.

Ashley said, "Mom, don't look at me with that strange face. We just feel comfortable with each other as friends, nothing serious. I am learning a lot from him. He knows far more than me. He is very good in art too."

I said as a matter of fact, "He should be. He is in college and three years older than you."

"Mom, he starts his summer internship in Hartford. It's a paid job at the Traveler's Insurance. Looks like he needs money for his tuition."

I said, "Oh, that's good. Dartmouth is an expensive school. He will need at least fifty thousand dollars a year for tuition if he doesn't have a scholarship. I have been to Hanover many times. It's a little more than a two – hour's drive from here. A quiet neighborhood. Winter is colder there and summer's sticky. I had a boyfriend from there when I was in college."

Ashley's face was brightened suddenly, "You had a Dartmouth boyfriend? You've never told me. Looks like it ended sadly, that's why you didn't marry him."

"It happens. Boys come and go, as my father said. It's nice that you met Tim, but you never know what is going to come. I hope everything's going well between you two. I liked him."

Ashley said, "Mom, we are different. He is conservative. He doesn't say anything lightly. He's very responsible. Always watching what he says."

I responded, "That's very good. I think his dad is the same. Maybe he learned from his dad."

That week, the three of us went to a Japanese restaurant in Milford. People say it is run by a Chinese couple, but I cannot tell Chinese from Japanese. To me, they all look the same. As long as the food is good and price is right, we can enjoy ourselves. I offered, "Tim, do you drink? A beer or Japanese wine? Ashley, what about you? I like to have a beer with dinner. It's pretty warm today."

Tim said, "A beer, please. My dad and I are not real drinkers, but we drink beer after golfing together."

"Oh, does he play golf? I couldn't imagine. I thought he'd always be reading. Is he a good golfer?" I said.

Tim smiled, "He taught me the game and put me on the high school golf team, but I am better than him. I can drive, but my short game is not good. I realized I cannot be professional, so I gave up early and concentrated on my studies."

Ashley said, "Mom, buy me a set. I want to take up the game too. Playing with Tim would be fun."

I smiled, "Golf is a very difficult game. It needs real patience and composure. My dad tried to teach me, but I gave up quickly. I am too hot for the game." We moved on from one subject to another. I asked Tim, "So how is your family? I guess your dad keeps himself busy." I noticed his face darken,

"He is not okay. The church is not quiet."

I asked him, "What do you mean by that?"

He said, "I don't really want to tell you what's going on, but my dad was drawn into an ugly fight. He is not a fighter. He doesn't want to be in a conflict. That's why he is in agony."

I was thinking about his face in the Amazon. He seemed to enjoy nature, but occasionally he looked so troubled. Tim's account of the events in their church makes me understand why he looked so unhappy.

Ashley added in, "They have English service. Do you want to go there, Mom? You can meet good friends there and listen to his sermon. Tim invited me."

I hesitated, "I don't have a strong faith. I am not religious. Honestly, I don't like people who are too religious. My mom's family were all Catholics in Cuba. She still goes to church every Sunday, by herself. She cannot bring my dad. He prefers watching Yankee games and drinking beer. My mom complains. I said to my mom not to bother him. Let him do whatever he wants. Religion is a personal choice. Nobody can push you into it. I am not sure whether to go to the service or not. Let me think about it. If I decide to go, I will let you know in advance."

Tim said, "Don't think too hard on it. English mission is quiet. It is totally different. People like my dad's sermon. The English congregation started from a handful and now has grown to be about forty. Elder Tom Curtis does an excellent job. He helps my dad a lot."

I was tempted to join, but I wanted to mull over it. I know me. Once committed, I am all in. We had a good dinner. Tim and Ashley held hands and walked to my car. They looked happy. I wished I had someone like that.

Dear, Young,

I know now that you are a pastor, but I like to call you 'Young.' You never said you were a pastor in the Amazon. I am glad I met you there. When we met, we were all strangers, but nature drew us closer. I like to believe that our encounter was more than a coincidence, maybe we were fated to meet. People meet and part in the course of their lives, but some people meet again. Ashley and Tim are getting along well these days. I guess Tim did not tell you yet. A few weeks ago, we three had dinner here in Milford. Tim is a charming young man, brilliant, responsible, and a man of his word. I wish I had a son

*like him. Tim said your church had an English service.
Tim invited Ashley to the service, and my daughter wants
me to go with them. Can I attend to your service? I think
you won't say no because you are a pastor. Tim said you
have many, American parishioners and that they like
your sermon. No doubt, you are good on the pulpit. I
am sure you are a thoughtful, intelligent, and persuasive
person. I am not a religious person, and my knowledge
of the Bible is very limited. I wish you could inspire me.
If you felt comfortable having me, I would be there next
Sunday. I got your email address from Tim.*

Best Regards Elena Reynolds

I got an answer from him.

Dear Elena,

*You are not a forgotten person. Nature connected us,
two unknown persons so that we can be natural friends.
I didn't know Tim sees Ashley. I have a good image of
you two. You look so natural, as green as trees, deep as
Amazon, and as free and gentle as winds. As you may
remember, we met a brother and sister who sold shell
ornaments when our canoe touched on a tiny bay. They
looked so innocent, pure, and unspoiled from polluted
civilization. I hope Ashley and Tim cultivate their friendship as the Amazon children have. I will talk to him
when he comes. I remember people through their image.
I was deeply impressed by your spontaneous and natural
spirit. You spoke like birds and walked like a wild cat. I
noticed you paid great attention to the changing colors
of nature when you took pictures. I am sure you have
wonderful images. Can you send me some of those? Of*

course, I welcome you to my service. I may not be the pastor you might have imagined. I am not an evangelist. I am a flawed pastor (I cannot tell you everything now. I am going through difficult time as a clergyman and my church is in turmoil. But English service is okay). I need a person like you. I want every one of my church members to be like you – unbiased, honest, and natural (I am using the word, 'nature' so many times because I really like it). Maybe you can 'save me' from disaster. I am looking forward to seeing you. When you come, please contact Elder Tom Curtis. He is a great man and a real Christian."

> *Yours,*
> *Young Park*

I read his e-mail twice. A few phrases caught my attention, "a flawed pastor," "church is in turmoil', "save me from disaster." I heard from Tim that Young was experiencing an ordeal, but I had no idea how serious the problem was. And how can I save him? Who is waging war against him? Why? For what? Is there any conflict between the Koreans and the Americans? Am I ready to fight if I see something ridiculous? Many questions crossed my mind. I felt a bit uncomfortable. But, I already said I would be there. When committed, I'm all in.

I went to his church with Ashley the following Sunday. It was about half an hour's drive from my home. It was a decent sized church, built in a good location. A bunch of Koreans were leaving the church with their Bibles in their hands when we arrived. They looked grim. They talked to each other, but I couldn't understand what they were talking about.

The size of the English service was about forty, as I

had heard. It was a mix of young and old; about twenty were young and other twenty, fifty or older. That puts me between the two groups. Service started at 11:30 a.m. and lasted forty minutes. Pastor Park's sermon was compact, lasting about 18 minutes. His message was simple but comprehensive. He employed precise language as I had guessed. He spoke excellent English, even though he was not born in this country.

At the end of his sermon, he said, "When we are a bit transparent, we may find people who are struggling in a similar situation. We enjoy a growing fellowship with God and become more aware of our own brokenness and inadequacy. Then, God is able to use us more fully to help others. Let's allow God to strip away any pretense and let us consider how we may spur one another toward love and good deeds. God doesn't want us to wear a mask. When we are open and true, people will trust God to meet their needs too."

After the service Young approached me and introduced me to elder Curtis. He looked in his 50's and had a benevolent expression. This was the man who Young described as a genuine Christian. He said, "Welcome! I heard you were coming from pastor Park. You met in the Amazon. How nice it is! Is she your daughter? She is so beautiful like her mom. So, what's your impression?"

I said, "It's my first time here. I generally liked the service. Looks culturally diverse and it reflects our neighborhood."

Curtis wanted to have a private talk with me. "The English mission is a minority in this church in terms of the number of parishioners and tithing. There are considerable cultural gaps between the two groups. Pastor Park is more respected by us than by the Koreans. This church is currently going through serious internal conflict. I believe some unreasonable parishioners are making trouble. I don't see how it will end, if they never reconcile. We need open communication, as pastor said at the end of his sermon, but the other party is not listening. It's sad, but I heard it's happening to a lot of Korean churches."

I didn't respond to him. I just said I felt sorry for the pastor, and added, "I believe he is a genuine person. I have no doubt he is open, honest, and responsible. I don't understand why he is not respected. It is my belief that a good pastor is a good pastor, regardless what ethnicity and culture he represents." I told him I would be a regular member and try to figure out how to help the church and the pastor.

That night I wrote this in my diary.

"I found the man, finally. He is so different from Orlando. Orlando was hiding, he lived in the shadow. He lived in the human woods like a wolf, looking for prey. His religion was power. I was looking for a man with a pure heart. I found one in the Amazon. Unfortunately, his body and soul are tied by a mysterious specter. He is a complex, multi-layered man. He is struggling. He needs a fight, but he hesitates. His integrity told him not to fight back, to love thy enemies. He might lose the battle. He wanted me to "Save" him. How can I do that? I don't want to fight anymore. I had a long fight with Orlando. I am tired. I am no longer young and vigorous. I have a feeling that I might be drawn into another war. Oh, God, please don't invite me into another conflict. Helen, you foresaw this in the Amazon. Why don't you come here to save him? They cannot kick around an 88-year old, real Christian. God, please save him. He may not be a perfect pastor. But he is a great man."

Chapter 14

I Found Her

2003, Westchester, New York
Young Min Park

I find you finally. But, too late. I am abandoned, tired, my wings are broken. Why didn't you come to me earlier? I was looking for you all my life. I found you in the deep Amazon. By the time I met you, my body was hit by Indians' arrows. No part of my body is safe. My soul is injured. My wife has lost her valor. Her wings are broken too. She cannot fly. My mother is an old woman now. She cannot push me anymore. She's lost energy. My dear father is gone. Everybody around me is gone or injured. I have a son, Tim. He is strong. He will support me when he graduates from college. I have a daughter, Sarah. She is a good girl. She is helping her mom.

I have you, Elena. I heard you are injured too. You already had a good fight. You won it. You recovered your freedom and dignity. My injury is too deep, like a soldier whose body was tattered in the war. Elena, where have you been? Why do you come now? Why didn't you answer my call? Why? Why? Why? The only hope is inheriting the spirit of the Amazon. We need its enormous energy, its secret power, and its miracle to overwhelm all my enmities. Elena, do you have the spirit of the Amazon? Can you save me? Not my job, my soul.

After I delivered that sermon at the English service, I was alone in my office. I sensed the unfriendly gaze of pastor Kim and the Korean secretary. I assume they are spying my every move. I am surrounded by enemies. They might report everything to Huh. He is their boss. I am their prey. I was thinking about Elena. I felt sorry for her. She came to the church at the worst time. I felt shame. Why should I show her my miserable face? I looked at myself in the mirror. There I found a defeated man. A pale, listless, middle-aged man, who was exhausted. I took out a note pad and scribbled.

Elena, Elena, Elena. Curtis. Curtis. Curtis. My struggle. My faith. My weakness. My fate

I threw it into the waste basket. I didn't know if Kim was staring at me. I have only two front eyes. I don't have an eye in the back of my head. I shut my door behind me and wept. I cried not for me. I cried for the people around me – my family, Elena, my people in the church who support me. I left church and drove home. Kim and the Korean secretary were still there.

My wife was home. We haven't slept in the same room since she was injured. She suggested it first, "I don't want you to hear my groaning. Please use the other room until I recover completely. She hadn't asked me to sleep together again since. I was happy to sleep by myself. I can dream freely, get up in the middle of night to walk around, and read books without bothering her sleep. Now it is our new norm.

As I came in the door, she asked me, "How was the

church? People still bother you, I guess. I left early. I was not feeling well."

I said, "It's the same. They wouldn't change their attitude overnight. And you know what? I have a strange feeling. I think I am on their radar. They watch me with naked eyes."

My wife responded, "Oh, God. Please stop them. If they go extreme, God will renounce their bad behavior with His mighty power. Lord, please save us." She was confronted with a new revelation, "Somebody told me today that they are preparing another disclosure of your faults. That's like a Spring Offensive in the war. They are tireless fighters. They are good at it and enjoying it."

Tim came home. We closed the door to my bedroom and discussed about what was going on at the church, and about Ashley. I started, "I heard you were dating Ashley. She seemed like a good girl. She looks like her mom. It's no problem with me. Actually, I welcome it. Her mom, Elena came to the service. She seemed strong, articulate, and decisive. Elder Curtis might ask her to help me as a volunteer on Sundays."

Tim studied my face and said, "Dad, are you okay? How is the church going? I don't expect them to loosen up on you. Ashley is an attractive girl. I like her a lot. Her mom and us had dinner together a few weeks ago. Dad, don't tell mom. I often meet her coming home from Hartford after work. By the way, Traveler's Insurance pays me handsomely. It helps me with my tuition. Elena is a strong and caring woman, as you thought. She divorced her Cuban husband five years ago.

I said, "She came a bit too late. Time is not on our side. It's pretty hard to reverse the tide. Now they watch me 24 hours. I think they have many spies. They dug out our past and vowed to keep doing it. It's a dirty war. They behave like gangsters. The only way to defeat them is by bringing the case to the court. English mission people believe that's the only option left. It's perfectly legal. A court decision is final and nobody can argue. I am not ready to go for it yet, but I might. A law is a law. Meantime, your mom and I will keep praying."

Tim was thinking seriously and said, "Dad, have you considered quitting the ministry? I am very sorry to say this. I ask this because you don't seem to be enjoying your job. I also know you didn't want to be a pastor. Grandma pushed you. You considered switching your major to English, but mom blocked it. You again attempted to study other areas of your own interest in Houston, mom again opposed it. Dad, I am very sorry to mention this. I think your heart is not on preaching. It's not your passion. You wanted to be a writer, or a scholar, or a journalist. It's late, but not too late. Why don't you announce that you will be resigning within a year? By the time I graduate, I can fully support your study. They may want you to quit immediately, but you can propose a plan where the assistant pastor will gradually assume your job. Then, they can cut your salary and benefits considerably. Dad, I am awfully sorry to suggest this, but I think you will be free."

I was stunned. I thanked Tim. This was exactly what I wanted from my childhood. As Tim said, it's late, but still I can do it. I am only fifty years old. The question is whether my wife would approve of it or not. I think it's an uphill battle, but it's worth fighting. I said to Tim, "Thanks. I will seriously think about that. I may need your help. We have to persuade your mom." I held Tim's hands. I embraced him.

He threw his body to me, sobbing, "Sorry dad. I suggested this because I love you so much. You are the most honest and honorable dad. I don't want you to be destroyed by evil people. You are important. You have to survive. You quit your job, but not for them. It's for you. You can achieve your dream. Your dream is not ministry. It's not a defeat. It's winning. You have to win the battle. For yourself and for me."

Tim is the best son. I am never the best father, but he thinks I am. We had dinner together. Sarah is now a good cook. She studied recipes and asked questions to her mom. Tim and I had a glass of wine. We had nothing to celebrate, but I was in better mood. Tim and I looked at each other and exchanged smiles. My wife and Sarah didn't understand our smile.

Two days later I was a little bit late for church. I was sitting at my desk when someone knocked at my door. It was Deacon Chung who understands me. He gave me a flier. I lost my words as soon as I read it. It said, "Pastor Park appealed to elder Curtis and a new American woman, Elena, to help him. We found solid evidence. He knows he doesn't have support from Korean members. Now he is relying on Americans. What a coward! And he admitted his lack of faith. He should resign right now, otherwise he will be expelled from this church."

This is ridiculous. I never asked for any support from English members. And how did they know Elena? She has been here only for a couple of weeks. Deacon Chung said, "I think pastor Kim searched your waste basket and gave it to Huh. Kim pledged revenge after his brother was fired from Yonsei University.

I called elder Curtis and told him what had happened. He was furious and rushed to the church. He doesn't understand Korean, so I explained what the flier was about and how they got my scribble. He called the police immediately. Soon, two detectives from the Westchester

Police Department arrived. Curtis told them about the flier and provided the background information. The detectives called Kim and the secretary and questioned them for about an hour. The police said to them, "We are not arresting you today. But, if it happens again, you will be detained. This is a serious invasion of privacy. You cannot dig in someone's waste basket and use it to slander them. We will ask for a restraining order in court. Please understand clearly. Stop this kind of behavior. It is against the law."

Curtis called Elena and told her what had happened. She was extremely mad. It was beyond her imagination. If it had happened at her school, the person involved would be fired. A church should be a holy place. How can such a dirty trick be permitted? She was determined to fight against these bad people. Whether they are Koreans or Americans doesn't matter. A bad person is a bad person. She hadn't clearly understood what was going on at the church, now she had grasped the whole picture of the conflict. She jumped into the fight to save me. She sent me an e-mail that night.

Dear Young,

I call you Young because I respect you as a person, not as a pastor. I didn't know about church practices, especially Korean churches. From now on, every action in your church will be monitored by the authorities. I will report any illegal activities to the police. If they don't like it, let them complain to the police. You need police protection. They should learn a lesson the hard way. This is America. Everybody should follow the law. I was not ready to be actively involved, but it has grown so ridiculous that I cannot ignore it. I hope this episode ends soon. Give my regard to your son. I think Ashley likes him dearly. They deserve a good relationship. That's their privilege. They should be happy. I guess you have many untold stories. If you tell me your deepest thoughts that would help me understand you and your conflict. We fight to win. Please do not surrender.

From Elena.

The whole incident complicated my plan to quit the ministry. It was a forcing delay. The court restraining order chilled the spirit of our church. People left one by one. Now, only half remained. Church members were too tired to argue who was right and who was wrong. They just moved to another church. The other group blamed me for the loss. They never realize their faults. Tim came home the following week. We sat down again.

He said, "Dad, things are going to the other way. Now the authorities control our church. The battle line is clearly drawn. It's good and bad. They cannot use bad tricks anymore. But, everybody's the loser. You still can propose early retirement, but Curtis and Elena will vehemently oppose it. They believe the bad people should pay for their ugly fight."

I said, "I'd like to quit, but it's not the right time. I have to wait till it quiets down." Tim looked at me with a worried face.

Chapter 15

Confession

February, Milford, Connecticut
Elena Reynolds

I wanted to know about his past, his present, and what he will do in the future. His past is a question mark. I was anxious to hear from him. I wanted to hear his heartbeats. I sent a message to him. "It's Saturday. Can you come to Milford to see me? I won't take too much of your time. I know you need to prepare for tomorrow's service. Elena."

He answered right back. "Okay. I will come. Let's me have your address."

I wrote back, "Thanks. Watch out. Somebody might follow you. If that's the case, approach any police car and pretend to be asking directions."

I was nervous. I cleaned my house and thought about what I should wear. My heart was pounding. We met for lunch at the same Japanese restaurant where Tim, Ashley, and I had dinner. At twelve I arrived there. He was waiting for me. He looked relaxed and seemed happy to see me, with an expression like a high school kid. He was an older version of his son, Tim. I asked to him, "How was the drive? Did anyone follow you?"

He said, "You guessed exactly right. After I pulled my car out of the parking lot and headed north, someone followed me. I intentionally turned to the south, New York bound, and drove about five minutes. He was still following. I stopped next to a parked police car and asked directions. Then the car behind me disappeared. I turned back north and came to you."

I said, "Good job, Young. Who was following you?" I gave him a big smile.

He said, "I don't know. It must be one of *those people*. They never stop their bad behavior. They are so used to it. They don't feel shame."

I said, "It's been almost five months since we made the Amazon trip. The Amazon was amazingly beautiful and abundant. There were plenty of dangers, but we were safe because we had a good travel guide. He kept us from danger."

Young said, "Now you are a guide and I am a traveler. You can protect my journey."

I said, "Actually, in the Amazon, you were a guide. You already knew about the jungle because you had read a bunch of books before the trip. Especially, The River of Doubt. It's a classic." He said, "I was overwhelmed by its spirit and fierceness. I can see now why people adventure in the wilderness, risking their lives. Theodore Roosevelt was a real adventurer. He couldn't sit back and relax. His whole life was a challenge."

At the end of lunch, Young asked me, "I saw you took lots of pictures there. Did you make a photo album?"

I responded, "I did. I made a slide show too. Do you want to see it? It's at my house." He didn't answer immediately. He hesitated. I studied his face. He was in deep thoughts. He remained silent. I nudged him, "What are you thinking? Don't worry. I won't kill you."

He answered, "Are you sure? You might kill me. My instinct says a trouble lurks there."

I was shocked by comment, "Why should I hurt you? I do care for you. I am trying to protect you. I like you, that's why I invite you here. You are thinking too much. Let's go to my house and take a look at the pictures of the Amazon." I pulled his sleeve. He followed me like a kid pulled by his mom.

I showed him about one hundred images. I divided the pictures into four different sections: water, rainforest, birds, and people. He said they were all good shots and recommended I plan an exhibit. I was considering asking the Firehouse Museum of Milford. He mentioned, "You've captured the excellent colors of nature. Nature constantly changes its image and color. Rivers change their color thousands of times a day. You took really good shots. Look at the hummingbirds. Remember, we saw the birds in the valley. You asked me about hummingbirds. I said they sing in a low voice. They fly low."

I answered, "Yes, I remember that clearly. You told me you were a hummingbird. You live in the rainforest and sing sadly."

Young said to me, "Do you remember the chorus of frogs? I had never heard such a loud, concerted singing by any animal. It was amazing. I guessed thousands of them were singing all together. They silenced the birds' singing."

I agreed, "Yes, it really was. It was a great piece of music."

"And we saw the native people. The old man who collected juice from rubber trees, the toothless guy who climbed the tall tree, and a brother and sister who sold ornaments. We also saw the Meeting of Waters. The picture clearly shows the two rivers refusing to mix."

I showed him floating houses and the people who lived there. It was almost four o'clock. I looked him in the face and asked, "Young, you seem not to enjoy your job as a pastor. How did you become a preacher? Tim told us a little bit, but I want to hear it from your heart. Why are you tormenting yourself? Can't you be a simple, happy person?" I demanded his answer. He hesitated again. I pushed him again. He reluctantly told me his past. He told me that his mom pushed him to become a pastor, he considered switching his major, but it didn't happen. His wife saved his college graduation and helped him with his struggles as a pastor. I asked more, "Why didn't you resist? I could tell you didn't like your job when we first met in the Amazon. I didn't know you were a pastor. You didn't want to be called as a pastor. That's why I always call you "Young". You confessed to me that you don't believe in Jesus' Resurrection. I assume you don't believe in His Second Coming either. I myself never believed." It was clear that I had touched the most sensitive subject.

He looked at me, knelt down, and confessed. "You are the only person who has asked me without any hesitation. I don't believe in His Resurrection and Second Coming. That haunted me all my life. My mom first doubted my faith, but she now thinks I believe it. My wife doesn't. Tim knows I don't have a strong Christian faith. He wanted me to quit preaching and study something else. He promised to support me." He sobbed. He wept like a kid sitting before his mom. His weeping became sobbing. He looked like a disciple looking up to Jesus confessing his sins.

I wiped his streaming tears with a tissue. I held him tightly. I kissed him. He seemed surprised. He looked at me with a frightened face. I kissed him again, not as a mom, but as a woman. I whispered into his ear, "Young, I was looking for you. Where have you been? I searched all over to find you. You are a genuine person. You have a beautiful heart. I hear your heartbeats. I love you."

He said, "I was looking for you too. Won Oak snatched me and made me a pastor. She saw great potential in me as a preacher. Her dream was to become the wife of a renowned preacher. Now, I know I am in deep trouble. I confess my sin. I've misguided my parishioners for the last twenty years." His face was all tears. His tears were not just water. It was a deep well full of regrets. I embraced him and pulled him to my breast. I felt my body trembled. He hesitated. Hesitated. And hesitated.

He grasped me. He kissed my lips, my forehead, and searched my body. He is finally answering my desire for intimacy. I felt my lower body wet. I took off his clothes. He undressed me. He was inside of my secret part. I moaned with pleasure. He poured all his energy into my body. I held him tightly and said, "I love you, Young. I really do. Don't leave me. Be strong. Face reality. Don't hesitate. Don't think too much. Just live your life. Every day is important. Whenever you face any trouble, think of me. Trust my love. Ashley loves Tim dearly. She is dreaming about her marriage to Tim. I know I cannot marry you. Now you are mine. I am yours. We are in the same boat. Rowing side by side."

He sat on the couch. He didn't talk. He looked at me. First like a stranger, then like a friend, and finally as a lover. He murmured, "This was my dream. I've been dreaming from my childhood to meet a girl like you. My lifelong dream came true. I hope it will last. I really do."

I said, "A girl? That pleases me. Yes, you are an innocent, lovely boy and I am your girl. We will wander unspoiled land, hand in hand. We love nature and nature loves people like us. Because we are pure in our hearts." He had to leave. He said goodbye. I said, "See you soon." He turned back and looked at me. I saw his tears.

He left. He left so many unspoken words. He left me with a strong impression. He left me lots of questions. He left me more sadness than pleasure. I was looking at the couch we had made love on. I hadn't even closed the curtains. No shame. I was in a hurry. My body was waiting for him. I opened my body and heart for him. His body wanted me. His mind was trying to block him. I lured him. He succumbed to my lust. He knelt before me and confessed his sin. Is it really a sin? I think not, because I don't believe those religious lies. I think lots of pastors don't believe in His Resurrection. Who can believe it? Jesus came out of a tomb and went to Heaven? And He will come back to this world and wake up all the dead? It's a nonsense. Then why did I go to his church? I was there to see him. But, for him it's a big deal, because he is a pastor. The fact that he didn't want to be a pastor doesn't matter. He said he always quoted the Bible. It's not his words, but God's words. But, it came from his mouth. If he was not sure, he shouldn't have said anything. He should not be a pastor. He knew his sin, because he is an honest person. Many other ministers blindly quote the Bible without any qualms of conscience. They habitually utter lies or they don't even think they are lying. They are parrots. He cried in front of me. Is he a weak-minded moron? Other people might think so. I do not. His deep conscience made him cry. His words are poems. A distilled collection of words. His speech touches people's hearts because it is so sincere. Bad people in his church might think they can beat him with lies and conspiracies. He knows he may lose the fight. He prefers an honorable defeat to a dishonorable victory. His conscience and dignity precedes his faith. Does he cry before God? He might not, because he doesn't truly believe in God. He knelt before me because a woman he loves is more important than a God he doesn't worship. Who am I? Am I Satan? I induced him to make love. Am I really a bad woman? I don't think so, because I wanted him. I wanted to possess him. Now what is going to happen to us? Will he shun me? Will we have more sex? What if he refuses to see me? Do I have to lure him again?

Then I heard the sound of the garage door opening. I was surprised. It was Ashley. She wasn't supposed to come home till late this evening. "Mom, what happened to you? You look distracted. Has someone been here?"

I answered, "No. No one was here. Didn't you say you would be late?"

She said, "I did. My friend Sherry didn't show up for the meeting. She doesn't feel well. It was boring without her. So, I came early. Mom, I am going to Hanover tomorrow to see Tim. There is a winter snow festival there. I might come home real late or perhaps the next day. Is that okay, Mom?"

I said, "What do you mean real late? Or might not come home? You mean a sleep over?"

Ashley replied, "We already kissed. If he holds me, it's hard to say 'No'. He would be mad then."

I studied her face. I couldn't find any guilt. I guess she's ready to open her body to Tim – as I did for Young only an hour ago, in this living room. The difference is they are young and fearless and we are old and careful. And Young is a married man. More importantly, he is a pastor. I said to my daughter, "Why don't you take a quick shower and we can go out to eat."

She was excited. "Which restaurant do we want to go to? Japanese?"

I answered, "No, not tonight." "Why not? I like the place. Food is good and it's not that pricey."

I said, "I want to have a steak tonight." I didn't mention Young and I were there for lunch. I didn't lie to my daughter. It's a secret.

Chapter 16

After Confession

Westchester, NY
Young Min Park

I was in my office. There were watchful eyes, but I didn't pay that much attention. Nobody asked me where I was. I closed the door and sank into deep thinking. I knew what had happened. My body told me something unusual had happened for the first time in my married life. I tried to regain my calm. Suddenly, I missed Elena. What is she doing at this moment? Is she thinking of me? Why did I weep before her? It is the first time I knelt and cried in front of a particular person. I even didn't cry this much when my father passed away. My tears were my confession. I bore my sin to her. Why her? She was not a priest or a nun. I don't have a convincing answer. I confessed to her because I liked her. I believed she was the best person to understand and forgive me. She actually accepted my confession. She opened her whole body and put me into her. She absorbed my sin. We are sinners. She didn't care. She did what she wanted. She seemed happy to have me. What about me? I made another huge mistake. Do I regret it? Of course, I do. That's why I hesitated and hesitated.

The bigger issue was my confession. I told my long-kept secret to a woman. I could not tell my wife or my son. I can never admit to our church people. That's a death sentence. I'd have to resign from the pastor's position immediately otherwise, I would be expelled. Do I think all pastors firmly believe in Jesus' Resurrection? Probably not. But they will never admit that to their people. Neither will the parishioners ask the embarrassing questions to their pastor. Only nasty people or idiots would do it. So pastors don't have to say whether they truly believe the Bible or not. If anybody raises any doubts, they would answer "The Bible said that." That's the best answer one can give as I did at the Houston church.

Then, why did I confess to her? Am I an idiot? Yes, and no. Yes, because I shouldn't say that to anybody. No, because my confession gave me some freedom. Is it big a deal? Why don't I lie like other people? Why do I believe conscience is more valuable than faith? Maybe, I am an honorable and good man, but not a religiously faithful person. My enemies in the church are saying my faith is false. How can they prove? They cannot scan my heart. They cannot use a polygraph to support their claim. It's conscience. Nobody can guess.

Do I believe Elena will tell my confession other people? Absolutely not. I have a good instinct. I can tell good people from bad immediately. Did I confess to her because she is pretty and sexy? Probably, but a bigger reason is the trust. I have no doubt that she is an honest and articulate woman. She was in our tour group for 12 days so I had a good opportunity to watch her. She is as natural as the Amazon. My problem is not my faith. I lied to my church people. I pretended to believe in

Resurrection. I misguided them. That hurts me. Would I open another church if I were kicked out from this church? Absolutely not. I will never do that. I am not a hypocrite. I cannot say that I have never lied, but I have lied much less than other people in the church. What if someone asks me of my relationship with Elena? No chance. Nobody will know that. We have tight mouths.

I was thinking about what elder Curtis said. Resurrection and His Second Coming theology will be changed in the future. But, when? I don't believe it will come any time soon. Change in theology is always slow. The clergy are narrow-minded, stubborn people. There's only one-way communication. If someone raises any issue, he would be condemned by the whole church. The church enjoys freedom of religion, but there is not enough freedom of expression in the church. Curtis encouraged me to be trailblazer. That's impossible. I am not that strong. I don't have followers and I don't have a strong conviction. Then what is my choice? Quitting the ministry is an option. I cannot deceive other people and myself any longer. There was no easy answer. I was tired. I came home and went to sleep right away.

It was early February. Outside was snowy and cold. We had had more snow than any other winter in memory. El Nino hit northeast hard. Vermont, Massachusetts, and New Hampshire were buried by snow mounds. Tim didn't come home for many weeks. Mountain roads were impassible and treacherous. Massachusetts already broke its snowfall record and snow piles was so high that people could not find places to dump more. My efforts to clear our driveway left me sweating. Sarah helped me and my wife offered assistance, but I yelled at her to go inside. She was too weak to do snow removing work. Whenever it snowed, church members were called for shoveling. Since most of the congregation were old, we needed to hire day laborers to do the job.

The church maintained silence for a few weeks. They might have thought it was too cold to fight. March came. Still, snow was all over and the temperature hovered in the teens and twenties. One Sunday it finally warmed. As I approached the pulpit to deliver sermon, a group of people screamed, "Pastor, we don't want to listen to your sermon. You are Satan. We know you don't believe in Resurrection and His Second Coming. That's the foundation of Christianity. Get out of this place. If you don't, we will drag you out."

I was shocked. People shouted. Parishioners stood up from their seats and scrambled. Somebody yelled, "Call police. Is this a war zone? Are you street gangs? God is watching. It's a shame." And then, suddenly someone screamed, "pastor's wife fell. She is not getting up. Call an ambulance." People rushed to her and some women members brought water to her. It was a mayhem. I was still standing shocked at the pulpit.

I said, "I will give you three words: respect, forgiveness, and love. Amen. This is my sermon today."

When the police arrived, some members were still pushing each other. Police heard both sides' argument and arrested two people, one from each side, charging disorderly conduct. They were released later on that day, but they have to appear in front of a court. When I walked to my car in order to go to the Westchester Medical Center, where my wife was, I found the tires had been slashed. "Looks like someone did it on purpose. It's a crime. Who did this and why?" I asked for help from a young deacon.

He said, "This shouldn't happen anywhere. How could this happen in a church? Do they have any conscience? Are they criminals?"

I called AAA to tow my car to a nearby service station and replace tires. Another member volunteered to drive me to the hospital. Won Oak was in the emergency room. It didn't look like she was in immediate danger. The initial test results of her EKG and blood test were not serious. A hospital staff member said they needed further tests and advised me to visit again in the late afternoon. I rushed to church to deliver the English sermon. Elena gazed at me with a concerned face. I guessed she knew what had happened earlier. I didn't approach her and she kept enough distance from me. After service. Curtis and I asked her to help as a volunteer on Sunday. Curtis said, "We need someone to make contact with the English members and do some paper work. Our church has a few helpers, but their English is limited. It's not time consuming. Only a few hours' work."

Elena looked at me and said, "Is this what you want, Young?" I nodded. She said, "When should I start and what are the hours?"

Curtis answered, "Please be at church by 10 a.m. You will be done by 1.PM. Can you start today?"

She gave me a faint smile and said, "Yes. I will do it." Elder Curtis, Elena, and I entered the church office to tell pastor Kim and the Korean clerk that Elena would work as a volunteer. They looked at her indifferently and said nothing. Elena looked confused, but extended her hand to introduce herself, "I am Elena. Nice to be working with you. I am a volunteer. I'll only work 3-4 hours a week."

I told the Korean secretary to arrange working space for her. she said, "We don't have any extra desks or a laptop. Let her sit in your office."

I said, "She cannot sit in my office. And I think we have more desks in the storage. I think she can use her own laptop."

Curtis expressed his disapproval, "Lady, you don't have to be nasty to her. We all work together for the church. I'll make a working space for her." I noticed Kim was staring at us. He didn't say anything. He just gave us a cold gaze.

I went to the hospital at five in the afternoon. My car was fixed. Sarah was there. "How is your mom? Did Tim call?"

"She is waiting for a CAT scan and echo. Tim is on the way home and will be here soon." We waited for two hours.

When the test results came the emergency room doctor said, "She can go home now. Nothing is serious, but she has problems here and there. Her heartbeat is irregular. She should go to cardiologist. Her blood pressure is high as well. It appears to have been a nervous breakdown. It comes from excessive stress. She has to go to a psychologist for checkup. She needs complete rest for the time being. She needs someone to watch her. Further stresses can deteriorate her condition. I don't know the source of her severe mental issues. If you tell me, I will recommend it to the authorities to eliminate the cause." Sarah told the doctor what had happened that morning at church. He said, "I will report this incident to the police department."

The next day, the police visited church and warned us not to fight again for medical reasons. Won Oak is not the same vigorous woman anymore. She doesn't talk, occasionally cries, and complains of repeating nightmares. We were concerned. She wanted to visit her parents in Korea. "My mother is sick again. I don't think she will die soon, but you never know. I want to be near her for a few weeks. Sarah has been absented from school to take care of me."

I couldn't say no to her. I told her to check after her health over there. She left for Korea planning to stay for three weeks. She told me at the airport, "Take care of yourself. I am tired. I have no energy. I cannot fight anymore." She looked at my face sharply and said, "Be careful of everything. They are nasty. You are under their surveillance. They never get bored of fighting. They enjoy it. They use toxic mixes of demagoguery and nonsense. They are anxious to destroy you. Don't dig your grave. I will pray for you." She held my hand and wept. I watched her disappear into the departure gate. She called me the following day from Seoul.

I received an email from my sister two days after my wife arrived in Seoul.

Young Min, it's me. Sorry I couldn't write to you for a while. I met your wife yesterday. She looked sick and thin and that made me worry. I heard what was going on in your church. Mom told me a little bit, but what I heard from your wife was beyond what I imagined. I know you didn't want to become a pastor. As you know, I protested to our mom. As time passed, I really wished that you were enjoying your job. Obviously, that was not the case. Mom visited my house a few weeks ago and asked my kids whether they were going to church. My husband is a non-believer and I don't push him. That's his choice. We were discussing our children's religious education. I wished to send them to church, but he didn't want to. We decided to let our kids decide for themselves. They said they didn't want to go to church and we didn't bother them anymore. Mom asked my husband why he didn't go to church. He said he didn't believe in the Resurrection or His Second Coming, and said so without any hesitation. He told mom, "I've never believed it. I am not sure Jesus was resurrected and I haven't heard of anyone resurrected in last two thousand years. I don't think He is coming back to rise the dead. Last month, one of the employees in my company stole millions of dollars. He was a deacon and he always said he had been a good Christian. I am not saying his religion is an issue. But, we all were greatly disappointed." Mom was shocked to hear that. She didn't say anything else and left our home. Young Min, don't grind. Church is vitally important to you, but don't take it as Do or Die. My husband was promoted to a director and he is making a good money. I am still giving voice lessons. It's my money. I can support you if you choose to quit ministry and studying for your Ph.D. I will not tell mom. Please take my suggestion seriously. All I want is your safety and happiness. You are my only brother and I love you dearly.

Your sister, from Seoul.

I wrote back immediately. "Dear sister, Thank you very much for your suggestion and kind offer. As my wife explained to you, I am in trouble. Some of the elders are trying to kick me out of the church. They are employing all kinds of dirty tricks. They uncovered my weak belief. I don't believe in Resurrection or His Second Coming. I should not be a pastor, but made a wrong choice. I feel like they are counting my days in this church. Tim urged me to quit ministry, but my wife didn't agree. She said we could not surrender now. It's a war now. I don't mind losing the fight, but people who support me don't want me to give up. I am in a big dilemma. I don't know how to deal with it. If I decide to leave the ministry, I will ask for your support." I hesitated for a moment thinking whether to send it or not. I looked around, checking if anybody was watching me. No one was there. I pushed the SEND button. I didn't know this email would cause another big problem.

We had an elder-deacon meeting two days later. Huh's group immediately attacked me. "We have solid evidence that pastor Park is not a Christian. He doesn't believe in the Resurrection or Second Coming. We have an email confession. How can a non-believer be a pastor? That's ridiculous. He has deceived us for the last twenty years. We obtained an email that is proof of this. A correspondence between him and his sister in Seoul." People were shocked. They read the mail distributed by Huh's people. They highlighted my admission of non-belief. Elder Huh cleared his voice and continued.

"Pastor Park is also trying to destroy our church using Americans. They called the police, two were arrested, and he hired an American woman to watch pastor Kim and the Korean staff. They complain that she is rude and doesn't know anything about our church. This is our internal matter. Why call police? The number of our church members is declining every week. We've lost more than half. There's only one exit. Pastor Park should go. If he keeps reporting to police, all Korean members will refuse his sermon. We all will walk out during service. We will give you a ten-day notice. We will have an all church members' meeting in two weeks. We will vote to expel you."

I was astonished. How do they uncover my email to my sister? I was careless. But, stealing someone's mail is a crime. I guessed that either pastor Kim or his church staff stole my password and hacked my mail. Some church members raised this issue. I know the silent majority of my supporters have left the church in recent months. Now, the bad people control this church. Only the hostile fighters will stay and they will kick me out and plant Kim as my successor. That's their plan. They are pointing a gun to my head. They fabricated facts to indict me and stole my mail.

I said, "I realize the seriousness of the dispute. Continued controversy is destroying my family, dividing Korean and English members, and we are degrading God. I am imperfect, flawed, and I know who I am. I am responsible for it. Please give me a break. I am exhausted. I will think about what the best solution is. I don't want to be a burden for this church. I recommend pastor Kim to deliver sermon next week. I don't feel well. My wife is sick and so am I. I need a rest. I will take a trip alone. I will be out of touch. I will be back one week before Easter. If I feel okay, I will be on the pulpit. If I am sick, Kim will deliver Easter message." I noticed a broad smile on Huh's face. He grinned. I also saw pastor Kim's smile. They knew they had won the battle. I had finally surrendered.

The Last Sermon

I realized my days were numbered. One week — two weeks — three weeks — four weeks. I couldn't count anymore. I made up my mind. I decided to confess my non-belief to my people this Sunday. I made the draft of my speech and printed out about 200 copies. I cried in my office as I wrote my final sermon. I read it over and over again. I felt a sharp gaze from the church staff. It

236

was mid-March, a few weeks before Easter. I ascended
to the pulpit.

> Dear congregation. I love you dearly. This will be
> my last speech in this church. It is not a sermon.
> It's a confession. I know some of you will be
> infuriated with what I say. You can beat me badly,
> even kill me, but please do not call the police or
> an ambulance. Just leave me alone. I don't deserve
> your respect and protection.

(At this moment I noticed Huh's people moved up to
the front pews. I couldn't continue my talk immediately.
I paused a minute.)

> Dear people. I am confessing my sin. I don't
> believe Jesus was born of a Virgin Mary. I don't
> believe in Resurrection and His Second Coming.
> I don't believe Jesus is the Son of God. I believe
> he is the Son of Man. I think he is the greatest
> teacher in human history, but I never believed
> he was God.

(I noticed people were shocked. Some people whispered,
"Oh, my God. How can we say he has been our pastor?
"There were commotions. People looked at others' faces
in disbelief.)

> I am so sorry to say this. I have misled you for so
> long. Please accuse me, beat me, and tell me I am
> a hypocrite. Don't forgive my sin. I am a sinner.
> I believe in God. My mother gave me her love of
> God. She prays every morning, every evening, for
> me and for this church. She is a real Christian.

She believes in Jesus Christ, his resurrection, second coming and everything in the Bible. My father was a good Christian too. He lived in God's words until he passed away. My parents made me a pastor. I was not much interested in theology study and considered quitting. My wife pushed me to continue. I was forced to become a pastor. I repent my past mistakes and spiritual malaise. I shouldn't be your pastor. I apologize deeply.

(I heard someone said, "Pull him down. I don't want to listen to his sermon. He is a damn liar.")

Please let me finish my speech. After I became a pastor, I was aware of my failure, but I was not brave enough to give up ministry. I was a coward. I didn't have the courage to confront you. Let me say it this way. I don't believe in everything in the Bible, but I still believe in God. Bible was not written by God. It was made by people based on folktales and legend. It doesn't have a solid scientific base. There are too many mysteries and contradictions in the Bible. Most of people believe it blindly, but unfortunately I cannot. I tried to change my thinking, but I couldn't. I don't believe God made the world. I believe in evolution theory. I believe most parts of Bible, but not everything. I think we shouldn't interpret Bible literally. We need to understand the whole context. The Bible was written two thousand years ago. Times have changed. We are living in the internet era. We have to take the Bible accordingly. Look at the decline of churches in Europe and here in the U.S. Even in our church, English mission and Korean services are different. God teaches us reason too. But you only like to believe in mysterious powers. I believe you like to believe in His Resurrection because you wish to live after you die. I don't believe in eternal life, no heaven and no hell.

(At this moment, a group of people came to the podium. One grabbed me by my shoulder and someone hit me with a stick. I was bleeding. I covered my face with my hands. I saw people pushed and punched each other. Someone yelled, "Call police.")

I shouted, "No, don't call police. No ambulance either."

Some young men protected me and carried me to my office. When I passed by the cafeteria, one woman threw an egg at my face. She yelled at me, "You're not a pastor. Go to Hell." I made it to my office. Two Korean female staff members looked at me, but they did not protect me.

I heard Elena crying, "Oh, my God! Are you okay? You want me call an ambulance?"

I said to her, "No, never. Don't call. I am okay. Please give me water. I will be fine."

This is the remainder of my speech. "Dear congregation. I have served more than twenty years at this church. I never said that I didn't believe in resurrection and second coming. I just quoted what Bible said. But, it came out of my mouth. I am a sinner. I will resign as pastor of this church in one month. In the meantime, I will not deliver sermons. Please find my replacement as soon as possible. I am so sorry. I love you. I stayed in my office for about an hour. Elena brought water, and I drank. I washed my face. I told Elena to go home. She looked at me with a deeply concerned face. We went out of the office about 4 p.m. She went to her home, and I drove to mine.

The church had a special meeting the next day. Huh's group accused me of non-belief and voted to expel me from the church. I was told to leave within two weeks, not the four weeks I had asked. I was relieved. I found peace of mind. It was humiliation, but better than guilt. My journey as a pastor had come to an end. The Ship was sinking. I was the captain and the only passenger. I didn't want to be drowned with someone else. I didn't want to hurt anybody. I was thinking about the hummingbird in the Amazon. They live in the shadows of the rainforest, singing sad songs. I am an injured hummingbird. I have fallen from a tall tree. I will be the prey of monkeys. I felt helpless. I knew my days were counting faster than I imagined. I hoped no one in my family knew what had happened at church. I told Elena and the Korean church staff not to tell my family what happened today. I created all the problems, and I should pay the price. It was my fate.

Chapter 17

Is This A Honeymoon?

Milford, Connecticut
Elena Reynolds

A short e-mail was waiting for me when I woke up in the morning. I am not an old woman, but routinely go to bed early, before ten, and get up at about six. School starts early, it's the teachers' life cycle. The e-mail was from Young.

"I am taking a few days off. I am so tired. I will wander around the Catskills. Maybe I will go to Cooperstown. My church had a meeting yesterday. They gave me a two-week notice. I said I needed a short break. My wife left for Korea. She is coming back in a few weeks. I will be out of touch. Young."

I wrote back right away. "I want to be with you. I cannot let you go by yourself. I am not sure you are okay. You were hit by a stick and bleeding. I can take a week of vacation. No problem. I have a substitute teacher. If you don't want to come here for security reasons, I can meet you somewhere in the Catskills. Just give me the address. "

He responded in ten minutes.

Are you sure? Aren't you trying too much? If everything's okay, let's meet at Emerson Rest Area on route 202 at nine tomorrow morning. Let me know.

I answered immediately.

"I am okay. I got the address and mapped it out. See you then. Be careful. Someone might follow you".

I had some lingering questions, but I didn't ask him. I was just happy to spend a few days with him. I told Ashley that I was going to a teacher's conference for three days. When I arrived at that rest area, he was already there. He is very punctual. Ten minutes earlier than the appointed time. I discovered his punctuality during our Amazon travels. I knew at the time how responsible he was.

The rest area was pretty big. He was eating his breakfast in the cafeteria. There was also a gift shop and a small clothing store. I looked around the area, checking whether anybody had followed us. There didn't appear to be any Asians there.

The Catskills is only an hour away from where we live but felt like we were in another world. He said, "We drive one car from here. I asked the restaurant manager whether it was okay to leave a car here. She said it shouldn't be a problem. They have somebody watching the parking lot." I locked my car and joined him. Young seemed relatively peaceful this morning, and that relaxed me.

I teased him, "You look great today. And youthful. Remember, I told you that you looked like my younger brother? I am excited to be having a trip with you. I feel like we are having our honeymoon." I quickly glanced at him.

He smiled, "A honeymoon? Maybe it is. Even though it will be short. By the way, did you tell your daughter?

I told Sarah I would be away a few days. She said it would be good for me. She is seventeen now. Tim's very busy this week. He has to finish his group project. So, nobody will bother me this week."

I smiled and said, "Ashley didn't even ask where I was going or for how long. She has an exam next week. I think she has been more motivated since meeting Tim."

We took West 202 toward Margaret County. Young seemed to know this road. He said, "I used to drive this road years ago. Our social club had golf outing at Hannah Country Club, up north. Cell phones didn't work there. It's surrounded by high mountains."

I said, "Did you bring your golf clubs? I am not good, but I can hit the balls. I am pretty athletic. I bet I can run faster than you."

He said, "They don't open before Easter. It's too cold, and the golf course is covered by snow. You can ski there, but no golfing."

I said, "Maybe we could sleep at the ski resort tonight. A room with a fireplace. That would be romantic." I touched his hands. They were warm. He held my hand. We looked at each other and smiled. I really felt like we were on our honeymoon. He stopped his car at a cliff. He wanted to go down and take a look at an abandoned house below. He said, "There is a stream down there. The water is clear. It tells the ancient stories of the Catskills. And there is an abandoned house by the lake. I considered buying it, but gave up."

The water was ice-cold. Young washed his face, but I couldn't even touch it. I said, "It's too cold. I cannot even wash my hands. We should come here during summer. Are we coming back?"

He didn't answer. He was thinking. He finally spoke, "This water tells us the long history of the mountain.

They see the Catskills waking up in the spring, turning richly green in the hot summer months, dropping their autumn leaves in the flowing stream, and freezing over during the harsh winter. They are reading the history book of the Catskills and reciting the mountain poems. If the Amazon river is an orchestra, this is the sound of a violin. Listen to it. It's so beautiful." I was amazed by his wild imagination.

We saw a little pond nearby. There was a single white swan swimming there. I was sure there must be fish there. We walked around the lake. The water was shimmering under the cold, blue sky. "It's so peaceful and beautiful here. I wish I could live here. Not year-round. During the summer."

He said, "Why not all year? I can enjoy my life here. Nobody will bother me. I can live with animals in the mountain. They will be my friends."

There we met an elderly man who was fishing. I said, "Hi, I am Elena, and this is Young. He's been here before. He was interested in that house. He even considered buying it."

He looked at us carefully and said, "What's your last name, Elena? Young, I am sure you are Korean. I was in the Korean War. I can tell Koreans from Chinese or Japanese."

I said, "I am Elena Reynolds. I was born in Cuba. I came here at age two."

He said, "I am Tom Reed. I was born here in Catskills and have lived here all my life, except those years I was in the war. Reynolds is not a Cuban name. Is it your husband's name?"

"No, it's my father's name. My grandfather was a sailor." I said.

He said, "That's interesting. By the way, do you want

to look at the house? It belonged to my friend, Fredrick Middleton. After he had died, there was a huge flood here, so his son abandoned it. You can go and check it out. It's a wild animal's place now. If anyone asks whether you have a permit, just mention my name. I know the town officials and everybody knows me here." As we moved towards the house, he said, "I got to go. I didn't catch anything, but my friend is waiting for me at the pub. Have a good time. If you have any questions, go over to the Town of Shandaken. It's only two miles from here.

The house stood on a plain of the Adirondack Mountain. As we walked toward the old white house, we shared a strange feeling. What if somebody sees us? The owner of the house might bring out a gun and shoot us. "Hello, is anybody here?" We yelled. No answer. The front door was latched. We entered through the back door. A frightened squirrel darted off. There were bird nests. The mother bird watched us, ready to attack if we hurt her babies. There was a living room and two bedrooms upstairs. There was a rotten couch in the living room. I cleaned it off and we sat down. It was cold, but quiet. I held Young and looked into his face. He was deadly serious again. I held him and kissed his lips. He kissed me, took off his heavy coat, and wrapped us together. I searched his body. I was ready to accept him. He pulled me in and took off my underwear. My body was waiting for his entry. It was wet and hot, despite the cold. He didn't hesitate this time. He poured all his strength into my body. I moaned with pleasure. I said, "This is our honeymoon. This abandoned house is better than a five-star hotel. I wish we lived here together. If not now, someday in the future. I love you, Young. Remember? I never called you "Pastor." I don't like a pastor. I knew you were not a true pastor when we met in the Amazon. In your heart, you are not a pastor. In my heart, you are not a pastor either. If I knew you were a pastor, I would not love you. I love you because you are a sensitive and good man."

Young said, "You know me now. You know everything about me. You have great instincts. We should have met earlier. Too late now. We should have met twenty-five years ago. We were in the different country then. God didn't bring us together. You came to me when my wings were broken. I cannot fly now. You are the only person I love now. I am giving my soul to you. That's the only thing I can offer. Of course, I like our intimacy. It's more than sex. Our bodies met because we are truly looking for each other. I heard the happy song your body sang. It was a more beautiful than any soprano's singing. Today, the birds watched our love. They are witnesses. And the mountain heard the music our two bodies created. I am happy. I fear it is not going to last long. We met too late, Elena."

I stared at his face. He was crying. I said, "It's not too late. I am a courageous woman. I will fight for my happiness. Don't be pessimistic. I will fight for you until I die. Don't die before me. Let's leave this world together. Never give up. He held me and cried. I wiped his tears with my handkerchief.

We went deeper into the mountain. We started in Sullivan and arrived at Margaret County that night. We were hungry. We asked the Emerson Rest Area to recommend the best hotel in the area. They said, "Nothing special here. They are all the same. There is a good one near the lake which is quiet and has a good view. And they have a fireplace in each room. I guess you need one in this weather." We ate at a diner. I had a steak, and he ate fish. It was a good meal; we really enjoyed it. I put all the charges on my credit card as a precaution.

The cottage we checked into was warm and spacious. It had a king-sized bed. I was cold and wet, so I took a shower first. Hot water melted my frozen body. Young took a quick shower and changed his underwear and shirt. He didn't bring much clothing, but he had extra socks. I prepared a fancy dress, a sweater, a nice warm coat, a couple of good pants, and jeans. The fireplace was ablaze. It was pitch dark outside. We had no place to go. The whole mountain was sleeping. We sat in front of the fire. Our bodies grew warm. I took off my top and pants. He put on his pajamas. I kissed him.

He said, "It's pretty warm here. You can take off your clothes."

I said, "I did. I only have my underwear on. Why? You want me naked?" I noticed he was thinking hard about something. "Young, throw all your worries into the fire. Burn and forget them. Today's important. Don't think about tomorrow. You can think about tomorrow when it comes." Young looked at me intensively. I brought my face close to his and said, "What do you want from me? Do you want to discover every part of me?" He nodded. I took off my underwear and stood naked in front of him. You can have everything. My body, my soul, it's all yours. Just don't disappear from me."

He came closer and closer to me. He got onto his knees and looked up at me, like a boy praying to Jesus Christ. He said, "I can touch you. I can hear your voice."

I said, "Yes, you can have me. Young, don't leave me alone. Promise me." I pushed him onto the bed. I was tired but happy. I woke up in the middle of night. He was moaning and screaming. He was sweating. I asked, "Are you okay?"

He said, "I had a nightmare. My father called me from far off. I said to him, 'Don't call me. I am not ready to join you.'" He fell asleep again. I put a blanket on his stomach. He told me once that his stomach was always cold and that it interrupted his sleep. I slept like a rock beside him.

The next day, we drove to Cooperstown, home of the baseball hall of fame. Cooperstown is in the deepest part of the Catskills, in Otsego County. I had been here with my dad when I was young. It was summer. We went to the Hall of Fame, ate at the best restaurant, and visited the museums and parks. We had attended a concert too. I have a fond memory of this town. The town was still sleeping. Restaurants were empty, the museums closed, and the parks were not yet ready to open. We checked into one of the best hotels in town. It had a magnificent Federal-style edifice with a breathtaking mountain view. It had an upscale indoor/outdoor pool, a health club, whirlpool, and a sauna.

I made a dinner reservation for the best restaurant in town. I fixed my face and made-up as beautifully as I could. I put on my best dress and most expensive coat. Young was really surprised at how I looked, exclaiming, "Oh, my God. Who is this? Are you Elena, my lady? I can't believe my eyes. You are so beautiful."

I was happy, "Yes, it's me. Your lady. Now, you should dress up. Did you bring a suit and tie?"

He said, "No, I didn't. But, I have a nice jacket and a clean shirt."

I said, "That's okay. We are not going to a dance party. Let me see. You look gorgeous. Everybody will think you are the most handsome man in the restaurant. We are a nice-looking couple. No other couple is more beautiful than us. You look very intelligent and elegant. I have the best man in the world." I tried to cheer him up. I wanted him to keep me. Not just for me, but for himself.

We had a very good dinner. After we had come back to the hotel, he took a shower, and I went to the sauna. Then, we went slipped into the whirlpool and had a water massage. He looked happier and praised my beauty. 'Elena, you are the most beautiful woman I've ever seen. I knew you were pretty in the Amazon. Why did you hide your beauty there?"

I said, "I didn't hide. You hadn't discovered it".

He said, "I hadn't fallen in love with you then."

I answered, "That's okay. It's the past. Today is what's important. Now, you should keep your love. Don't abandon me like that house was abandoned." He didn't answer. I kissed him. The kiss is the language of our body. I threw my body into his arms. We slept together holding each other. We had planned to go back the next day. I awoke in the middle of the night to discover he had grown ill. His whole body was hot. I was scared. I searched my bag and found some Aleve. I was thinking about calling a doctor but decided against it as I figured out it could cause some trouble for us. I prayed for his recovery. "Lord, please help him. He doesn't have a strong faith, but he is a good man. I am not a believer, but I am an honest woman. Please help him and save our love. Please give him a chance to prove himself. He can help others with his intelligence and imaginations. Please, Lord. Amen." I watched him carefully. He was sweating. I put cold towels on his forehead. He seemed to be getting better slowly.

He was still weak in the morning. We stayed another day. On the fourth day of our trip, we came down from the deep mountain. The real, harsh world was waiting for us. We parted at the same rest area where we met. I said to him, "Young, our honeymoon is over. Our relationship will continue. We are a couple, although an unmarried one. Be strong. Never give up. When you are in trouble, please remember me. Don't forget my body and my soul." I cried. He wept too. We held each other and kissed. I didn't know it would be our last kiss.

Chapter 18

Don't Come to Me

Westchester, New York
Young Min Park

When I came home, Sarah welcomed me with a bleak face. "Dad, I am relieved you are home. I was scared by myself. I felt as if someone was haunting me. Dad, are you sick? You look terrible. What happened to you? You have a scar on your face. Where have you been? I called you a couple of times. You never answered. Someone called home twice. As soon as I picked up the phone, that person hung up. I have no idea who called. Mom called from Korea, so I know it was not her. You look very bad. I think you need to go to a doctor."

I said, "That's okay, Sarah. I was deep in the mountains. My cell phone didn't work there. I am sick. I think I have the flu. I need rest. What did mom say?"

Sarah answered, "She was just worried about you. She said she had bad dreams about you. I think she will come home sooner than she planned. Maybe next week. Dad, are you hungry? I will make chicken soup for you.

Dad, I am good at cooking now. Maybe not as good as mom, but pretty good."

I said, "Chicken soup sounds great. I will wash and take a rest." I took a long, hot bath. I was exhausted. I still felt dizzy and nauseated. Sarah is a good girl. She wants me to go to a doctor. No need. I don't have to take care of myself anymore. I was thinking of Elena. Did she arrive home okay? She should. No reason not to believe it. Why am I thinking of her? I should forget everything and everybody – even Elena. I won't call anybody and won't answer anyone's call. I don't need communication with anyone. I ate the soup Sarah made. It was so good. Then, I went to sleep on my bed. I felt so comfortable. I woke up after three hours of sleep. I opened the window. Chilly winds rushed in. They were waiting for me. I closed the window. My wife called me again in the evening. She asked me where I had been and how I felt. She asked me what was going on at the church. I said, "It's getting worse. Anything can happen."

It became so quiet. No one called. No one came. Even birds didn't knock on my door today. It rained in the evening. It whispered to my ears. It carried someone's messages. Maybe it's hers. She said she missed me. I said I missed her too. But, I cannot see Elena anymore. I have kissed her for the last time.

I once again invited sleep. Once again, I had a nightmare. My father came to me through dense fog. He was calling me. I answered. I was trying to locate him. I approached him. He was mad. "Don't come near me. It's not time yet. I tried to catch his sleeve. He hit me with a stick. I woke up sweating. I took another pill and ate more chicken soup. I opened my laptop. I found some junk mail. Nobody had sent me any serious mail during my absence. I am a forgotten man. Everybody shuns me. They knew I would be gone. They declared victory. They only need to wait for two more weeks. Then, the church will be theirs.

That night I had another dream. I saw my mother. She looked very old and noticeably weak. I asked her what made her so miserable. She didn't answer. She began running away from me. I was trying to catch her. She was faster than me. She looked scared. I kept chasing after her. She disappeared into the fog. She met her husband there. He chased her away too. She was crying with all her force. It was so loud and fierce that I snapped awake. I was soaked in sweat. I took another pill and ate more chicken soup. Sarah is a good girl.

I was thinking about my son, Tim. I wished he would marry Ashley. I thought they would be a good couple. Elena would be happy. She would think of me whenever she saw Tim. Tim is a copy of me. He said he would take good care of me. Thank you, my son. But, I don't want to be a burden. Not even on you. I know you love me. It is too late. I don't deserve anybody's love. I am a sinner. I have to pay the price. How? I will figure it out. I was thirsty. I drank a glass of water. It was boiled tea water. I liked the water. I had another glass. I slept again.

I did not go out the next three days. I stayed home, took coughing medicine, and ate the soup Sarah made. She seemed less worried about me and went back to school. As I regained strength, I walked around the block with a heavy coat on. I didn't want my cough to draw the neighbor's attention. I thought about whom I should meet before it was too late. A few names came up, but I decided not to call any of them. I hoped they wouldn't call me either. I have nothing particular to talk about.

Won Oak came home one week before Easter. Sarah and I picked her up at the JFK airport. The airport was full of travelers. People from all over the world arrived and departed. They seemed frozen in the cold winds. It was an unfriendly wind – a clear warning signal telling them that New York was not an easy place to live. I had the same apprehension when I first arrived, almost two decades ago. I realize now that I've lost the most important battle of my life. I saw many Koreans. They looked relieved when they were greeted by their family or friends.

As soon as my wife saw us, she studied my face and said, "Are you okay? I was worried about you very much." She looked better than when she had left. I didn't answer her question. I couldn't. She continued, "My mother wanted me to stay longer, but I couldn't. Something pushed me to shorten my stay there. It was a strange feeling. I never dreamt when I was young, but I had a nightmare in Seoul. A woman kidnapped you at a rest-stop, dragged you to an abandoned house, and lynched you. You were screaming. She drove you into the deep mountain and tortured you. You were bleeding and tormented from pain. And then she ditched your body into a stream. You disappeared and were swept away in the current. The woman didn't look like a Korean; rather she was an American. She looked like one of our church members. She looked much younger than me. This was the worst nightmare I ever have had in my life. This bad dream made me come back early. I Don't want to lose you. I love you. You are my husband. You are wounded badly, but we still have a future together."

I couldn't look at her face. Her dream had told her what had happened between Elena and I. I felt guilty. It hit me really hard. I realized the last moments were approaching. I held her hands and said, "As long as we look at each other and smile, we are okay. Let's go home and have dinner. Sarah prepared it."

Sarah said at the dinner table, "Don't worry, mom. Dad is fine. Tim will call you this evening. He is awfully busy this week. By the way, how are the grandparents?"

My wife said, "They complain of their sicknesses, but nothing alarming. They said every part of their bodies needed repair, like old cars."

Sarah laughed, "Our cars are still running well. So, they should be okay too."

That night, my wife told me that her mother had given her fifty thousand dollars. She declined, but her mom said, "I don't need that much money. You have a son in college, and your daughter goes to college next year. A pastor's income is unreliable, especially when the church is not quiet. If you need more, do not hesitate to ask us. I am ready to go into inexpensive senior housing. I am getting real old. I am a short woman as you know. Whenever I look in the mirror, I feel like I have shrunk."

I didn't say it, but this news gave me relief from my financial concern for our family. She asked me about the latest developments in our church, but I didn't elaborate. She was too tired to call her friends. The next day she learned I had taken a week-long vacation and that there was a swirling rumor that I had decided to resign from my pastor's position. She was shocked, "Did you really say that? Or are they fabricating the story as before? Don't resign. You did nothing wrong. They are the bad people." She had suddenly recovered her fighting spirit.

I opened my laptop. I wanted to write letters to whom I was concerned most. I was not sure whether to send them or not. I drafted a short message to my mom first.

Dear, mother. How have you been? ——— I hope you are fine ————-You loved me more than

I loved you. I knew you really wanted me to be a pastor. It didn't work out. I am a failed pastor. I misled people for the last two decades. ———— Dear, mom. I know you, and my father fled Communist North Korea for the family. You worked hard for us. I have not been a good son. I couldn't meet your expectations. Sorry, mother. I am really sorry—. Your son.

I didn't send this message.

To my son, Tim. I know you are busy this week. You will graduate next year and get a good job. You have been such a good son. I really appreciate. Go to graduate school, as you wanted. Don't worry about me. I don't want to be a burden on anyone. Not even for you —— I think Ashley is a good girl. She is just like her mom. They are genuine, natural, loving people. I hope you two love each other. Who knows? Maybe you two will be a couple. ——- Stay well, my son. Your dad."

I didn't click the SEND button.

To my wife, I am very, very sorry to leave you in the cold. I know you tried to make me a famous preacher. You thought I had a great potential. It was partially true. Yes, I can sharpen my message and deliver it the most effective way —— But, that's not enough. I lacked faith. You knew me from the theology school days. You have tried to calm me down and instill faith into my heart. —— I was not a simple person. I have been a complicated, stubborn man. —— I was not a good husband —— I was —— I was —— a bad husband. I abandoned you. Now I am leaving you. ——Love Sarah and Tim. — They are good children. Much better than me —— Sorry wife. I am very sorry. — Please forgive me

Your husband.

I didn't send this mail.

To my daughter, Sarah. Thanks for the chicken soup in my final days. It was the best food I've ever have. You are a great daughter. You are as kind as your mom. The difference is, you are not as possessive as your mom. I want you to listen to your mom. No doubt, you will. Love your friends and neighbors ——— Love Tim. Meet a good guy. Be happy. Your dad.

I didn't push the SEND button.

Dear parishioners, I thank you for your support. I know some of you didn't like me and pushed me to the brink. ——— I apologize for my sin —- I am paying the price —- But, believe me —- I tried to be a man of integrity — I know it's not the main issue —- I should not have become a pastor — My mom made me —- Now I am leaving you — You can still accuse me of my sin —- I repent my sin —- Sorry, sorry and sorry.

I hesitated more than ten minutes. I decided not to send.

I considered drafting more messages to my sister and

some of my friends but stopped. I thought it was enough. Finally, I wrote a message to Elena. I will send it on Easter Eve. She will get it next morning —— She will know what has happened to me. I truly loved her. I have no doubt she loved me. She will miss me as much as I miss her. I love you, Elena. I am so sorry to leave you behind. You pleaded to me, "Don't leave me." I have to go first. I have to pay the price.

Chapter 19

We All Are Liars

West Port, Connecticut
Elena Reynolds

When I opened the door, all was quiet. Ashley was not home yet. I checked every corner of my house, nothing stirred. I was tired. I took a hot bath and changed my clothing. It was a memorable trip. Ashley came home around five o'clock in the afternoon. She seemed surprised to find me home, "Did you come early?"

I said, "No, it's about the right time. Was everything okay here?"

"Nothing special. Nobody called you. Mom, how was your conference or vacation?" she asked.

I answered, "It was okay. Actually, more than okay. It was fantastic. I had a great time." I was thinking about the moments with him.

Ashley said, "That's good. You look tired. Take it easy."

I said, "I should. I need a full rest. I don't have to go to work until Monday. Then, Easter break comes.

I have plenty of time to relax. Ashley, we go to church on Easter."

She answered, "Of course. It's Easter. Even non-believers go on Easter. They become Christian for two days a year. On Christmas and Easter. And, we will see Tim's father."

I laid down on my bed. It was so comfortable. I closed my eyes. I was thinking about him. Did he arrive home okay? He was sick, has he recovered now? When his wife is coming home? Did he feel guilty for what we did? How is the church? He looked so sad and unstable. I hope he can get out of all his troubles soon. He confessed to me that he had not been a true Christian. He said he misled his church people. I hope he doesn't think too much. He is not the only one lying. We all are liars. All politicians lie. They are natural liars. All businesspeople lie. They cannot make a profit if they don't lie. I have no doubt some pastors lie, even if they don't know they lie. If they don't lie, they cannot survive. Young, you are too honest. You don't have to feel guilty. We are all sinners. Don't hurt yourself. Don't rush your decision. You don't have to be perfect.

I really worried about him. I saw a great anxiety in his eyes. Can I see him before Easter Sunday? I don't think he wants to see me. Should I send him a message? Should I knock on his door unexpectedly? I laughed, imagining how surprised he would be. I decided not to bother him for the next few days. He needs time to settle. He has to regain his strength to fight.

I slept well. Young dreams a lot, but not me. I spent time all by myself for the next few days, with a little shopping. I bought a shirt for him for Easter. Ashley wanted to go out to eat, but I declined. We ordered Chinese food and shared it at home. I checked my telephone messages. Elder Curtis had called. He didn't leave a message. I decided not to call back. He may ask me where I had been the last few days. I felt lonely that night. I missed him. I knew I don't own him solely. I have to share with another woman. It was our fate. I could not answer him when he was calling me. He could not find me earlier. We should have met earlier, in Korea or any other place in the world. I should have met him before he married his wife. Then I could have become his wife. I wouldn't have had to meet the Cuban man and be snatched by him. It's our fate. Maybe it is late. No, it cannot be too late. Anything can happen in our lives. Be patient, Young. Think about Tim and Ashley. I hope they get married. We should be at their wedding as parents. Tim would dance with me. You should dance with Ashley. And then I will tell my daughter we are in love. It's not normal, but who cares? I don't care much. I don't want to lose you. You are so important to me. You are my light. Young, be simple. You are not a good liar. You don't know how to lie. You are a terrible liar. I was so sleepy. I slept well again.

Ashley, Tim and I had another dinner, right before Easter. They seemed to be in love. Tim will graduate next year, and Ashley has started her studies in education in U Conn. I didn't ask about Tim's father because I now know him better than Tim. I tried to find Young in Tim's face. They look alike, but they are fundamentally different. Tim is a simple man. He was born in the U.S. and raised here. He is a normal American boy. Ashley is a typical American girl. They fit perfectly. Young is different. He was born and schooled in Korea. He has been surrounded by Koreans. He was pushed and kicked by Koreans. He tried to escape, but he was caught. If he were born here, like his son, no mother would push him to become a pastor against his will. He would be a writer or a professor. He would not meet his wife, Won Oak. Maybe I would have had more of a chance to meet him. What can we do now? It is a history. We cannot turn back the clock.

Ashley said, "Mom, what are you thinking about? I noticed you have been changing lately. You are thinking too much. Be simple, mom. Live today. Tomorrow is another day."

I smiled. "'Don't think too much.' 'Live today.' Tim, you should tell that to your father."

Tim became abruptly serious, "I do every time I see him. He is too complicated. But, I am proud of him. He is a good man. I will tell him again tonight."

I said, "I fully agree with you. Please tell him. Tell him not to grind." I didn't say that I loved him, of course. I hope Tim finds out about our love later in his life after he marries my daughter. We had good dinner. We missed one person. Young. We, the four of us, should eat together. When I approached my car, I glimpsed those two kissing. I murmured, "We kissed too. Many times." A sudden sadness engulfed me. They will kiss again and again. Can we? I was not sure.

The Day Before

Young Min

It was Easter Eve. The weather forecast said a severe storm was coming on Easter Sunday. I got up at about seven in the morning. I did my routine: I walked around the block for forty minutes, then ate breakfast with my family. Tim was home. He told me last night not to think too much. He said, "Dad, you are too hard on yourself. It's not Do or Die." I didn't say much. I opened my computer and deleted most of the emails. Before I left home at about four in the afternoon, I told my wife I might be real late so not to wait for me. She looked at me with a suspicious face but didn't argue. She was too tired from her trip to fight with me. I hugged Tim and Sarah and left home hurriedly. Nobody stopped me.

I checked my car: tires were replaced, the check-engine sign flashed, as it had since a few days ago, but I was sure it was a false alarm. It's an old Sonata, close to one hundred fifty thousand miles, but still running well. There was about a quarter-tank of gas left. I threw a white blanket on the back seat. I put on my heavy coat and headed to church. The church was quiet. I saw Kim and the Korean female staff. I told assistant pastor Kim that I was still not feeling well and asked him to deliver the sermon for Easter. He seemed happy. I told the Korean staff that I would be at church until eight in the evening. She said she and other church people would be here to prepare for Easter service. I closed my door tightly and opened my church computer. I wiped out all my e-mails. I opened my desk drawer and threw away anything unnecessary. And I sent a text message to elder Curtis telling him to deliver English Easter sermon tomorrow. I suspected they were watching me. I closed the blinds. I sat on my desk. I was thinking about my twenty years here. There were good times, but mostly I struggled. I repented my sin. I scribbled some words like 'Faith,' 'Resurrection,' 'His Second Coming,' 'Conscience,' and 'Integrity.' I threw the paper in the waste basket. Somebody may search it tomorrow, but that's okay. Before dark, I walked around the church. I came across some people. I hugged them, and they looked at me with troubled faces. They sensed I was leaving the church soon. I peeked the conference room, where I was tortured by them.

All of the controversies started over the education center. I am still confident that I was right. The fight is over. I lost, and they won. I still believe my conscience is more important than their disguised Christianity. But, it's a gone issue now. I've reached the point to give everything up honorably. I went outside to look at the grass and the trees. I bid farewell to them. I particularly loved a pair of oak trees nearby. There were some bird nests. I couldn't see the mother birds now. The baby birds might have grown up and flown away.

Some church members said to me, "Have a nice evening, pastor. See you tomorrow. Happy Easter."

I answered them, "Happy Easter, too."

At 8 o'clock in the evening, I closed my office door but didn't lock it. I didn't have to. I turned the lights off and checked everything. I was heading north. I had dinner at a rest area near Exit 17, Highway 87. I checked my wallet. I had only ten dollars left after paying for the meal. I killed about an hour there. I had my cell phone and my private laptop. I deleted all my e-mails except one. I sent my final mail to Elena at 10:00 in the evening. I confirmed, hitting the SEND button. I was sure she would not check it until late tomorrow. She told me she would not checks mail after 9 p.m. I stopped my car near a creek. It was dark. I couldn't see the water, but I could hear its singing. It sounded awfully sad. I took out my cell phone and threw it in the water. All my memories will flow along the water. Nobody will recover my phone records. Only the wind and stream know my last hours, but nobody will ask to them what I did. They don't communicate with nature.

I stopped at Route 202. There was a deeper stream there. I took out my laptop and threw into the water. Now, all my records were gone. They will not be able to find them. Even if it's found, it is not a big deal. Nothing special is stored in there. I arrived at this spot at about 11 p.m. I know well this place. I have been here twice. I came here with Elena only three weeks ago. There was a wide stream down the valley. There is an abandoned house across the lake. We spent about an hour there.

I stopped my car. I confirmed that my driver's license, registration, and insurance card were in the car. My car was registered to the church address. I prayed. I repented my sin. I told myself I was not the right person to deliver the Easter message tomorrow. I prayed for Elena. I cried. I said I was sorry to go first. I was ready. I turned on the engine. My story ends here. I will jump over the cliff with my car. I will die with my beloved Sonata. I hope my car doesn't catch fire. The gas tank is almost empty.

Who Killed the Pastor?

I Killed My Son

Young Soon Choi

I came home from New York three days ago. I am very
tired. It was difficult traveling for a seventy-eight-
year-old woman. I received a phone call in the middle
of the night. It was my daughter-in-law. She was crying
and couldn't speak. I knew instantly that something
terribly bad happened. I was numb.

I asked, "What happened? Did someone die? Otherwise, you wouldn't call in the middle of the night."

She said, "Mother — mother — my husband — he — died."

"What? Who died? My son? How?" I couldn't
say more.

She said, "He killed himself. Sorry, mother. I am
so sorry."

There was a long silence between us. We just sobbed. I
held the phone line tightly. Real tight. She said, "Funeral
comes in three days. Please come with your daughter.
Call the airline tomorrow. Mother, very sorry." Then
she hung up.

I lost my words. I drank a glass of water, then wept.
Cried. It was three in the morning. I hesitated for a
moment. Should I call my daughter? I did. She was astonished. "What mom? Young Min is dead? When? Why?"
I heard her sobbing.

"Your sister-in-law just called. He committed suicide." I said.

267

She responded, "Suicide? Why?"

"I met my daughter-in-law only ten days ago, here in Seoul. She came to see me before she returned to the U.S. I held her hands and said, 'Protect my son — your husband — I can imagine how much he has been hurt. There are many bad people in the world. Even in the church. Fight if you have to.' Then she left. Now, I heard this sad news." I couldn't go back to sleep. My daughter called a travel agency the next morning and reserved a seat.

It was cold in New York. It felt colder than when I had visited twice before. My grandson was waiting for us. He sobbed as soon as he saw us. We attended the funeral the next day. I watched my son's face. His face was broken. I couldn't look at him. I just cried. Someone held me. I came back to Korea three days after my son was buried.

Now, I am at my place here in suburban Seoul. I live in senior housing. I was asking this question to myself so many times. 'Who killed my only son? Who killed my pastor son? Who?' Finally, I got an answer. It was I. I killed my son. It was I who pushed him to be a pastor. I shouldn't have done it. I should have listened when he said, "Mother, I don't want to be a pastor. I have no faith."

I was wrong. I should have died before him, my son. I visited my husband's grave yesterday with my daughter. I cried, "Young Min died. He killed himself. No, I killed him. I am guilty. I should die first."

I heard my husband's voice, "I told you so. I told you not to push him hard."

My daughter said, "Mom, what can we do now? It's too late. Young Min is gone. It was no one's fault. It's his fate. We just pray for his lasting peace." Yesterday, I sent twenty thousand dollars to New York. No one works in his family. My daughter-in-law told me she would go back to work once settled. I don't need anything. They do. I will send them all I have. I killed my son. I — am — guilty. I will be crying every day until I die.

I Killed My Husband

Won Oak Park

My husband was buried. It was so cold. My body was shivering. My daughter put a heavy coat over my shoulder. I was exhausted. I didn't eat for a few days. Sarah made chicken soup. Tim went back to school. He has to study hard to graduate and get a good job. He said, "Don't worry mom. I will support our family." Sarah goes to college next year. She already said she would go to a state college. A week has passed. I still feel his presence. His suits are in his closet. His socks are in the drawer, his shoes in the shoe box, his smell lingers, and I found his fingernails yesterday when I vacuumed.

The Church stopped supporting us. We have to move out from this house. We have no choice. Thank you, both moms. My mother gave us fifty thousand dollars, and my mother-in-law sent twenty thousand. They are all good mothers. Only Korean mothers can be so kind. He didn't leave any words to me. He just disappeared into the darkness. His silence was the answer. I know him. He might have had thousands of words to say. Somewhere he might have left messages, but I couldn't find them. I knew how much he had struggled. He should blame everything on me. I was the one who made him a pastor against his wish. I seduced him and got pregnant before our wedding. It was my fault. I took away freedom from a brilliant man. He has been a man of honor. He always wanted to be an honest loser, not a dirty winner. I told him, "Don't think too much. Be simple," thousands of times. He didn't listen. It was him. I wished I could change him. I am guilty. I killed my husband. I had loved him as soon as I met him at school. I failed. He paid the price. I should be blamed for his death. I should have let him quit ministry and study what he wanted in Houston. I should have understood his lack of faith because I knew him more than anybody. Sorry, my husband. I killed you. Your honesty killed you. Your conscience killed you. A good person had to go first. Bad people stay. Sorry, honey. I will meet you someday.

We Killed Our Pastor

Lots of churchgoers missed pastor Park. The church members who left the church because of the controversy missed him the most. They thought bad church people had killed pastor Park as the Roman soldiers had killed Jesus. We should narrow down our differences with Love of God. Elder Huh and his people disagreed. He might say, "Who killed him? Nobody killed him. He killed himself. He knew he didn't believe in Jesus's Resurrection. That's why he committed suicide on Easter Eve, not to give Easter sermon." Huh, might be right. He never admitted his flaw as a human being, as Christian, and as an elder. Huh looked happy. His soldiers killed the enemy. Now he can control the whole church.

John Kim, who had become the principal pastor, gave the sermons now. He said at the end of a service. "Now our church has restored calm. We have nothing to argue about. Pastor Park's death gave us an opportunity to heal our wounds. Parishioners who left, please come back. God is calling you. What has happened was God's intention too. God believed our church needed a new order and a new messenger. Pastor Park's death opened a new door. He killed himself for this church."

Few people seemed in agreement with him. When the service was over, people left without saying a word. On the next Sunday, fewer people came to the regular Sunday service. None of the Americans came to English service. English mission was discontinued. That surprised Huh and his followers. They are losing the church by winning an ugly battle. He tried to bring back lost members, calling every former member. One person told him, "You are one of the people who killed pastor Park. Everybody knows you are responsible. I will never go back to the church." Many other people echoed this sentiment.

The church sent an official letter to Young Oak telling her to move out of the house and terminate all benefits immediately, citing a tight church budget. They didn't even pay for the funeral, nor severance payment. This was a surprise for most of the church people, not just for Young Oak. Some women members brought food to her.

She told us, "We are okay. My parents help us. Take care of the church people. Pastor Park died for the church."

Young members said, "Pastor Park gave us great sermons. Now who will lead us? We don't think Kim could do it and we don't understand his English. Elder Curtis is not coming anymore. How can all this happen in our church?" Nobody could answer the question.

Won Oak started work as a missionary for a Queens Korean Church. She taught Bible on Wednesday. She said, "Everything is in the Bible. Read it every day. Little by little. Just believe it. Do not question or think too much. Take God's word as it is." She was talking to her husband.

I Killed My Father

Tim Park

Easter break was over. I came back to school. I met Ashley's family on my way to school. We held each other and sobbed. Ashley said she loved me more after my dad's tragedy. We ate together with her mom. Her mom didn't say much; she Just stared into my face. I knew she was trying to find my dad. Ashley is now a college girl. She looks prettier and more mature than before. She whispered in my ear, "Tim, my mom is devastated. I think she loved your dad. She thought she found the man she was looking for."

I said, "Really? How did you figure it out? Or is it simply your guess?"

Ashley smiled, "Woman knows woman. I knew she liked him since they met him in the Amazon. And guess what? I think your dad came to my house once to see her. I saw him. I was eating ice cream with my friend in town, and he passed by in his car. Mom thought I would come home late that evening, but I returned early. When I entered my house, my mom looked not herself. She seemed like she was missing something. Don't tell this to your mom. We miss your dad too. I am so sad." She really cried.

I said, "I assumed they liked each other. I am glad they found each other. But, it was too short. My mom doesn't know, and I will never tell her. I don't want to hurt my mom." Ashley said she wanted to visit me at my school, but I told her 'not this time.' I needed time to reflect on what had happened.

First, I blamed my dad. He shouldn't have killed himself. He was too sensitive, excessively beyond control, and he was too self-centered. His self-esteem was too high. He loved himself too much. TOO MUCH. Everything too much. That tied his hands and his mind. I knew the dangers. I promised to help him after graduation. He couldn't wait. He was impulsive. When he left home on Easter Eve, I saw something ominous in his face. He rushed out of the house. I was thinking of following him, but I didn't. I should have done it. I shouldn't have trusted him. He was more dangerous than I thought. I misjudged him. It was my fault.

I killed him. I should have pushed harder, to persuade my mom and make him quit the ministry. I was not brave enough. I dearly loved my dad. He was a good dad. He had a great imagination. My grandma and my mom contributed to his early departure. They shouldn't have made him a pastor. His heart was not there. Why didn't he resist? Now he's gone. I cannot see, touch, or even argue with him anymore. I am sure he attempted to leave his last words to me. He never was a simple man. He was too complicated. His mood swings were too wild. He hated and loved himself. He wished Ashley, and I would get married someday. "Dad, why did you do that? Why didn't you wait for me?" I looked at a picture of us on my desk. He and I were playing golf. It was our common sports. I always beat him. No more. He beat me badly.

I Killed My Love

Elena Reynolds

It's late April. A high – pressure system over Atlantic Canada produced cold air, winds, and occasional rain across the region. Where is the sun? I want to go out to the beach and take a walk. It's Sunday. I don't go to church anymore. I am not a real Christian. Three weeks have passed already. I was shaken, broken, and my heart sunk. I felt like I was treading water. The water was too deep and rough. The current was fast like some parts of the Amazon. Indians shot arrows at me. One pierced my heart. I staggered. I had to get up. I tried to resume my normal life. I went to school and taught my students. My fellow teachers asked me what made me look so devastated. I couldn't give them an answer. I just said I was not feeling well lately. Milford Firehouse Museum sent me a letter asking whether I was interested in exhibiting my Amazon photos. I answered, "Thank you, but not now." I needed time to reset.

Ashley asked me an unexpected question the other day, "Mom, did you love Tim's dad? You look like the saddest person in the world. You look like a widow."

I stared into her face. I said, "Yes, I loved him. I cannot hide. Maybe I am sadder than Tim's mother. He was the man I was looking for since my girlhood. As soon as I found him, he was gone. It's too short. My heart is broken. But, Ashley don't tell Tim. Promise?"

She hesitated for a moment before stating, "I won't. I respect your love."

I sensed that she might have told him already. That's okay. It's not a big deal. It was the one hundred percent truth. And, he is not here anymore. Looking back, I had many chances to save him. I knew he was not a pastor in his heart. I knew he considered quitting the ministry and studying more. And, I knew he feared the worst. But, not being his family member, I couldn't aggressively handle the issue. I was not able to block his fateful trip to the Catskills that night. I knew Tim urged him to quit and start his Ph. D. I should have joined Tim and financed his study, but it was too much for me as only his other woman. I am an articulate, courageous, and fearless woman, but I have limitations.

If I knew he would kill himself at that cliff, I probably would have taken drastic action. I didn't realize he had intentionally taken me to the valley and stopped at the abandoned house. I was just excited to have him. It was a short, but unforgettable honeymoon. I regret now my foolishness. I should have protected him from danger. Helen told me to save him. I was naïve, not aggressive, and I thought too much. Yes, I always told him not to think too much, but I thought too much. I was too careful. I should have been fearless. I was a coward. I killed him. I killed my dear love. I lost my chance.

I opened the door in the late afternoon to check the weather. It was raining. I put on my heavy coat and boots. I drove to the West Port Beach where I had wandered in my childhood. The water was cold. I remember the same cold water at Catskills. Young had plunged his body down into the water with his beloved car. He died there.

I looked at the Long Island Sound, far away. Seagulls

were circling the cloudy sky. I was looking for him in the sky. I was frightened. He was not there, not in the heavens. He is under the ground. He didn't believe in Heaven and Hell. He is resting in his hut. There is no pain, no anguish there. I should visit him soon with Tim and Ashley. I can talk to him even if he cannot respond. I walked to my car. A little bird flew near me and said something. It was a hummingbird. The bird sings in a low, lovely voice. I welcomed the bird, opening my hand out to it. The bird flew away from me. It was Young.

I Cried the Most

Elena Reynolds

One month had passed. It was early May. The grass was fresher, and the air was much warmer. Tim, Ashley, and I visited Oakwood Cemetery in Mount Kisco, Westchester County. Young's grave was not finished yet. On his burial day, I couldn't look at it carefully. It was so cold, and my body was trembling. We left the cemetery hurriedly as soon as his casket was lowered. There are a few other funeral processions today. Every day people die. Many families were visiting their loved one's graves with flowers.

I stared at his grave intensely this time. He was sleeping in the quietest part of the memorial park. That's what he wanted. He did not like a noisy café, crowded bar, or packed restaurant. For him, quality of food didn't matter that much. The atmosphere was more important. The cemetery was not well manicured. It looked rather natural. I believe that suits him too. There was no headstone there yet. I looked around. Many other people were resting in peace. I checked their names. There were some Korean names. They came to this country seeking better lives, worked hard, and died here. They wanted to be buried here because their families live here. Dead people cannot say anything. The living decided where they should be buried. There was no tree around the grave. It makes it easier for the memorial park to maintain their grounds. Birds are not welcome. We brought two bouquets of flowers. Tim and Ashley wanted one and I wanted my own. Tim bowed to his father in the traditional Korean way and poured a glass of white wine to him. Ashley bowed her head to pay tribute.

Tim murmured to his father, "Dad, are you okay? You must be lonely. You have friends: the wind, cloud, snow, and rain. You live with nature. Now you don't have to think too much. Grandma gave us money. Don't worry; we are okay." He held Ashley's hands and said, "Dad, I love Ashley. I want to propose to her when she graduates from college. Do you approve?" He listened to his dad's response. Tim said, "Of course you would."

I laughed. Ashley looked very happy. It was my turn. I sat in front of him. I put my hand over the grass and whispered to him, "It's me, Elena. You said you liked my name when we met in the Amazon. I liked your first name, Young, because you looked so young and I wanted you to stay young forever. You also liked my last name, Reynolds. You said it just sounded good. You were that sensitive about words. Words were your toys. You sported with words, especially English. You were excited whenever you discovered proper words or the best description. You interpreted your Korean poems into English for me. Young, you have an indefinite amount of time now. Produce good poems and stories. Tell me your stories; I will write a novel in your name. We will be co-authors, Elena Reynolds and Young Park. You have work to do. I'm giving you homework. Use your imagination and don't waste your talent. I will be here again and again. I will check on you. See you next month."

Tears came down my cheek. I heard him reply, "Thank you, Elena. We can produce a great piece of work TOGETHER." I was looking for the hummingbird.

I couldn't find one. Then I realized that the hummingbird cannot fly or sing anymore. The hummingbird is gone. I cried more than Tim. I cried the most because I loved him the most.

The End

Afterword

This is my second novel written in English. Two years have passed since I published The Mountain Rats, a collection of short stories. It was pretty well received; lots of people encouraged me to keep writing. Who Killed the Hummingbird? is a long story.

This story is entirely fictitious. I've never heard this kind of episode in my life. It came out of my pure imagination. I do believe there are at least some pastors who don't believe in Jesus Resurrection. And also I believe they continue preaching despite their weak faith. As I said in this novel few church people would ask this embarrassing question to their pastors. If they did the pastor would say "It's in the Bible." I heard whenever pastors delivered their Easter sermon they said, "The Bible said Jesus resurrected."

I have been thinking about this fundamental issue and how to fictionalize it for the last several years. I know some of you never agree with me. Some might refuse to think about this question. As Won Oak says, "That's what Bible said. It's not your saying." Young Min is a complex, multi-layered person. He was not a pastor in his heart. His mother made him. His wife pushed him.

He couldn't withstand all the heat he received from his enemies. He was a terrible liar. His integrity killed him.

There are not many perfect marriages. Young Min thought he was snatched by Won Oak and Elena believed she was robbed by Orlando. They were dreaming about meeting "the right person." When they met in Amazon, it was already "late." They fated to be met, but their relationship ended in tragedy.

A few pastors told me I would be a great preacher if I decided to be a pastor after they heard my non-religious speech. I thought they were really impressed by my concise and persuasive speech. They thought I was a good communicator. I said to them, "Thanks, but I have no faith." If I became a pastor, I would be Young Min. I attended Sunday service for many years, but stopped once I realized I was not a true believer. But, I do respect other people's faith. I think the church exists for people. When people and society change the church has to be changed accordingly. When the change is not coming timely, then conflicts arise. This story reflects a glimpse of contradictions.

I probably will not create another story on religion. Writing a novel is a meaningful work, but it is an awfully difficult task. It is doubly hard for a non-native author like me. I may produce one or two more stories in the future if circumstance permits. I always thank those you have supported me. I know I didn't meet your expectations. I never thought I am a gifted writer. I just do what I love so much. The description of Havana and Amazon is based on my trip there. I traveled Amazon twice.

I thank Sue Chung who kindly read the rough first draft. I especially thank Dr. Kaye Kim who spent so much time to read and corrected many mistakes. I truly appreciate her love of literature and unselfish help she gave to me. The whole process was painful, but I am happy to share my imaginations with readers.

Boklim Choi, August 2016
Port Washington, New York

About the Author

Boklim Choi is a journalist-writer. He worked for over twenty years in print media and broadcasting in the United States and Korea. He has published two poetry collections and two novels in Korean. He has also published a golf essay collection and still contributes essays to a Korean paper. This is his first full length novel in English. He was born and raised in Korea. He graduated from Yonsei University in Seoul and received his Master's degree in communications from City University of New York. He lives in Port Washington, New York, with his wife. He has three grown daughters.